THE REWILDING

ROBERT EVANS

CRANTHORPE
— MILLNER —
PUBLISHERS

First published by Cranthorpe Millner Publishers (2025)

ISBN 978-1-80378-290-4 (Paperback)

www.cranthorpemillner.com

Cranthorpe Millner Publishers

Printed and bound by CPI Group (UK) Ltd
Croydon, CR0 4YY

MIX
Paper | Supporting
responsible forestry
FSC
www.fsc.org FSC® C013604

For Louis and Emilia.

ONE

Nathan clambered over the moss-covered rocks. He was angry. His parents could try and ground him if they wanted; it wouldn't work. It hadn't worked! He was out. He was free and off to explore the woods. So what if he had broken his sister's phone! She deserved it! She was on the thing too much anyway, even Dad said so. She was always recording herself doing those stupid dances and pulling those faces that made her look like a beaver's anus.

Nathan pushed a branch away from his face. His unkempt hair already had small bits of twig and leaf in it. He loved being outside. It was the one place where things just seemed so easy for him. He knew he wasn't particularly sporty or smart like his sister, but he knew how to build a fire. He knew how to build a shelter. Spending a night out in the woods would be easy. That would give Mum and Dad something to think about: a night worrying about where he was and what their lives would be like without him.

Although Nathan felt like he had been walking for a long time, he was not really sure how far he'd gone. He had never ventured this way before. Even though he didn't live far from the stretch of woods he was traipsing through, he had always been driven to a set route before. The Cubs always had their preferred camping destinations, and Dad always liked a hike with some sort of hill in it. He considered it a pointless ramble if he hadn't exhausted himself climbing something.

Nathan took his bag off his back and sat down on a fallen

tree trunk. It must have come down during the gale last month. He rummaged through the bag until he found what he was looking for, a Mars bar. Bear Grylls might have been his idol, but he was not quite ready to look under rocks for worms and insects to eat.

It was greying overhead as the sun began to think about going down for the night. Nathan knew he'd have to find somewhere to build a shelter soon. That was fine. He knew what he was doing. He'd borrowed his dad's penknife to cut branches with and had been sensible enough to bring a sleeping bag.

Nathan stood up again and crammed the empty Mars wrapper into his pocket before setting off again. He hadn't gone far when he came across exactly what he was hoping to find – or at least close enough to claim that it was exact. A tree with overgrown lower branches which now hung so low with the weight of them the tips almost touched the floor. Nathan could work with it, easily.

Taking out his dad's penknife, Nathan set to work chopping at a nearby branch with the intention of building himself some sort of canopy over the natural frame the other branches provided. At first, he tried to hack at the branch, but it didn't achieve much; a few scratches in the bark. Not what he'd expected. Realising that that wasn't going to work, he tried to saw at the thing. That proved equally ineffective. Maybe the stupid knife was blunt? It was not as if the branch he had chosen was that thick, yet all he had managed was to gouge a small divot where the tree's white flesh showed through. Nathan decided to try and snap the branch instead. It proved irritatingly flexible.

Nathan let the branch go and sighed. He looked around to see if there was a branch that looked more accessible. As he was so intent on making a shelter, he didn't take much notice of the quiet that was beginning to descend on the area. The birdsong that accompanied most evenings was lessening.

Deciding that, as it was summer, a shelter was less important than a fire, Nathan set about collecting bits of kindling. Fire was always the most important key to survival; everyone knew that. The shelter was just a distraction really. Besides, Nathan knew he could get a fire going effortlessly enough. He was always making them at home, ever since he had learnt how to at Cubs and then discovered his dad's old flint. It seemed to always get him into trouble even though he had them under control every single time. It was not as if he was irresponsible – he was not some sort of fire-starting maniac. He was simply honing his skills.

Nathan was arranging some larger sticks to form a box over his kindling when he heard a branch snap in the distance. The sound echoed through the trees. He froze. He listened.

Nothing. He couldn't hear anything. It was probably just an old branch that had finally given up on life. Even so, Nathan felt his heart beating a little faster. He pulled his dad's penknife a little closer and made sure the blade was out before continuing to crisscross the sticks over one another.

There was another snap. Quieter this time, but closer as if something had been deadened slightly against the dirt. Nathan listened again, his heart starting to pump into his throat. His hand found its way over the handle of the knife and lifted it slightly as he listened. This time, he was sure he could hear something there. He was sure that he could hear breathing in the distance. Then again, the blood pumping around his ears and the thumping of his heart made him less sure that he was hearing correctly.

His eyes were transfixed on the direction he thought the

sound was coming from. It was definitely the direction the branch snapping had come from. He wanted to run but he couldn't. He dared not move. It was likely just a fox or possibly a deer. There was not exactly much wildlife in Scotland to be scared of. Nathan knew this. His head knew this. His brain knew this. However, his imagination seemed oblivious. So was the rest of his body.

The noise got closer yet stayed out of sight. His brain told him that any animal that came into the small clearing was likely to run as soon as it saw him. Even so, his hands shook slightly.

Plucking up what little courage he could muster, Nathan let out a short sharp bark. He intended to scare away whatever was coming. It would easily send a deer skittering away or cause a fox to turn in another direction.

His shout reverberated slightly through the quiet of the trees in the still summer air. Nathan listened. The sound of distant movement had stopped. Maybe the animal was considering whether it had heard correctly. Nathan let out another bark. This time slightly longer. This was his territory and animals could stay away for the night, thank you very much.

The unmistakable sound of feet, paws, hooves or whatever it was started again. Only, they weren't moving away. And they sounded like they were moving quicker.

Discovering that the initial paralysing surge of adrenaline had decreased slightly, Nathan sprang to his feet and ran. Somewhere in the back of his head, there was still a rationale that there was nothing in the wilds of Scotland that could harm him. The rest of his head didn't care for the fact. He leapt over branches. He slalomed trees. He dared not look back.

He didn't need to look back; his ears were telling him all he needed to know. Heavy feet pounded behind him. They were accompanied by guttural breathing. Nathan started to sob as he

4

ran. He had never run so fast for so long. He had never known that he could do so. And then he stumbled as something heavy hammered his feet from under him. He felt the air forced from his lungs as a heavy weight pushed down upon his small and insignificant body. And then he knew nothing.

TWO

Steph Patel licked the end of her thumb as she continued to read through the articles she'd collated. There was a one-day-old cut on the end of her it caused by a tuna can lid. The wound had closed but was irritatingly placed.

This was the fifth article she had found on the subject, and it was enough to pique her interest. Like much of the material she researched, it was put together by a small-town paper, local to the area. They were always like that; large papers wouldn't have touched the subjects with a twelve-foot barge pole.

Steph squinted as she read. She was tired. She'd been at it for a couple of hours. This would be the last one and then she would decide what to do in the morning.

The article spoke about an eight-year-old boy in Scotland. He'd been out exploring but never came back. A search party was sent out, and they were fortunate enough to find him. Unfortunately, what they found was not in one piece. The boy had been ripped apart by something. A local 'wildlife expert' had exclaimed how the wounds and lacerations to the boy's body were not from any creature native to that part of the world. Police had written off murder as there were bite marks all over the body with no use of a weapon evident. The family of the boy were devastated, of course. Et cetera, et cetera.

The idea of a monster causing such harm was clearly thought of as preposterous, but people rarely seemed to consider an animal that had been released somewhere it shouldn't. This always baffled Steph. Moreover, people didn't fully understand the damage wild animals could inflict, so they struggled to get their heads around incidents when they occurred. Steph understood well enough. She'd seen things. The worst was seeing a fully grown gorilla tearing a man's arm off.

Steph's business covered the sensational as opposed to the easily explained (although she would try to rationalise the sensational), but that was more due to what people wanted rather than her own opinion. To her it was just as interesting to find an unlikely but perfectly reasonable and digestible explanation for something rather than something so out of the ordinary that it would shatter people's belief in what was real. Steph had never actually found something so extraordinary. She had alluded to the possibility of it as that was her job. She was good at her job. It was why she was going places with a six-part documentary series in the pipeline. Certainly, that was what her agent would have her believe.

Steph ran her index finger along her teeth. It was probably a large cat of some sort. The type that had been kept as a pet by some criminal or other that had either escaped or been released when the owner was bored of it. Pablo Escobar had inadvertently been the creator of a hippo population in South America. They'd had a big impact on their surroundings. However, even less dangerous creatures could have an effect.

Some genius had introduced an American grey squirrel into a London park. The result was that the red squirrel had been pushed almost completely out of England just a hundred years later.

Steph shut her laptop and yawned. Was there enough there to justify paying for a flight to Scotland? There was an article in it for sure, but was there a book? She would have to do a lot of digging when she was out there and pad things out with all sorts of interviews. It could be tricky to make it stretch. Then again, she had an audience; her last book's sales said as much. Besides, she could always knock something up on the Loch Ness monster if needs be. That was a subject where all the work had basically been done for her but seemed – for whatever reason – to still spark people's interest.

Screw it. She'd do it. She'd told her agent that she was working on something, so she should probably get on and change the lie into a truth. A half-truth.

She opened her laptop again and looked up the cheapest tickets to Scotland she could find. One day, she was sure, someone would pay for her to fly places. They'd probably fly her out in comfort too. If they wanted her there so badly, they would at least book her into business class. After all, she imagined, it would be based on a business deal so it would be fitting.

Steph shook herself out of her head and paid for the tickets. She wondered whether her parents would be annoyed knowing she would have been relatively close and not called in. She could do that on the way back. They wouldn't know. She could hire a car and drive down to Sheffield as a surprise. That would win her points.

Steph yawned again and looked at the black travel case she kept under her bed. Then she looked at her wardrobe with its door hanging open and a couple of shirts tumbling down from one of the shelves. She rubbed her eye with the palm of her hand. She'd pack tomorrow; it wouldn't take long.

Steph arrived at San Francisco International Airport earlier than she needed to. Although she was a messy person, she at least knew she was punctual. Punctuality was what most people noticed. That was the impression she liked to give. It helped that she didn't work in a job that required a desk or anything static, where her shadier habits would be noticeable to others. Not that she'd ever wanted a desk job. It was why she had trained to be a field biologist rather than the dentist her mother had suggested so strongly she become.

As usual, Steph breezed through the check-in, flew through security, grabbed a McDonald's breakfast despite promising herself she would not this time, and sat and read her book. It had been nine months since she started it, but she was determined to finish it even if it killed her. She should have just picked up something trashy that she would enjoy. Now she was stuck with a classic she thought would make her seem *more intellectually insighted*. She thought it might make her more attractive to any single men potentially looking for something more than a one-night-fling. Not that Steph would have turned down a fling. But at what cost would this fling come? The book was painful!

Steph put down the book and picked up the magazine she'd bought. It was a waste of time but less of a slog.

It was to Steph's displeasure that she found herself sitting next to one of those social types when she got on the plane. The seatbelt sign had hardly been turned off when the man seated next to her turned to engage her in conversation. The man was smiling as if a long-haul flight was something to be happy about. His hair was turning white, but wrinkles seemed to have mostly missed crevassing his face apart from where they marked out his happy nature.

"What takes you to Scotland?" the man asked.

"Work," Steph replied, fiddling with her bag.

Through her peripheral vision, she could see the man nodding.

"Oh, and what's your line of work?"

"Biology." That was half true.

Steph pulled a notebook from her bag along with a Parker ballpoint. Her grandmother had always insisted one should have something good to write with. She'd always written with a fountain pen. Steph could understand why as they wrote much smoother, but they lacked the practicality of a ballpoint, especially when traipsing around the wilderness.

"What kind of biology?"

"Field biology."

Steph started making notes on her pad. There wasn't much aim to their content, but she hoped that the action would be enough to dissuade the man from further attempts at conversation. She was wrong. The man was apparently irrepressible.

"Gosh, field biology sounds exciting," the man said, leaning back.

"I suppose it is, not that what I do is perhaps as academically smiled upon as that of colleagues I know," Steph replied before grimacing. She'd said more than two words. She'd flung the door open; she knew it.

"Why do you say that?"

Stuff it. In for a penny, in for a pound. She put her pen down.

"I don't go to study normal phenomena exactly. I could do; I have the qualifications to do so. However, I suppose I go where the money is. I do what is popular."

"What do you mean?" the man asked, frowning.

"Well, let's put it like this: there are a large number of people who go into the study of plants and animals, but could you really tell me any you know or what they do? No. Unless you are in that line of work, you just know they study animals. That is to be respected. I respect it, I do. But and here is the thing, where do they get their money from?"

The man opened his mouth slightly before deciding there was nothing to come out of it except a stumped exhale. He shrugged.

"That's my point," Steph continued. "If you're really lucky you might be picked up by a television company. You might fall into studying a species of animal that has some sort of commercial value to some private company – I'd rather not get into the details – but the chances are you will end up studying a species of plant or animal that, although it furthers human knowledge, is not massively interesting to the wider society. Someone must pay you for your work. The idea of driving around the savannah following big animals sounds cool, but who is going to pay you to do it? Why you? Why not someone else as there are enough people about? And what are they getting out of it that is of value to them?"

"I don't know," the man replied slowly, clearly unsure whether Steph was inviting him to talk or not. She was becoming more fervent in the way she spoke.

"Precisely. So like I said, I go where the money is. I find niches where there is a hunger for information that people are willing to pay for?"

"Like studying monkeys in a lab or something to help cure brain tumours or...?"

Steph, for the first time, turned to look at the man who shrank slightly.

"I am a field biologist, not some sort of Dr Frankenstein of animals."

"Right... sorry."

"No, I go and study unsolved mysteries of the animal kingdom," Steph continued. "I go out and try to come up with a plausible explanation by studying the natural environment including both the flora and fauna. Sometimes I do not find an exact answer but that doesn't seem to matter exactly."

"And who... who pays you for that?"

"The public does, I suppose," Steph said. "People love a mystery – if you excuse me for stating the obvious – so I give them real-life ones that involve animals. Obviously, I include relevant information to educate the reader..."

"Reader?"

"I write books. I found an agent who was able to sell my particular idea to a publisher who has since discovered my niche to be lucrative enough. Nothing massive, but it pays a lot better than if I went to simply study wolverines or something similar for whatever reason. Actually, there is the potential for a documentary series for me on one of the animal channels which would really get things going."

"Which one?"

"I am not at liberty to say."

There was silence for a minute. Steph contemplated picking up her notebook again. The man noticed.

"So what's the mystery you are investigating in Scotland?" he asked.

"The death of a boy," Steph replied, a little too matter-of-factly for the man's liking. "He has been attacked by something that shouldn't have been there or by someone who found a way to make it look like that. Supposedly, it was near a large fenced-off area. I am not sure exactly why the area is fenced off, only that it belongs to a private company working on some sort of environmental project... potentially. I'll be honest; I haven't managed to find much about it. Again, this is part of the reason I'm going. Sort of like an animal murder mystery if you like."

THREE

Steph got off the plane, went through passport control and made straight to collect her luggage. She waited impatiently for the conveyor belt to start. How long could it take to chuck some bags on a truck and throw them on a belt? Steph tried to look intently at a pillar when the old man from the plane meandered over to the luggage reel. She had given him enough of her time on the plane.

It didn't take long to rent a car and drive out of Glasgow. What did take a while was navigating the roads through the Trossachs towards the village of Calnally where the dead boy had lived.

It was hard to keep her eyes open due to jetlag and, once or twice, Steph had to swerve to stay on the right side of the road, which happened to be the left. Perhaps she should have spent a night in Glasgow to recover a little bit. But time was precious. Besides, she would still be jetlagged in the morning so she might as well endure the pain now, or so she thought.

Calnally was a rather picturesque little place set against the natural beauty of the surrounding wilderness. Well, what counted as wilderness for Britain. Living in the USA had given Steph a broader understanding of what wilderness truly was. Alaska had been a crazy experience. You could easily get lost there and not even your remains would be found – a great selling point for Steph.

Being a village, Calnally didn't have many places to stay. After the third car had screeched its horn at Steph for swerving onto the wrong side of the road, she realised she needed to find somewhere quickly. She needed to rest.

There were one or two places that made most of their business through ramblers and the type of holiday goer that wanted to escape town life. In the end, Steph chose a hotel attached to one of the local pubs. She had long since discovered that the best starting point to get information was from locals who liked to chat. Drinking tended to induce conversation. The pub was a no-brainer.

Despite her eagerness to get to Calnally, Steph was in no rush to begin work. After getting her keys and hauling her luggage up two flights of stairs, her head hit the pillow. She slept. It was two in the afternoon.

Having awoken after seven in the evening, Steph forced herself to get up and go downstairs. She knew lying there would be dangerous, as it would become difficult to get to sleep later. The carpet leading down the stairs was patterned and worn slightly in the areas over the lip of each step. Steph supposed there was not much reason for the place to stay at the cutting edge of floor fashion. It likely had little impact on those who chose to stay there.

Although allowing the carpet to age didn't inspire comfort, the authentic old-fashioned bar area did. There was rich oak panelling halfway up the wall, whilst a deep blue patterned wallpaper covered the rest. A few mounted antlers adorned the wall, along with other game and a couple of old flintlock rifles from years gone by. To one end, high-backed brown leather chairs surrounded the fireplace.

Steph made her way to the bar. The room was occupied by a few small groups, chatting the evening away after early dinners, but there was no queue for drinks.

"What can I get you, dear?" asked a middle-aged woman,

her dark grey roots beginning to show under her dyed blonde hair. She smiled good-naturedly.

"A gin and tonic, please," Steph replied, looking around the room.

"Coming right up."

Steph hauled herself up onto one of the padded barstools and leant on the surface of the bar.

"So what brings you all the way up here?" the woman asked after having taken Steph's room number.

"Up here?" Steph asked, pouring the tonic over the lime wedge languishing in the gin below.

"Your accent gives you away."

"Oh, right, yeah," Steph said, taking a sip. "I'm from Sheffield originally but I've lived in the States for the last nine years."

"Oh, I love America," the woman sighed. "Everything seems so much bigger out there."

"Yeah, I guess so."

"So what brings someone over from America to the middle of nowhere? You have enough nowhere over on the other side of the ocean if you wanted some seclusion."

Steph smiled and took another sip of her drink.

"Work."

The woman nodded and then picked up a newspaper and an old ballpoint. She was halfway through a crossword which she now lay on the counter. Steph couldn't help peering over.

"Five letter word beginning with T, fourth letter M; the clue's *better*," the woman said without looking up.

Steph thought for a second.

"Trump?"

The woman put pen to paper.

"Well, you certainly trumped me with that one; I've been

on it for ten minutes."

Steph gave half a smile as the woman began reading the next clue to herself, her lips moving but no words coming out.

"Is this a quiet sort of place?" Steph asked.

The woman looked up momentarily before looking down again.

"I suppose so. People come on walking holidays around here and a few who like to escape the city, but otherwise, it is mostly locals. It's not like people would come to stay here for Ben Nevis or Loch Lomond if you get my understanding. Too much of a distance still. They want it on their doorstep."

"I get you," Steph replied, swirling her glass slightly. "So it's quite a cosy village then? Most people know each other?"

"I suppose it is a bit like that, aye," the woman replied, putting pen to paper once more. "Although, it's not as if everyone knows everyone else intimately, even if news travels fast enough between people. Par for the course in any small place I suppose."

"I suppose so," Steph said. She wasn't quite sure how to tackle the subject she really wanted to. Death could be a delicate subject. "Sorry, but seeing as you work in a bit of a local hub, I was wondering whether I could ask you something."

"Local hub?" the woman chuckled, looking over to a couple of older men relaxing in the chairs by the fire. "What was it you wanted to know?"

"I couldn't help overhearing a couple of people talking about the death of a boy a few weeks ago. I looked it up and supposedly he was attacked by an animal or something?"

The woman pursed her lips slightly. For a moment Steph thought she had hit a dead end, but her face then broke into a sad sigh.

"The Tierney boy, Nathan," the woman said. "Was found

dead a few weeks ago, but supposedly, when they found his body it had been attacked by an animal – the poor wee lad."

"That's terrible," Steph tutted.

"Oh, it's awful," the woman continued. "I don't know the Tierneys personally, but you can only feel for them. Apparently, he had run off after an argument. They had no idea he was even missing until they checked his room to see whether he had gone to clean his teeth. The next thing you know, the police were everywhere looking for him; the whole village was on alert. It's not usual for something like that to happen here."

Steph could sense that the woman was starting to settle into her role as a storyteller.

"Who found him?"

"Someone walking their dog discovered his body; a complete mess is what they said."

The woman shut her eyes and shook her head slightly to emphasise the terribleness of the event.

"Did the police not find anything?" Steph asked, thinking about all the research she had done into the police's likely theory of events.

"Nothing that made much sense," the woman said before dropping her voice slightly. "They concluded that it was a hunting accident... poaching accident is what was said, I think."

"Poaching?"

"They suspect someone was out hunting deer, using dogs – some still do practice it I suppose – and the dogs got ahead, sensed the boy's movements and just saw red, as if some instinct kicked in. I don't believe it."

"You don't?" Steph frowned.

"No... usually hunting dogs are very well-trained. Unless

it was some gypsy who didn't know his elbow from his arse, hunting dogs are usually well-trained and wouldn't go after a boy. I'm sure one could train their dogs to hunt someone, but who would be loitering in the woods with his dogs on the off-chance there is a young boy to hunt? That wouldn't make sense either."

Steph had little knowledge of how a hunting dog was trained or what sort of people even kept hunting dogs these days. However, she supposed the woman was right; it was unlikely that a dog was the culprit.

"Of course," the woman continued, causing Steph to look up, "it all happened not too far from the fence."

"The fence?"

"It's what we call it. A large stretch of fence marks the land owned by some billionaire. It's electric too! As if even the thought of people crossing his land is too much to bear thinking about, even though he has miles and miles of it!"

"A billionaire owns that tract of land? But I thought it would belong to the people; a national park or something similar?" Steph asked, swirling her drink. She already knew some of this, but it was good to get the local perspective.

"Bought it from the government somehow. Must have given some politician some amount of money to make it worth their while. It was never a national park, but it was as good as. Now you can't cross it. Like a bloody military base!"

"Who owns it?" Steph asked. This she had little idea of.

The woman turned towards the two old men by the fire.

"Jock!"

"What can I do for you?" one of the men asked, turning to reveal a thinning head of hair and a warm smile.

"Who is it that people think owns the fenced-in land?" the woman asked.

18

"Ah, people think it's that business chap who owns all those technology companies," Jock replied, looking to his friend who nodded. "The one who had that allegation made against him and then went off the radar. That's what they say, anyway."

"Do people not know for sure?" Steph asked, turning to Jock.

Jock shook his head. "Nobody has seen him, dear, apart from one man and his dog which is probably where the rumour came from that it's the technology man."

Technology man? Steph mulled this over in her head.

"How long ago was this allegation against the guy they think it is?" Steph asked.

Jock turned to consult his friend in a lowered voice before turning back.

"Must be around the turn of the millennium. Just before or just after; I can't remember which. Something to do with a young girl and some cocaine or something along those lines. You know what these rich types are like. Didn't like the media attention so went missing. Now it's possible he is hiding out here where nobody gives a shit about his Hollywood antics."

Steph thanked Jock and finished her gin. She thought about having another but decided instead to have an evening stroll before going back to bed for an early night. She was still tired.

It was dark as Steph explored the streets and studied the looming hills that surrounded the village. They were nothing more than large shadows in the night.

It was funny the perception most people had as to what went on in Hollywood. Or, even more amusing, the assumption that any American with money must have something to do with Hollywood and not Silicon Valley.

Steph suspected she knew the man they were talking about, although the likelihood of him owning a lot of land in the middle of Scotland that he had fenced off from the public seemed somewhat improbable. If it was who she was thinking about, then he had been in the public eye and described as a bit of a dot-com playboy from what she had read somewhere. She was young when he'd been at his most famous so she had no recollection of events that may or may not have been reported by the British media.

Kelvin Handle had been a major name and face in the past as he capitalised on the world's move towards a digital revolution. He had been as big a name as Elon Musk was today. He seemed to show his face everywhere and lived life – or so gossip journalists would have had people believe – like a rockstar nerd. Then it all went wrong. He appeared to be in the middle of an accusation with a seventeen-year-old girl and a spiked drink. There was a court case. The jury found in favour of Kelvin. Although he'd been seen with the girl and it was his house party, enough video evidence proved he'd not been in the same room when the drink had been poured or even drunk. People didn't care about the verdict. Mud stuck. Then he just disappeared from the public eye.

Steph vaguely remembered watching a trashy television show late one night called *Where are they now?* which was as vacuous as it was addictive to watch. Kelvin featured in a segment that went over the case and then went on about how he had disappeared off the face of the earth – journalists couldn't find him, and his companies were either tight-lipped or as in the dark as everyone else. The only evidence for his continued existence was the acquisition of a mixture of other companies from genetics to pharmaceuticals.

Nobody was really interested in him anymore though.

There had been too many new cases of celebrities getting in trouble that were more relevant than some guy from over two decades ago. Even so, Steph could understand his wanting to stay out of the way of journalists, but buying up land in Scotland from the government and fencing it off? That seemed unlikely.

Realising that her feet hurt and that her knees were beginning to knock, Steph called it a night. Once again, her eyes shut as soon as she hit the pillow. Her sleep was glorious. Until three in the morning. Then she lay awake, waiting for morning and cursing her jetlag.

FOUR

After a breakfast at a local café – a classic fried breakfast; something the Americans hadn't quite mastered – Steph decided that she wanted to go and see the location of the boy's death for herself. She needed to explore the area and start asking herself the questions she should as a biologist.

She bought herself some lunch to put in her backpack and began walking in the direction the barwoman had told her about the previous night. It didn't take long to find her way in amongst the trees.

The land was undulating. She was surprised a little kid had persevered with the walk. Even if he hadn't gone that far, it was still tiring work. That said, Steph loved it. It was miles better than being stuck behind some desk waiting to die.

Every so often the trees would clear revealing some wide-open spaces. But at the altitude she was, there were always trees over the next dip or around the next corner of whichever rocky hillock she tried to circumnavigate.

She sat down against the base of a tree and took out her water, notebook and a pen. She sipped the water and then began writing. Her pen first began to jot down the names of surrounding trees: oak and birch. Then she penned potential food sources as well as observations of the size of the land. Could the land support wildlife? Easily. That was the type of thing most of her readers wanted to know.

She had written a whole book on the alleged Alaskan Bigfoot and its supposed activities. The premise of the book orbited around the notion that the area where all the sightings were meant to have occurred could comfortably support a large primate if one was so adapted to the climate. As far as she was concerned, it was not her job to say whether there was or wasn't such a creature, just whether one could survive with the right adaptations. The reader could decide for themselves what they thought.

For herself, Steph started jotting down a list of a few native animals to Scotland: badger, fox, deer and rabbit. It certainly wasn't the African savannah. It wasn't even the American Rockies. Unless the boy had already been dead, there wasn't a native animal that could have caused the damage. A rabid badger might deliver a nasty bite, but it was unlikely to tear a child limb from limb.

In terms of Steph's audience and what they would want to know, could there have been a non-native animal roaming the wooded valleys? There was always the chance of the hunting dogs theory being true, but it seemed unlikely. It would have been rather exceptional.

Steph laughed. The idea of hunting dogs killing a child in Scotland being described as an exceptional case when she was busy trying to investigate the potential of the land to house rare and exotic predators tickled her.

She got up and carried on. As she walked, she took out a printed piece of paper that had one of the media reports of the boy's death. It said that there had been bite marks on the boy as well as clean lacerations on his legs – one of the parts of his body still whole. That also put the dog theory to bed in Steph's mind; a dog was unlikely to cause a clean cut to someone. They lacked the tools. They would bite and tear in a messy way.

Steph had watched wolves bringing down a young bison in Yellowstone once. They had exhausted the thing with their constant biting, ripping and yanking at its flesh until it finally succumbed to the inevitable. Nothing the wolves did could be described as clean though.

To deliver a clean cut, you would have to slash quickly through someone's flesh with something sharp enough not to drag too much. A knife would cut. However, if it had been a knife cut on the boy, the coroner would have identified it straightaway. The boy's death was still reported as being under mysterious circumstances. The police were not claiming murder, but the boy had clearly not dropped dead of his own accord, and yet there were no wild animals sufficiently large enough to bring him down. They were stumped. Steph got it. It would have been quite a thing for any member of the law who wanted to be taken seriously to suggest there could be something else out there. Most people didn't want to be perceived as whack-jobs. They toed the socially acceptable line. The fact that the boy's death fell the wrong side of the line... well, that was just too bad.

Eventually, Steph found what she had been hoping to find: the fence. She walked up towards it and looked left. Then she looked right. She could see no end either way; it just trailed off into the distance or deeper tree coverage.

What really interested Steph was that the woman behind the bar had been right: the fence did have an electric current running through it. However, the wired parts of the fence that had the charge running through and that were buzzing slightly were not on Steph's side of the fence. They were on the inside.

Steph got up close to the fence and peered through it. The inside looked similar enough to the land on the outside. However, there were some notable differences. The tree coverage was thicker on the inside of the fence. Also, the layout of the trees appeared less natural, as if they had been planted.

They were young Steph also noted. Young and yet large enough to create a partial barrier to sight. But for what? Steph strained her eyes to try and focus on a spot which seemed to cut through the trees. Nothing. Not anything of note. Or was there?

Steph was not completely sure but it was possible that she could see a section of metal fencing further back. She could not be certain as it was such a small area she was looking at and then it became engulfed by vegetation again. It could just be branches that at the couple of hundred yards or so were playing tricks on her. But why would they look metallic?

She reached into her bag and pulled out her binoculars. She put them near the wire fence in one of the gaps and then tilted them before looking through one-half of them with her right eye and shutting her left as if she were using them like a telescope.

Through the magnified sight it looked even more like a section of fencing. Two fences? Why? And how come the people at the hotel said nothing about it last night? Did they even know? Perhaps not. It was not exactly obvious. You'd almost have to be looking for it to find it.

It was odd. Having an electric current on the inside of a fence suggested keeping something in rather than out. Having a second fence suggested you *really* wanted to keep something in. Steph had seen things before that were vaguely similar, especially around military bases, but nothing quite like this.

She looked around to see how she might be able to get over the fence. There had to be a tree she could climb to jump over. It was not as if the fence was a ridiculous height; maybe eight or nine feet. It would not be the most comfortable drop-down, but even a rolled ankle would probably be worth it.

As Steph walked along its perimeter, she noticed no obvious

tree from which she could launch a scaling of the fence. It was frustrating. Could she go under it? Not without a spade. She was sure that someone must have gone over the fence before. There had to be someone who had been curious enough to try it. Perhaps it was worth asking the woman at the bar again. It was Friday so Steph suspected there might be a few more people looking for a drink and open to a conversation.

Steph began studying the gap between the outer fence and where she presumed the inner fence must run – she had lost sight of it as she walked, allowing it to be swallowed by the vegetation once more. She sighed. There was something definitely worth pursuing about this fencing. Just the double fence alone would spark an interest in her niche audience.

The light was starting to fade slightly as dark clouds gathered above. Steph looked at her watch. It was too early for the light to be fading which suggested rain was likely on its way. She was about to turn away from the fence when something caught her eye. Something didn't look quite right in one of the trees. It was as if there was a knot showing on the trunk where there shouldn't be one. Maybe a slight deformity in the bark? Steph strained her eyes. They yielded nothing. She took out her binoculars and peered through using only her right eye once more. She blinked. She lowered the binoculars and then raised them again. Steph snorted at what she saw.

In the tree was, when observed carefully enough, the unmistakable outline of a lens. It was true that people put up camera traps in forests to observe wildlife – Steph had used this method enough times herself – but they were rarely so well hidden. This one looked as it if was in the tree itself. It was only on closer inspection that Steph realised a fake bark had been placed around the exterior to blend it in with the tree even more. That certainly explained the mildly deformed look.

Questions. This first small expedition had left Steph with more questions than answers. That was a good thing as far as she was concerned. The worst thing she could have encountered were answers straightaway which would clear things up in a succinct way, But that wouldn't sell any material.

Wincing up at the sky, Steph hauled her bag onto her back and headed off.

FIVE

The hotel bar was busier that evening. Even so, there wasn't much more chatter. Perhaps the pelting rain outside had helped dampen things.

Steph was relieved to see the same woman behind the bar as before. She also noted that Jock's friend was by the fire again as Jock leant against the bar ordering a couple of ales.

"Cheers, Jackie," Steph heard Jock say as he grabbed his drinks and returned to his companion.

Steph sat at the bar and looked around as she waited for Jackie to finish serving a woman. The woman kept turning around to her table to double-check that she had got the order right. Steph rolled her eyes.

A few couples were talking quietly over glasses of wine. Like Jock and his friend, other small groups were enjoying some local ales. In the corner, however, two men seemed slightly apart from everyone else. They had positioned themselves so that they could see the whole room rather than having their backs to people. One of the men looked somewhat weathered but otherwise jovial; a large grin decorated his face as he talked. The other looked surly beneath his heavy black locks that were flecked with the greys a tired life brings. The surly-looking one flicked his eyes up. For a moment, Steph was caught in his gaze until he looked back down into his half-drunk pint.

"Oh, my goodness!"

Steph spun around to see Jackie, the bar lady, staring at her.

"You look as if you've been deep-sea diving!"

"Ah, well, I did get caught a bit in the rain," Steph replied, taking off her sodden jacket and hanging it on a hook under the bar.

"Here!" Jackie thrust a clean tea towel at Steph.

"Thanks," Steph replied, running the towel over her long black hair.

Having given the now-soaked towel back to her host and been given a whiskey – Jackie assured Steph that it would warm her more than gin – Steph began to open up her line of questioning once more.

"I'd heard someone say they thought there were two fences," Jackie replied after serving a man who kept looking at his watch, then the window and then his watch again. "But I didn't really pay much attention to it. Just seems like one of those things that isn't really true. Why would someone need two fences?"

That was what Steph wanted to know.

"And it is electrified on the inside. Do people know why or...?"

"I can't say *I* do. I'm not really one for rambling too far off the beaten track if you get my meaning."

Steph sighed as Jackie set about making more drinks.

A moment later, Jackie put a tray on the bar with two ales and a whiskey. Steph looked puzzled.

"Take this over to Jock and Harry; they enjoy a ramble."

"But there are three drinks?"

"The whiskey is for you; you still look blue, and I'd rather not have you coming down with pneumonia."

Steph smiled. She was not a whiskey drinker. She'd forced the first one down. Even so, she was not going to look a gift horse in the mouth. She carried the tray over to Jock and Harry, who proceeded to fuss over pulling up another chair and seating her between the two of them.

Jock was all too delighted to divulge everything he *knew* about the fencing and the land within. Some of it was first-hand information, but much was second-hand blended with his and Harry's conjecture. Even so, it gave Steph something to chew over.

It appeared there had been a small handful who had braved getting past the fence – Jock seemed unsure on whether the second fence existed, and Steph decided to keep her own knowledge to herself – but the outcome was mixed. One was never seen again. Another two claimed there was nothing really in there but some wildlife project and a man wanting a bit of privacy.

"There must be housing inside, as there are a few people who work there," Harry said. "Also things get delivered there. I've seen the trucks."

"Work there?" Steph frowned.

"Of course!" Jock snorted. "It's a bloody great piece of land. It will need tending to in some way, especially if some rich bugger lives there. They always need people looking after them."

Steph nodded thoughtfully.

"Do you personally know anyone who works there?"

Jock shook his head.

"Not on a personal level. But I recognise the faces. Like those two in the corner for example."

Jock then nodded over Steph's shoulder. She turned to see the two men in the corner she had clocked earlier. The surly one noticed her looking again and held her gaze until she turned away.

Steph tried to ascertain from Jock and his friend exactly what they thought the two men did, but neither man seemed certain. They kept themselves to themselves. They weren't oblivious to the locals' dislike of the freedom of the land being taken from them – dislike from those old enough to remember the fencing not being there. They didn't need to get involved in the dislike.

Jock and Harry's thoughts on their jobs ranged from tree surgeons to general handymen. Essentially, Steph gained very little in that department from them.

Jock and Harry finished their drinks, and Steph accompanied them towards the bar as they headed to the exit and their wives who would be "likely to take away their drinking privileges if they were too late". It was only nine.

"Well?" asked Jackie.

"They knew a bit."

"Thought they might," Jackie smiled. "Hey, you haven't drunk your drink! Come on. Your body will thank you for it."

Steph grimaced as she put the peaty liquid to her lips. It was then that she realised the two men from the corner were leaving. The slightly older one smiled at her as he walked past, whilst the other, despite his earlier looks, ignored her as he left. Steph considered following them, but the rain was still hammering outside, and she had rather little thought about what she would achieve by following them then.

"Do you know anything about those two?" Steph asked.

"Which two?"

"The two that just left. The older-looking one with the smile and the other who looks like he doesn't know what a smile is."

"Ah, those two. Not really. I know they both work on the land on the other side of the fence, but everything they do seems to be a secret. That or it's really as boring as they make out it is."

"What do you mean?"

"Well, on the odd occasion I have spoken to them, they just claim that they look after the land. Just like any forestry commission. They don't come here often so it's hard to strike up any sort of relationship."

"Do you believe them?"

Jackie shrugged.

"They haven't really given me a reason not to. People tried to ask them about the death of the boy though. They seemed as upset as anyone else but were as full of questions themselves about it all. That was probably the most I have heard them talk to me in actual fact. They didn't know anything themselves though and it was not like I knew anything, so it was hardly a conversation destined to go anywhere."

Steph nodded again and, her mind distracted, sipped her whiskey. She took too big a sip and coughed. Jackie laughed.

"So where do they get in?" Steph asked.

"What do you mean?" Jackie frowned.

"To the fenced-off area. There must be some sort of gate or entrance or something."

"Oh, I see what you mean. There is meant to be some sort of gate thing – I am only going on what others have said – about five miles from here. If you take the main road south out of the village, you will see a road to your right after a few minutes of driving. It has no signs or anything because it just leads to the gate, or so people tell me. I obviously pass the road if I drive out, but I've never bothered going down it. Others have though. Curiosity and all that. They say they always get turned away at the gate."

"What kind of gate."

"Some big metal security gate with cameras and whatnot, where deliveries come in and out."

"Deliveries?"

Jackie laughed.

"Yes, deliveries! I'm not sure people that live in there go and sweep their local supermarket for their weekly shop."

Steph nodded. That made sense at least. Although much of what she had gathered so far did not make sense. Even the stuff that did, did not really join together in any succinct way.

She decided that she had two potential options going forward. She could get someone to drive her out to the gate to investigate it. Or she could find some way of getting past the fence. One way would see her definitely turned away. The other could see her done for trespassing as well as, in a roundabout way, turned away. She knocked back her whiskey and sucked it in between her teeth. She was getting the hang of this drink.

SIX

It had been a straightforward decision for Steph. It had not been easy to eventually find a tree that was simple enough to climb whilst also overhanging a section of the fence. However, she didn't have the threat of rain rushing her this time.

A bit of vomit jolted itself up her oesophagus as she landed with a thud.

A damp spot engulfed Steph's knee as she rose from the ground. Slowly she began walking forward, speeding up a little only when she was satisfied that she was moving freely and that the fall had done no damage.

She pushed past bushes and rounded trees until she could see what she had been looking for. Ahead of her was the second fence, but beyond it?

Steph made her way closer. She was not sure what she expected to see exactly but her heart was beating faster all the same. She could see that this fence also had an electric current running along the inside although it had a barbed, backward overhang. Someone really didn't want whatever was inside the fencing to get out. Not that Steph assumed they wanted anyone to come in either, but the work had definitely gone into keeping something in.

The trees rustled gently overhead as Steph approached the fencing. She tried her best to quieten her breathing, holding her breath in an attempt to calm it. All she achieved was a more acute awareness of her beating heart. She stood and stared through the mesh. Nothing.

Frustrated, she grabbed her binoculars and looked through them once again. Still nothing. Her heartbeat was calming naturally. The anti-climax was the perfect remedy.

She pondered what to do. There were plenty of trees but none that would help her climb over the barbed overhang. Mathematically speaking, she suspected there was a good chance, out of the thousands that littered the landscape, that there was a suitable tree that could get her over; but how far would she have to walk to find it? There were miles of fencing, and how long would she really be afforded between the fences before she stumbled across a camera? Now she thought about it, how long would it take her to find a tree that could take her back over the first fence? She put that thought to the back of her mind for the time being. One issue at a time.

She decided to set up camp where she was until a better idea came. Perhaps there would be something to observe close to the fence?

A large protruding tree root offered her some elevation from the ground as she sat waiting. She sighed. Then listened. Listened to the sound of the forest: the birds, the wind and tiny rustlings.

Having chosen to sit and wait, she became acutely aware of how sour her stomach felt. She was a rubbish drinker. She always had been. Two-day hangovers were not uncommon for her on the rare occasion she let herself unwind. She knew she wouldn't actually vomit, but that also meant that she knew she would have no sudden release of the acidic feeling in her stomach. It would go when it was ready and not before.

A loud rustling caused Steph to snap her head up. But which side of the fence had it come from? The inside of the fence. No. Yes. Two sounds? The dominant noise was coming from her side of the fence. It was getting louder, the unmistakable whirr of wheels on dirt. But the first noise?

Steph looked up in the direction of the wheels and then back to the fence. A herd of deer erupted from the undergrowth and leapt their way frantically along the fence line. At the same time, a couple of quad bikes burst over a small ridge and between two trees to Steph's right.

Part of Steph had hoped for this. She had wanted to be found. Although their timing was unfortunate. She spun her head back towards the deer who were darting back deeper into the trees. Something had spooked them. The way they were moving showed signs of panic.

The soft engine sound pulled up beside her. Steph didn't look. She didn't want to take her eyes away from what was going on behind the fence.

"You can't be here!" a voice announced. Steph ignored it. She took a step forward, craning her neck. Everything was happening faster than she could process.

"I said..."

Steph spun around to glare at the man, intent on telling him to shut his fucking mouth. She was caught off-guard when she recognised the face. It was the surly-looking man from the hotel bar.

Steph was about to say something when the sound of something heavy crashing through the vegetation made her spin around once more. She was just in time to catch a glimpse of something large and almost grey-looking plummet back below the surface of the treeline. She only managed to glimpse the back end of it, but it was enough to fire her curiosity.

"What was that?" Steph asked the man on the quad bike.

The man pressed a button on his quad bike and sat up straighter. His companion, who Steph now noticed was the more amenable-looking of the pair from last night, did the same.

"Nothing, just some deer," the man replied, wiping a clod of dirt from just below his left eye.

"No, the deer were ahead, I saw them. That was something else!"

"It was a straggler."

"Deer don't tend to thud over the ground like that, do they?" Steph snapped with a sneer.

Running a hand through his hair, the man growled to himself, "For fuck's sake!" He then turned to his older companion who laughed at him and shrugged.

"Well, Davey, it's been a while since we had to bring one in," the man chuckled.

Steph watched in confusion as Davey bared his teeth to himself in frustration.

"If we had set the system up that I wanted, we wouldn't be too late for these kinds of things!" Davey barked.

"True," the other man shrugged. "But it would mean more people, and you know how the boss feels about all that." The happier-looking man then put a finger to his lips in a hushing motion. He laughed to himself and repeated the action in the direction of Steph. Steph looked on bemused.

"Fine," Davey sighed. "Get on!"

"Are you talking to me?" Steph asked, folding her arms, intent on holding her ground against... well, whatever she was holding it against. She wasn't quite sure.

"You!" Davey nodded sharply.

"I'm not going anywhere!"

"You bloody are!"

"I bloody well am not!"

Davey rolled his eyes and took a deep breath. Steph could see that the older man was finding the whole thing quite amusing. This annoyed Steph.

"Look!" Davey said through gritted teeth. "Either you get on and we escort you back or we call the police and have you done for trespassing."

Steph considered this for a second.

"What do you mean 'back'?"

"I mean back to the office."

"Office?" the older man laughed. "Office?"

"Well, Michael, what do you call it then?" Davey asked.

"I dunno... back to base?" Michael shrugged.

"What?" Davey smiled – this was the first and one of the rare occasions Steph would see him smile. "We aren't a bleeding army camp!"

"Could have fooled me!" Steph put in.

Davey turned on her. Steph raised her eyebrows. She'd have loved for him to have a comeback. That said, she was not letting herself become completely absorbed by the flow of idle talk. She was somewhat curious as to why she had been offered a choice between the police and going back to their... whatever they decided it was. Didn't they want to contact the police? Steph suspected not. Also having a chance to see a little more – she assumed that was what they were affording her, even if inadvertently – was too good an opportunity to miss. Not that they would know that.

"What would happen if I went with you?" Steph asked.

"That's up to the boss," Davey replied. "Probably reward you for your invasive curiosity rather than having you dealt with by the law like you deserve!"

Frowning, Steph decided to go and sit behind Michael. Davey muttered something under his breath that Steph could not quite catch. Michael was really laughing now.

"Some men know how to get the girl! Stick with me, Davey

boy, you might learn a thing or two!"

Steph held on, slightly concerned she didn't have a helmet. What had been running after the deer? It certainly hadn't been a straggler. And why was Davey such a miserable prick?

SEVEN

The quad bikes, much to Steph's annoyance, made their way to a secure-looking gate in the outer fence. An electric fob unlocked it, and they were soon on their way skirting around the outside fence. They continued to cover ground that Steph had yet to explore and – after what must have been fifteen minutes – arrived in a small clearing near the fence. There, Davey took his fob out again and pressed a button. To Steph's astonishment, the ground seemed to open ahead of them.

Steph couldn't help but be impressed. The opening had been so well camouflaged and the dirt, plants and dead leaves seemed to move with the door as if they were part of it. The men drove their quad bikes straight into the hole in the ground to reveal a well-lit tunnel. Steph looked over her shoulder and the daylight disappeared on her, behind its iron curtains.

They were not in the tunnel long before daylight at the other end began to make itself apparent. Davey slowed his bike at this point but left enough power running through the wheels to zip up the slope leading back into the world before stopping. Michael stopped behind him. A small square area of fencing surrounded the opening with a gate at one end. Davey pressed his fob again and the gate opened.

From there the small convoy followed a barely visible track through the trees. It was unclear where they were going until a large building loomed into sight. From what Steph could see, the building was a modern-looking house. A mansion really. It had tall glass windows fronting it and the type of timber cladding one would expect to see in one of those property shows where a couple with too much money tried to carve out whatever design was in their head.

It was odd. The place didn't seem right. It didn't fit with what was going on around it. The place looked, from the outside, like it should be a large family home in some equally large open space for some even larger-headed investment banker. Instead, it was surrounded by trees and ringed by another electrified fence. Once more Davey pressed a fob and they were inside the 'compound' as Michael would later call it.

If the location of the building seemed out of place to Steph, the inside did little to alleviate the oddness of it all. Steph walked into what she expected to be a grand hallway leading perhaps to one of those sweeping staircases that she used to see in the films her mother would watch incessantly. Instead, what she walked into was open plan, awash with the colour white and dotted with numerous green palms in large black pots. There was something clinical about it all, only broken by the varnished wooden pine that was spattered around the place like an afterthought.

In one direction, Steph could see a small cluster of computers, but nobody working on them. In another, she could see what looked like a large lounge area with an oversized television. There was a staircase, but it lacked the grandeur Steph had anticipated, its glass sides leading to a floor that wasn't visible from the ground level. Behind the staircase were two grand pine doors fitted with large glass windows. It was through one of those doors that Davey and Michael led her.

"What is this place exactly?" Steph asked.

Davey sighed.

"No doubt you'll find out; he always enjoys showing off."

"Understandable," Michael shrugged, nodding to a young-looking man holding a turquoise book with a golden sabre-toothed tiger on it.

"Who's *he*?" Steph asked, trying to look through the window of another door.

Davey ignored her. So did Michael. At least he didn't scowl about it.

The corridor ended by the doors to a small elevator. Michael leant forward and pressed a glowing blue button. The glass doors to the elevator opened and Davey ushered Steph inside. It was a cramped space and Steph noticed for the first time the mild body odour coming from the two men. She wasn't subtle in wrinkling her nose which caught the attention of Michael, who sniffed his armpit and winced slightly. Davey shook his head and muttered something unintelligible under his breath.

The door pinged open almost no sooner than the machine had started moving. Steph followed the two men down a well-lit concrete corridor. The concrete had been polished – it was on the floor and walls. It was different from the upstairs yet still retained that clinical feeling.

The walk stopped outside a heavy-looking wooden door with a large chrome handle. Davey took a deep breath before opening it. Steph found this odd but noticed that Michael found it mildly amusing, a smile cracking across his face. Everything seemed to amuse him. The door opened.

"Mr Handle!" Davey said, grabbing Steph by the wrist and walking into the room. "Your latest trespasser!"

Steph wrenched her wrist free and walked into a well-lit room. The walls were of the same polished concrete as the hallway, but there were bits of varnished pine furniture dotted around as well as a large desk at the end of the room under a giant skylight, which had soil scattered around the edges. Behind the desk, a man with a slightly receding hairline looked up. He frowned at first, his blue eyes analysing what was before him. Without warning, his frown lines vanished as he finished his analysis and settled on a course of action with which to proceed. He smiled. There was something off about the smile. Steph could not quite put her finger on it, but it was almost as if someone had told him when someone might smile and what it might look like, but he had never felt a genuine need to smile himself. That was Steph's take on it.

"At least this one is better looking," the man said, walking out from behind his desk. "Although is 'trespasser' the right word? Shouldn't we commend curiosity? It is how we develop as a species after all."

Steph watched Davey give a curt nod. He seemed somewhat more rigid in the presence of his boss, which was interesting as Steph would not have described him as being loose before. Michael still had his relaxed air about him. His hands were in the pockets of his green fleece gilet.

"So," Mr Handle said, turning on Steph, his smile lessening if not disappearing. "What brings you to my attention?"

"Because your goons brought me here," Steph shrugged, looking around the room.

Michael burst out laughing.

"I am not sure these two are really goon material," Mr Handle laughed. "What I meant was, what were you doing to make them think I needed to see you?"

Steph thought about it for a moment. There were a number of ways she could reply. Continuing to be obstinate in her replies was probably not likely to get her what she wanted. What exactly she wanted she wasn't sure. She just needed to know more. She would never be told everything; that was to be expected. She just needed someone to slip enough for her to have a ledge to leap from. She needed to feel she could reach a conclusion at some point. Readers always wanted closure. Often they would interpret their own closure, but that was their business.

"Well, Mr Handle…"

"Call me Kelvin!"

"Well, Kelvin, I suppose it was because I was hovering somewhere between your two fences on land which, according to – I believe he's called Davey? – I was not meant to be on. Obviously, I realise I climbed a fence – a tree to be precise – to get there, so I knew that I might not be welcome exactly. I just wasn't sure how unwelcome visitors were."

"There was an electric fence!" Davey snorted. "So very unwelcome!"

Steph ignored him although she could see that Kelvin Handle's smile had disappeared completely now. Instead, his face was one of pure focus, as if Steph were the only interesting thing in the room.

"However, when I was between the fences, I noticed something that drew my attention."

"Go on," said Kelvin, folding his arms and leaning back to perch on the edge of his desk.

"A herd of deer bounded by your inner fence – clearly spooked – and were chased by something that… well, something that I couldn't quite put my finger on," Steph said, keeping her voice balanced. "As a field biologist, I…"

"A field biologist?" Kelvin said, standing up again. Steph nodded but was unsure whether to continue. She sensed a mild change in the atmosphere of the room. Kelvin looked at Davey and Michael. There was an energy about him now despite his lack of movement. He had opened his arms up slightly and his eyes had widened. Steph turned her attention to the other two men, seeing Michael shrug and Davey frown even deeper – if that were possible.

Kelvin then looked mildly exasperated that Davey seemed unable to read his gesture which must have contained a whole dialogue somewhere in its subtly animated depths. He widened his eyes further and flicked his head at Steph and then up to his skylight. It clicked.

"What?" Davey spat. "No! Surely not! It's not ready!"

"Nothing is ever ready!" Kelvin replied. "There is never a perfect time for anything in the world. It is not how life works!"

"But there is a less perfect time!"

Although Steph felt she could read the room, she still had no idea what they were going on about. She chose silence as her means of interrogation.

"That's why I have made a lot of money and you, as much as I respect you, Davey, have not," Kelvin smiled. "Sometimes you can strike when the iron is hot, sometimes you just have to strike, see what happens to the pieces and then adapt as necessary."

Seemingly satisfied with his own wisdom, Kelvin strode back to the door.

"Shall we?" he said, pulling the door open.

"Never a dull moment." Michael winked at Steph.

Despite herself, Steph was quite enjoying it all. Nothing made sense exactly but then she had never expected it to. That was all right. That made for a better story in the long run. She may have been a field biologist and sought truth, but she was not so disillusioned to think that her money didn't come directly from an interesting story. A child being ripped apart was her hook. How it happened was the ending. How she discovered how it happened would be the middle. To have Kelvin Handle thrown into the mix was essentially another zero or two on her sales figures... as long as lawyers could do their jobs.

EIGHT

Kelvin navigated the party through the small warren of underground hallways. The property appeared far larger than the naked eye could anticipate by looking at the building on the surface. They walked fast. Everything about Kelvin seemed to be done at speed. His choice of clothing said as much, although jeans and a black jumper did not scream serious businessman. However, if this was the same Kelvin Handle that Steph assumed him to be, then he was indeed a very serious businessman. Perhaps that was why he was successful; he possessed an almost careless manic energy.

"I know what you're thinking!" Kelvin called over his shoulder.

"You do?" Steph asked, suddenly thinking she would have to admit her curiosity about his sudden disappearance from the Silicon Valley limelight.

"How did I manage to get so much work pushed through under the ground without people knowing? Money mostly. Keeps people quiet when you need them to and makes them work faster too. I got the idea from those London townhouses. Have you seen them?"

"No?"

"Fucking expensive things but finite in space up top. You must be wealthy to own one, but you don't really have enough space to show off! So what do you do? You dig down. That's what they've done but you wouldn't know it. Now these old buildings which look so fitting to the street are nothing more than fancy top hats for underground lairs that house swimming pools, bowling alleys, cinemas, etcetera, etcetera."

"And weren't there issues with neighbouring houses falling down?" Davey added, pushing Steph forward slightly when she tried to slow her walk to look through a window to a door.

"Luckily I don't have that problem!" Kelvin snapped.

The walk ended with their going through an automatic door which led to a room with numerous screens. Some showed camera images. Some showed red dots on maps. Others showed numbers which meant nothing to Steph but seemed to have meaning to Kelvin who studied them on arrival.

Satisfied with what he saw, Kelvin brought Steph to a table in the middle of the room. The table was a map of sorts. The type of thing one would expect to see at a property developer's building site displaying all the new properties and their location. This one showed mostly forest. There were undulating areas of relief, a river, the odd hut – or what looked as such to Steph – and the main house. Most notable was the double fencing.

"I realise it is a little old-fashioned, but it helps me build a picture," Kelvin said, not even looking at Steph. "Sure, I use technology too, but sometimes something simple helps shape something more complicated."

"More complicated than you think!" Davey muttered.

"Tell me, why do I employ you and your negativity?"

"Because I'm good at my job!"

Kelvin shrugged. And went back to looking at the diorama before him.

He snapped his head around and asked Michael, "What impact are the beavers having?"

"Minimal!" came the reply. "Too early to tell."

"Heading in the direction you expected though?"

"For now, but that could deviate off at any angle at this point."

"We can adapt," Michael said, frowning at a screen labelled X that showed nothing but a rocky slope covered with trees and dirt. A small plateau disrupted the slope partway up.

Kelvin waved a dismissive hand in Michael's direction.

Realising that Kelvin had become distracted, Steph said, "Why exactly am I here? I mean, are you going to warn me away or... I'm not really sure what is going on at all, to be honest."

Kelvin looked at her. His eyes scanned once more and then settled on a facial expression based on his analysis. He curled his lip slightly.

"I very much doubt that you don't know what is going on 'at all'. I am sure you have some sort of ballpark idea about what is happening here. Some of it might be right and some of it might not be."

"That still doesn't answer my question," Steph said, folding her arms.

"No, it doesn't, does it?"

Steph mindlessly grabbed at her upper left arm. Kelvin narrowed his eyes a little.

"Essentially, Stephanie, I know that you are from America – well, America-based – and your line of work often involves solving natural or supernatural mysteries using logic. Sometimes you will leave the answer up to interpretation, but I would assume that's mostly just a smart business decision. Something has brought you over here from the USA and I doubt it is a visit to your parents in Sheffield, followed by a scenic jaunt into Scotland. I suspect, although I cannot be certain, that it has something to do with the boy who died on the outskirts of the land my little project occupies. That seems to be the story that leaked more than others. Furthermore, two of my employees picked you up at the very moment you saw something chasing a herd of deer. I am sure they gave you some sort of semi-plausible story to explain what you thought you saw, and that is fine for the average onlooker. But you are not the average onlooker. That, in short, brings me to why you are here. Although I must admit, I didn't realise you were a qualified field biologist. I'm not sure how I missed that."

Steph's mind whirred. She could vaguely make out the sound of Davey letting out a growling sigh, but otherwise, her head was reeling. How did he know so much? Most of Steph's thoughts revolved around self-preservation. She was not sure they needed to, but neither did she feel safe. However, a modicum of rational thought hung onto 'the story that leaked more'.

"Why do you know so much about me? How?"

"I made my money in the tech industry," Kelvin shrugged. "When people say you leave a digital footprint, they mean it. More so for anyone who tries to market themselves online. It really is not as impressive as it seems; you'd be surprised – and potentially worried judging from your naivety of it all – at how easily the most ordinary of people can track down your basic information. And the speed at which it can be done."

He then crossed his arms again, biting his lower lip. "By the way, I realise that stories about myself are well-circulated – or at least they were – but they are not true. Not that it matters. People seem to care little for truth, which is why they can be vulnerable to manipulation by the media. Unfortunately, I was just on the wrong end of one of those distortions. It's why I stepped away from the light, as it were. Well, that and I grew up I suppose. At some point, you must stop partying and focus."

"And... and what do you know about the death of the boy?" Steph asked, deciding to battle her curiosity about Kelvin and stick to her task at hand.

Kelvin sighed. Steph noted how Michael had lost interest in the conversation completely and was looking at the various screens whilst Davey eyed Steph almost unblinkingly.

"That genuinely had nothing to do with what goes on here – as far as I am aware," Kelvin replied.

Steph waited, expecting more, but Kelvin seemed to have nothing more to say on the matter. Or nothing more he wanted to say.

"And what does go on here?" Steph asked. She'd skirt back to the boy later.

Now Kelvin's eyes lit up.

"Something wonderful!"

NINE

Kelvin had Steph sitting on one of the sofas in the main house. Five clipboards with papers faced her. Davey and Michael had been replaced by the young-looking man in jeans and a shirt – the same she had passed earlier – who sat next to her. A woman in her late thirties/early forties with long curly hair tied up in a knot sat next to Kelvin. She looked as if she'd been chewing lemons. There had been no formal introductions, which Steph found odd, however, she suspected that had something to do with the clipboards and content on them.

There was a small pause in proceedings as Kelvin checked through the clipboards. Steph took that moment to take stock. She had allowed herself to get wrapped up in the rapidly changing pace of things, terrified that if she slowed, she would miss out on some sort of lead to her investigation or the gap in a closing door. Now she had a moment to really think about it, she had moved recklessly fast. She had gone from trying to piece together some unfortunate story with vague word-of-mouth evidence, to being somewhere which was... well, what was it? With what had happened near the fence and the stories she had heard it was downright suspicious. And then there was Kelvin Handle! Journalists everywhere would give their left leg to be in her position – his story alone would bring in some game-changing money – and yet he was not even the most important thing to her.

"So," Kelvin began, satisfied with what he had scanned. "I said I would explain things, but before I do, I have some conditions."

"What do you mean?" Steph asked.

"You're not the first to get over the fence or see something that would raise suspicion. I cannot have things coming out until I am ready. I fully intend for things to come out – I think we're doing something truly wonderful here otherwise I wouldn't be putting my money behind it – but not until it is ready and *people* are ready."

Steph's stomach churned a little.

"So what happens to those people?"

Kelvin furrowed his eyes and snarled slightly before saying, "I give them money!" Amused at his own joke, he leant back and laughed. "That way I keep their silence. Everyone wins."

"And if they talk?"

"Ah, well. In that case, my lawyers will destroy them. And, of course, I stop paying them a monthly income. The turning off of the money tap is probably a bigger deterrent than the lawyers. It shouldn't be; my lawyers are vicious. However, I have never had to do that."

"But what about family members and things like that? Surely you cannot guarantee complete silence?"

"Money, I find, does a lot in this world," Kelvin replied. He looked out the window at this point, frowning slightly. "Besides, people often find they are excellent liars when they desperately need to be. Furthermore, most people who have the time to break into my grounds, do not tend to have children... or partners to blab to. Only one of them did, as I recall. Some journalist. I paid him and, so far, he has stayed silent. Had he not seen what he did, I might not have needed to pay him, but... he did."

"Just like I saw something?"

"Sort of. I am not sure that you're actually sure of what you saw," Kelvin replied. "Even so, this brings us here!"

He gestured at the clipboards.

The middle-aged woman snorted and looked around the room. Kelvin looked at her and shook his head slightly but carried on.

"First of all, let me begin by giving you the information I can provide without using the clipboards. We are working on a project to do with our relationship with nature. That's the official line."

"Right?" Steph replied. She wondered whether she would have a chance to subtly press record on her phone. She suspected not. This was not some plot-hole-riddled television show. She would be seen.

"Well, that is where I end for now," Kelvin said, sitting back.

"What?" Steph snapped. "Look, I don't know what kind of game you're playing here but…"

"But it is one that I cannot continue to play with you unless you agree to sign some documents," Kelvin interrupted.

Steph wondered what she had gotten herself into. Technically nothing, by the sounds of it. Not until she signed something.

"I don't sign things I haven't read!" Steph replied. Completely untrue. She had often argued with her father about being too busy to read the fine print on documents or the terms for downloading software.

"Essentially, I have provided you with five options," Kelvin said. "Depending on your degree of wanting to know things. Each one will require a certain amount of time from you whilst also providing varying degrees of information. I will even allow a predetermined amount of information to be disclosed by you for your own personal use."

"Doesn't that last part go against what you told me just a moment ago?"

"No, it doesn't actually. I will explain that though."

Kelvin then spent the next twenty minutes giving an overview of what each clipboard entailed. All the while, he kept looking at his watch and getting mildly agitated with himself if he slipped over his own words in his rush.

"Why me?" Steph asked. This received a hiss from the irritated-looking woman on the other sofa.

Steph eyed her a moment before continuing, "I mean, did everyone who made it over the fence receive this treatment or..."

"They received similar," Kelvin replied, suddenly checking his phone and flicking through things at a frantic pace. "Well, they were given different options to choose from in terms of keeping quiet, but I had no interest in their skillset."

He stopped and looked up.

"And my skillset?" Steph asked.

"Simple: biologist and thus respectable, but also you have an awareness of how to promote yourself. You aren't lost in your studies, know how to make connections and how people will take things. These skills could be useful to me."

"If you thought that was useful, why didn't you simply hire someone like me in the first place?" Steph asked, leafing through one of the documents.

"Eventually, I probably would have done," Kelvin shrugged. "Possibly even you, who knows? However, opportunities come when they come. Ideally, I would have waited longer, but you're here now so..."

Steph sighed. She knew what she wanted to do. She knew what was best for her career in the field. However, she also knew what was best for her sales. The obstacle to either consideration was time. Then again, when would another opportunity like this come up? Whatever the opportunity was. Kelvin had explained the contracts without explaining what she'd subsequently discover. Steph picked up the second clipboard from the right and signed the necessary papers.

"Good decision!" Kelvin said, standing up.

Steph stood up too. Kelvin grabbed her hand.

"Now I can formally introduce you to Martina Krochev, my head geneticist, and Daniel Pollard, a palaeontologist working under Krochev. What an unusual arrangement!"

With that, Kelvin started to walk out of the room, his phone in hand.

He stopped after a couple of feet, turned and said, "They will explain what you need to know. I need to take care of something pressing. Also I shall have Davey and Michael collect your things for you from the hotel."

"Collect my things?"

"That's right! I am even going to provide accommodation for you!"

Without waiting for an answer, Kelvin strode off. Steph turned to look at, who she assumed she now had to call, her two new colleagues. Daniel shook her hand warmly with calloused hands.

Martina nodded curtly and said, "Follow me."

Steph watched Martina stalk off. Daniel looked apologetic before holding out a supinated hand in the direction of his senior. Chewing her lip, Steph followed.

TEN

Steph was glad to find herself being taken somewhere of real interest. Not that the house itself was not interesting, but now she was getting to the real substance of its existence. She found herself walking through a lab, although this lab seemed to be missing something. There were microscopes, machines, jars with what looked like animal foetuses inside, as well as other bits Steph would expect to see. However, apart from Martina, there were no other scientists.

"Where are the people who work here?" Steph asked.

"I'm here," Martina replied curtly, not breaking her stride.

She ushered Steph through a door at the end of the lab that opened into a small office. Steph stepped inside, followed by Daniel. The young man seemed to take his cues from Martina and waited for her to sit down behind her desk before taking a seat himself. Steph followed his lead.

"Surely, you're not the only one who works in here?"

"Why?" Martina asked. "You think I need help from others?"

"No, it's just that... well, yes. Maybe you do need help as it seems a big operation and..."

Martina scowled until Steph felt her words shrink back down her throat.

"You don't know the first thing about real science."

Steph didn't reply. A small part of her burned with embarrassment. The comment felt too close to home.

"Yes, I have people work for me. Just two – Kelvin likes to

keep a small workforce for now."

"Where are they?"

"One is attending a wedding, and the other has gone to see his dying grandparent," Martina replied. "Not that it is really any of your business!"

Martina continued to glare. Steph gripped her hands together and rolled her thumbs over each other.

"So what exactly is going on and what is my job?"

It was best to get to the point. Martina was clearly not a conversationalist.

Martina leaned back in her chair and exhaled. She seemed to be studying Steph's face with an intensity similar to Kelvin's. Eventually she leant forward and rested her elbows on the table, her hands clasped under her chin.

"I will be blunt with you," Martina began. "I don't have time for games with words or whatever. I don't like that you're here. I think it is too early. I do not think you're needed as it can be sorted in-house. I don't know you so I cannot trust you and..."

Steph opened her mouth to interject but Martina held up a hand and raised her voice slightly.

"...I need trust. We need trust if this is all going to work. Maybe I will learn to trust you, maybe not. That is the way it is. Whatever the case, you are here now, so I will tell you what we are doing and what, I assume, Kelvin wants of you. If you have any questions after that, you can ask Daniel. He is much more... friendly."

Steph had many questions. She looked at Daniel who smiled affably.

"I shall try to be... what's the word again?" Martina said, looking at Daniel. "That one you say I am?"

"Succinct!" Daniel said.

"Yes, that! We are working on a large rewilding experiment. I am sure you have come across countless examples of this. Like when they put wolves back into Yellowstone, for example. Or how they are trying to bring back beavers in England. Anyway, we are trying to do that here by introducing animals that have been native to the land in the past and..."

"What kind of animals?" Steph asked.

"I told you, Daniel will answer questions; I am a busy woman! We are trying to bring back multiple animals at once which is why we need a large patch of land. We are trying to prove that the animals can survive, coexist and be sustainable on the land. Moreover, we need to prove that the animals can live alongside people, even the predators."

At this, Martina paused to examine Steph's reaction. Steph was not quite sure what her face said, but it was enough to make Martina smile slightly before she continued.

"We have some people living on the grounds with these animals. However, that is not all."

Martina seemed unable to help herself but smiled now.

"We are also working on something far more impressive! We have been able to bring back some animals which have not exactly been around for a while. Not long extinct, but dead all the same. Many have close relatives; however, we are the first to bring them back successfully."

Every ounce of Steph was dying to ask more. Her throat strained to be released. She could see that Martina was taking great delight in it all. Steph's eyes flicked left towards Daniel who gave a small nod.

"Your job – although I do not see what you can say that we have not already – is to help us establish whether it is all working or not," Martina said. "You will go out, do whatever it is you do that seems to make your opinion more valid than our own and come up with a report for Kelvin. Hopefully, it will say what we want to hear, but if it doesn't, it is no matter as we will get there in the end by doing what is needed to make it all work. If some animals work, great, if they don't, that is how it is."

Martina stood up at that point, satisfied that she had fulfilled her role in Steph's integration into the experiment.

"Now, I have more pressing matters to be seeing to. I shall see you around. Daniel, you can take it from here."

The pair of them watched her stroll out of the room without a backward glance. The door shut. Steph turned to Daniel who shrugged apologetically.

"She's a bit like that," he explained. "She tends to take the fat off anything if you get my meaning. Anyway, I bet you have a thousand questions, but I would venture to ask, would you like me to answer them whilst I give you a tour of the grounds – or at least some of them – or a tour of the rest of the house... facility... thing. Where we are now, might be a better description. It is all a bit how I imagine a high-end modern tech office to look like, except it also has a laboratory and..."

It was pleasing to Steph that Daniel was aware enough to read her facial expression.

"Yes, anyway," he muttered. "Grounds or house... place?"

"Grounds!"

"Good!" Daniel beamed, getting to his feet. "I was hoping you'd say that, as I can explain that better and it is so much more exciting. Probably far more up your street from what I hear too!"

ELEVEN

Daniel took Steph back through the main house and out into a small courtyard filled with basic-looking vehicles. There were a few quad bikes and what looked like a couple of oversized golf buggies that had been given a makeover. Although, Steph suspected they had a little more power than a golf buggy. They were also caged around the outside. It was one of those buggies that Daniel had taken the keys for and was opening when he heard a voice.

"And where do you think you're going?"

Steph turned around to see Michael walking lazily towards them. Daniel growled to himself.

"I was going to show... Steph, is it?" Daniel asked, turning to Steph. Steph nodded. "I was going to show Steph around and answer some of her questions."

"Ah, gave her a job, did he?" Michael replied, rolling his eyes. "I have honestly never seen a recruitment strategy like it. Wait for people to break in and then give them jobs!"

Michael winked at Steph.

"He hired me the normal way!" Daniel protested.

"Did he?" Michael asked.

Daniel paused for a moment.

"Well, sort of. He was sitting in on a guest lecture at my university and liked how I argued with the lecturer despite him being an esteemed palaeontologist and me being a 'wet-behind-the-ears little slug with my head in the clouds'. I think the two concepts are somewhat juxtaposed but... Anyway, we're going out to look around. I'm showing Steph where a few things are."

"Not without me you're not!" Michael said.

Daniel sighed.

"Don't you sigh at me. I didn't make the rule. If you don't like it, take it up with the boss. Anyway. Give me a moment to fetch some tranquillizers and I will be right with you."

Steph watched as Michael wandered back around the house.

"I did speak to Kelvin," Daniel whispered. "He said it was a loose rule. I go out without him all the time anyway. Besides, the rule doesn't make any sense with the cabins. Ah, you look confused. Don't worry, I shall explain that in a bit."

Steph considered the young man for a while. He didn't look like he was long out of university. Whether that was true or not was hard to tell as he had one of those boyish faces. He had seemingly struggled desperately to grow some wispy chin hairs to combat this problem, but if anything, it made it worse. He was wiry-looking, the type of build that suggested that no matter how much food he consumed, he was never going to gain a single pound. Above all, though, he had a kindly face. No wonder he was walked over.

Having returned, Michael sat in the backseat with a rifle over his lap. He assured Steph it only shot darts. Why he felt she needed reassurance on the matter was beyond her.

"So why did Kelvin give me a job?" Steph asked. She was going to test how accurate Martina's assumption was that Daniel would answer her questions.

"He thinks that you will be able to see whether the animals have tried to integrate," Daniel replied over the mild electric hum of the buggy. "He's rather a spontaneous person. Makes snap decisions. Says that's how he made his money in the first place and how he makes more still, so he isn't going to change his habits. I can't comment on that; what I can say is that I think he is trying something bold and exciting. Plus, he's a good boss. Has been to me anyway."

"And what counts as bold and exciting?"

"You'll see," Daniel replied, excitement etched across his face.

"And how does he know I am staying at the hotel?" Steph asked.

"What?" Daniel replied, looking away from the track momentarily.

Michael leant forward. "Because he knows everything; doesn't miss a trick. Davey possibly told him, but otherwise, he has his sources. He is a little like one of those medieval spymasters who has a person in every royal court across the Western world."

Michael sat back. Steph digested this information for a while. It made sense, she supposed. Even so, she did not like the idea of someone going to the hotel to get her things. It felt forced, controlling even.

They travelled through areas of trees as well as open heathland. There were slopes that Daniel made a point of avoiding, claiming that the vehicle would never cope with all of them in it. At one point, they crossed a bridge over a river where Steph could see trout swimming.

"We top up the river with trout from a farm," Daniel said.

"So what other animals do you have here?" Steph asked.

"Loads!" Daniel replied. "All those native plus a pair of beavers – they have just mated successfully. That's a common species to rewild in this country I know. Deer, wolverine, a pack of wolves, moose, a brown bear, a cave bear, a cave lion, and we would love to have mammoth, but it is hard to find a decent specimen where the DNA is useable. Oh and a small herd of European bison."

Steph put her hand on Daniel's arm. He turned as she gestured slowly to stop the buggy, words failing her. Daniel laughed as he gently stepped on the brake.

"How is all that possible?" Steph asked, having gathered herself. "I mean, getting permission for existing animals is one thing but... extinct animals? How is it even possible?"

"Money!" Michael put in, scanning the treeline.

Daniel shrugged then nodded.

"I suppose money does talk when it comes to a lot of things. It is how Kelvin managed to acquire this land as far as I am aware. All above board! Sort of; as far as politicians are concerned."

Steph tried to hide her scepticism.

Daniel pushed on.

"That said, I think it's all rather hush-hush. I think the Scottish government – British for that matter, although they care less – knows there is some sort of rewilding project going on, but not the full extent, even though they have signed documents acknowledging it... or someone has. What they are not aware of is the introduction of more extinct species."

Daniel stopped as if he thought he had covered the main parts. Steph looked at him.

"She probably wants to know about how an extinct species could possibly be alive today," Michael put in, shaking his head at Steph and grinning.

"Oh, right! Well, Martina is the one to ask for the finer details," Daniel said. "However, the gist of it is that they find intact DNA that hasn't been damaged by a thawing-out process. People wait for a specimen that has been frozen perfectly since the last ice age. The best finds are males with their testicles still intact. They then add the DNA to the egg of a close relative and develop a hybrid. The process is repeated until they arrive at a creature closer to the extinct animal. For the cave lion, we used a mountain lion – I know, smaller, but hardier; not that it seems to have prevented its large size. For the bear, they used... well, a grizzly I believe. It's basically just a larger bear. Although to me, it is fascinating."

"His job was meant to help us predict the behaviour of the animals," Michael added, nodding at Daniel. "But it's proving to be like getting a hot tip for the races from a snail."

Daniel frowned, but ignored Michael, instead staring out at the treeline. Steph turned her head to see a mass of shaggy brown fur come loping out from between two trees. Steph saw Michael smile. She studied the animal from afar. It seemed completely disinterested in their presence and sat momentarily on the grass.

"That's not the cave bear, is it?" Steph asked, frowning.

"Nah, the prehistoric version dwarfs that one," Michael said.

"So why do you have other bears here?" Steph asked.

"To try and create a more realistic dynamic," Daniel replied.

Steph scoffed. She saw Daniel roll his eyes as he started the buggy once more.

They drove for maybe another couple of miles; it was hard to tell. There was little that Steph could see in the distance. Everything was up close. They passed a herd of deer who skittered off as the buggy went by. She would have liked to have stayed with the herd. With so many predators about they were surely due an unfortunate amount of attention.

Eventually, Daniel stopped the buggy in the middle of a field scattered with rocks, heather and other plant life that broke up the monotony of the open space. Daniel then pointed to a clump of rocks.

"There!" he whispered.

Steph strained her eyes in the direction Daniel was pointing. She was not quite sure what she was looking at.

"He blends in well," Daniel said when he saw the confusion on Steph's face.

It was at this point that Michael handed Steph his rifle used for tranquillizing animals. Steph took the gun but looked bemused until Michael pointed to the scope at the top and moved Steph's finger away from the trigger. Steph nodded slowly, closed her left eye and raised the scope to her right.

It did little better for her than the naked eye, but at least now she could make out the outline of fur lying on the rock even if she could not yet distinguish the features properly. There seemed to be a patch of fur missing in one place or, at least, the fur seemed thinner.

"Has the lion been fighting?" Steph asked.

"Quite likely," Daniel replied. "It sometimes clashes with the bears. Not the cave bear – I don't think – but the others. None of them have come out on top yet, but they give each other a good bashing."

"Why's that?"

"Well, I dare say that's for you to tell us," Daniel smiled.

Steph considered this for a while. She supposed it was her job. She would be paid well enough from what the contract said; double what she would have normally earned. She assumed her salary would also be scalable as the work progressed. Then there was the matter of the death of the boy. It would be easy to get distracted by this new job which would be the envy of many of her peers. Yet even as she thought of it all, her gut groaned.

"Well, we can't stay here all day," Daniel replied, not taking his eyes from the rocks. "Davey will likely be back soon with your things from the hotel, and I have no doubt you will want to settle into your room."

"I'm still not really sure how I feel about that," Steph said, also not taking her eyes off the rocks. "It feels a little invasive."

Daniel grimaced.

"Kelvin sometimes can be a little like that. Time is very much an entity to him. I guess he assumes the quicker he can get you on-site, the sooner you can get to work."

"But what if I don't want to live on-site?"

"I suppose you could take that up with him; he wouldn't be able to stop you. He would likely just give you incentives to stay. Besides, it's actually pretty good in the house and grounds. I doubt you saw the pool or the other rooms with the gym stuff yet, and... well, I don't use the gym but I'm wicked at table tennis."

"Don't worry," Michael put in, scanning the land around them, "you can still head off to the pub for some alone time. You just aren't allowed to disclose what goes on here. The locals know the drill well enough by now. Gives you an air of mystery. I love it."

"You would!" Daniel said.

Michael laughed and slapped Daniel on the back. Shaking his head with a slight curl to his lip, Daniel started the engine again. The lion raised its head for a moment and then lay back down.

TWELVE

As they headed through a clump of trees, Steph noticed the ground to the side of the track was churned up. There were a number of prints in the muddy pits but one in particular caught her eye.

"You have boar here?" she asked.

Michael leant forward.

"Yep, more than was anticipated from what I can gather. By that I mean, I have been tasked with culling them as the predators aren't keeping their numbers down enough. They seem to find them too much of a pain in the arse to hunt. Make for great pulled pork though."

It was difficult for Steph to get a grasp of everything. If she were to do her job properly, she would need to know more precise numbers of animals, the size of the land where each animal tended to be found and where certain natural resources were.

"To be fair, we thought we had something that would have kept them in line," Daniel added. "It's a shame; I was excited about it."

"About what?" Steph asked, noticing a cabin off to the side of the track. There seemed to be a light on behind the window.

"We tried to bring back an entelodont," Daniel said, flicking his eyes momentarily towards Steph. "Sort of a giant warthog-type creature – vicious bastards."

"That was very black market," Michael put in. Not quite sure how Martina managed to get her hands on something like that and still be able to get DNA from it.

For once, Daniel seemed in agreement.

"Considering the climate of its time and the age of the creature, I can't see how such a specimen could exist," Daniel said, raising his eyebrows. "Even so, I had one to study and now I don't."

"What happened to it?" Steph asked.

"The winter took it I assume. It was not really adapted to survive in Scotland in mid-January."

"Don't you track them?" Steph asked.

"The big animals we do," Michael said. "We chip them. Not that the signal is amazing. It never gives us an accurate reading of where they are. Just a rough generalisation. You'd have thought that Kelvin of all people could afford better technology."

"I suspect he can," Daniel said.

"What do you mean?"

"I mean I think he has made sure that the larger animals cannot be tracked perfectly."

"Why? That makes no sense! He would have told me why. Did he actually say this to you?"

"No, but Martina said something about it acting as insurance."

Michael went quiet at this and sank back into his chair. He muttered something about Martina and Kelvin but too quiet for Steph to hear.

They pulled up to the house to find Davey sitting on an upturned log reading a book. Daniel let Michael and Steph out before parking the buggy back into the charging bay he'd got it from. Michael exchanged a few small words with Davey as he walked past him whilst Steph stood and waited. Davey finished the page he was reading, put a feather between the pages and shut the book.

"I heard you went and collected my things!" Steph said, unable to hide the disapproval in her voice.

"I did," Davey replied.

"You best have not looked through my stuff," she said, folding her arms.

"Why, do you have something to hide?" Davey replied, leaning forward on the log.

"No!"

"Because," Davey continued, "if you're worried about your snooping into the death of the poor little boy being interrupted, you needn't worry about me. I have no interest in it."

Steph swallowed. She scratched the ground slightly with her foot.

"So... so you did go through my stuff?"

"No, I spoke to Jackie at the bar. She said you'd been asking questions about it all," Davey replied, narrowing his eyes.

Steph played with the fabric of her shirt under her folded arms.

"Well, something definitely doesn't add up. I'm not even sure how the police couldn't know about what's going on here. Someone must have put two and two together and worked out that the animal could have come from here."

Davey smiled, took in a deep breath and then stood up.

"The police did come here," he said. "However, let's take a step back; you are assuming a lot of things. Firstly, you are assuming that an animal from here killed the boy. Secondly, you are assuming that the police hadn't thought to come here. Thirdly..."

He stopped and shrugged. "I guess just those two things."

"So they did come here?"

"They did. We showed them that all the animals had been accounted for, they were satisfied with the evidence and went on their way," Davey said, stretching his arms. "It's genuinely tragic that the boy died. I can completely see why people would be suspicious of us despite not knowing what goes on here. Yet, to my knowledge and Kelvin's it genuinely wasn't us. Kelvin even conducted his own investigation after the police."

"Why?"

"Why do you think? You're meant to be the detective!"

"I'm a biologist, not a detective!" Steph snapped. Even so, she bit her lip and looked at the ground. It was Davey's turn to fold his arms; the look on his face suggested he was enjoying himself. Steph found this irritated her more than it should.

She pondered everything she had seen. It had been a long day and she was tired, but the way Davey had spoken made her feel like she was missing something obvious. Something stupidly obvious. A large bird of prey screeched overhead in the fading light, momentarily distracting Steph. Then a thought started to spread.

"He is worried that something is going on that he doesn't know about because he is concerned about the DNA of the specimens getting out," Steph said suddenly, still looking down, pawing the ground with her toe. "He is, from what little I have seen, a man who likes to be in control. The police coming around will have disturbed him. He was worried that it genuinely was one of his animals that got out, although not because he was worried about his enclosure but because he suspected someone let it out."

Steph looked up. Davey clapped slowly.

"Well, more the black-market DNA thing," Davey said, "but I suppose the other stuff fits too. Anyway, follow me."

"Why?" Steph asked, straightening her back.

"Because I assume you want to know where you're sleeping, don't you?"

Steph watched Davey turn without waiting for an answer. He headed towards the entrance. Steph growled to herself, hoping an angry exhale would help her remain level-headed. She needed to keep her wits about her. Too much was going on.. The bird of prey screeched again in the distance.

Davey took her through the house to a corridor lined with oak doors. It still surprised Steph how large the inside of the house was compared with what she could see from the outside. Davey selected one of the doors and opened it, then made a sweeping gesture with his arm and waited. Steph walked past, making sure to hit him with her shoulder as she did so. She didn't apologise and was satisfied to hear Davey tut and walk off.

Steph walked further into the room. It was nice. Modest in size but, with an ensuite, it was comfortable. Like elsewhere, there was a lot of wood finishing, making it feel cosy.

Steph intended to make use of this time to herself to write down what she had seen and gather her ideas, as well as trying to get her head around the fact she was suddenly employed – something her parents would be all too pleased about. Instead, she lay on the bed and promptly fell asleep.

THIRTEEN

When Steph awoke, she found a note under her door: an invitation to breakfast from Daniel. He seemed to have taken it upon himself to help Steph integrate into the house. He gave her another guided tour of the rooms used for living as well as the dining room which was attached to a large kitchen. There was the freedom to cook what you wanted with groceries delivered weekly. There had been a chef, but he had fallen out with Kelvin when he wouldn't let him hunt one of the bison intended to feed the bears and the wolves. It didn't help that he had killed one of the two moose. They were meant to breed. Daniel then admitted he hadn't really come across the other moose for a while either.

It seemed crazy to Steph that such a place, which generated no money, could be kept up and running at such great expense. It was, in her mind, the ultimate vanity project. Not the worst. There had definitely been worse. However, it was the supreme.

Having eaten a small bowl of porridge and drunk half a coffee, Steph made a list of notes: a plan for the day. Then she scribbled half of it out. It would be impossible to do everything she wished. She supposed she should first consider her contract to Kelvin and, secondly, continue to conduct her own business.

The largest part of her, along with Daniel's enthusiasm, wanted to focus on the hybrids, the animals brought back from the ever-distant past. But then she stopped and thought. She scrapped that idea. It was self-indulgent. It made sense first to get a grip on the environment. She needed to go walking.

Nobody had really explained to her what the rules were regarding walking amongst the wildlife. She had been given some key cards and codes by Davey, so she assumed that she was free to make her own choices, that there was a level of trust once the contract was signed. Kelvin had come to her after all. Sort of. After she'd come to him. Anyway, he had offered her the job without any application from her. She supposed he must trust her. Trust her enough anyway.

What Steph wanted to do was head out for a couple of days. Camp overnight. Make the most of her time before coming back, consider her findings and then plan further. Without a tent or a good enough knowledge of the hybrids – she had settled on calling them that in her head as she did not deem them genuine pre-historic relics – she thought it would be sensible to return to the house for the night after the walk. Camping could wait.

"Where do you think you're going?" came Davey's voice as Steph opened the front door, her backpack over one shoulder.

"Walking!" she replied.

Davey sighed, swore and then told her to wait two minutes.

It was thus that Steph found that she would have an unwanted companion on the walk.

"I don't need you with me," she said as they walked through the woodland that patched the land, noticing the tell-tale signs of wild boar on the ground.

"You do need me," Davey replied. "Or Michael. Michael would have been better, to be honest, but he has the day off. He's gone to Edinburgh to look at the castle or something. Whatever these Americans like to do when they're over here."

"What do I need you for?" Steph asked. "I know what I'm doing. I know what precautions to take and when to be

73

sensible."

"But do you?" Davey sneered.

"What's that supposed to mean?"

"Well, here you are, suddenly wrapped up in the experiment of someone who has more money than he knows what to do with, when all you intended was to research how a boy died and whether there was anything unnatural and untoward. Or at the very least, allow your readers to feel that there could have been."

Steph stopped walking and narrowed her eyes. Davey also stopped and looked disinterestedly at his feet before quickly scanning the area.

"So you did look through my stuff!"

"Not exactly."

"What do you mean 'not exactly'? Either you did or you didn't!"

"You left a copy of one of your books on the side in your hotel room," Davey shrugged. "I borrowed it. Had a quick scan through – I didn't feel the need to read it properly. I just wanted the gist of your type of material and what you do."

"You stole from me?"

"It was interesting, with the Tasmanian tiger, how you mention land space, the credibility of individuals and their sightings, length of extinction, etcetera."

Steph pushed past Davey, which made him laugh. She could hear him walk after her. She tried to ignore him.

"All of what I said was true," Steph said after a while. "I didn't make anything up. I merely reported on what had happened and gave my take on the possibilities."

"I never said you didn't," Davey said, putting an arm across Steph's chest for a moment, studying the ground and then, once satisfied, moving off again. Steph tried to look at what had grabbed his attention but saw nothing. Then again, he'd seen nothing. Probably didn't even know what he was looking for.

"If it's so wrong for me to have been 'wrapped up in here', why are you here?" Steph asked after a few minutes more of silence.

"Because I, unlike you, was not earning as much before, so when I was offered a good payday, I took it," Davey replied.

"Took it to do what exactly?"

"Whatever I need to do. Primarily I was hired to look after the land as I have a background in forestry, but I will turn my hand to most things. I'm a quick enough learner."

"Seems odd," Steph replied.

"What is?"

"That you felt the need to say that you were a quick enough learner. Insecure?"

Davey laughed again.

"In this place? Definitely!"

They carried on walking. Steph decided, after some thought, that she couldn't spend the whole day trying to ignore Davey except for when she felt the desire to be petty. Instead she chose to make the most of his presence. Make the best out of... well, not a bad situation but an unfortunate one. It had come to her attention that there were a number of plant species alien to the natural surroundings. Davey explained that Daniel had suggested that there would need to be enough to satisfy the cave bear's omnivorous appetite, in addition to the number of prey animals.

"So what exactly does Kelvin think will happen with all of this?" Steph asked as they made their way from a treeline and up a gentle slope. "What is the point in it all?"

Davey stopped, which forced Steph to stop. She watched

him quickly scan the open space as well as the ridgeline up ahead, his bottom lip screwed under his upper jaw.

"He said something about bringing about a kinder world. Roughly along those lines. He believes that for the planet to survive, it needs to find a new balance... or revisit an old one. Whilst some rich people work on greener energy or space travel, Kelvin works in a different area. He thinks there is no need to work on something someone is already doing unless you know you can do it a thousand times better, or so he says. What he is actually picturing in his head, I am unsure of, to be honest. Although in my opinion, all these rich folk work on some sort of mental shit when they pass a certain wealth threshold."

"But what do you mean by 'a new balance'?"

Davey pondered this, panting slightly but not as much as Steph. Her bag suddenly felt very heavy.

"I think a new balance between humans and the natural world. He thinks people are already developing what is needed for a greener future in terms of energy and climate – although he appears frustrated at their lack of implementation, he seems to predict something more."

"What?"

"Well – and I am not saying I buy into this although I can see his point – what correlates strongly with most countries and a rise in education?"

"All sorts," Steph puffed.

"Yes, true, one being a fall in birth rates."

"OK?"

"Well, that means a lot of things," Davey continued, pausing just before the ridgeline. "There's a problem for the economists about a top-heavy population and how they might sustain the elderly with the age of death rising. However, Kelvin is interested in something else. An opportunity, as he sees it – I am not completely sure myself. We have encroached onto the wilderness in different countries for years. Our population has exploded like algae on a pond. We have built on it and put in place the infrastructure to deal with it all. Yet if the population decreases significantly – which it is already showing signs of in many countries – what happens to it all?"

Steph thought about this. She supposed the answer was obvious, but she didn't want to appear stupid by saying so and yet proved to be wrong – at least in Davey's eyes.

"It gets left?"

"Exactly," Davey said. "And it gets reclaimed by the wild. Wildlife is incredibly resilient; it has gone through mass extinctions before and always bounced back. It'll reclaim areas we abandon in the blink of an eye."

"What's your point?" Steph replied, looking around. "I don't see what this has to do with anything going on here."

"Of course you don't," Davey scowled. "Kelvin believes that the mood of people is changing to one of more cooperation and coexistence with animals, rewilding in other countries, the replanting of forests, people eating far less meat and people looking for alternatives to fur and leather."

"And so... so this is just an example of what Kelvin thinks life could be like in the future?" Steph frowned. "But with a dash of dangerous prehistoric predation thrown in for good measure?"

"I wouldn't say the predation itself is prehistoric," Davey replied, itching his arm.

Steph grimaced.

"Sounds a bit pointless to me, crossing a bridge we haven't reached and might not even arrive at. Anyway, even if he does prove a point somehow, what does it matter? What use is it to him to demonstrate that people can live amongst the wild?"

"That I am not quite sure of," Davey said. "Although men like Kelvin know how to pivot. I think that's why he got the prehistoric animals in. They were his insurance."

"Meaning?"

"Meaning if Kelvin is wrong about humans eventually getting closer to nature again, he can at least offer the opportunity to live amongst wildlife as a sort of holiday-type thing. With the extinct animals thrown in, he could make a bit of money back. Not to mention the rights he has to Martina's research."

Steph did not think much of his explanation. It felt weak. The only part that seemed to her to have any clout was the part about genetics. But why buy all the land? Was it pure vanity?

"Surely he won't regain the cost of the land with a simple holiday park?"

Davey was about to reply but put a finger to his lips instead.

FOURTEEN

There was a slight downward slope of open heathland leading to another treeline. To their right, there was an incline up a small ben. Grazing in the partially cleared field was a herd of red deer, with a large stag visible in the middle surrounded by a harem. Steph studied them. Something didn't seem right.

"They seem very skittish," Steph said.

"What do you mean?" Davey replied.

"Look at the edges. They are constantly moving and jumping as if they have seen something or think something is there. They seem agitated all the time. Is that normal for your herd?"

"I suppose so. I've never really thought about it. I guess I have become so used to it that it just seems normal to me. The deer are a good target for predators as they are easier than the moose or the bison."

Steph didn't reply but took her binoculars and tilted them to one side. She tried to see if there was anything that could potentially be bothering them or whether there were any patterns to their movements.

"Are the other prey animals that move in herds acting like this?" she asked.

"In their own way, I suppose," Davey shrugged, checking his tranquillizer gun. "I mean, the bison are a little more assured of themselves when we bring them in."

"Bring them in?" Steph put her binoculars down.

"Well, we can't do everything on-site here," Davey explained, checking a can of something attached to his waist. "Kelvin doesn't put all his eggs in one basket. He has a breeding facility. That said, I think he hoped that he wouldn't need them in the long run as the herds would be able to sustain themselves. He wants a 'natural equilibrium' here. I'm not sure that's the same for the prehistoric animals or whether he could breed them in the future. It's not my place to know, I suppose."

Steph chewed her tongue, looking at the deer grazing once more.

"How big is the whole area?"

"What do you mean?"

"I mean, how large is the stretch of land the animals roam in?"

"It's roughly seventy square miles; reasonably big."

Steph picked up the binoculars once more.

"I'm not sure it's big enough; some of the animals that you said you have usually have a territory bigger than that. I mean, a mountain lion can often cover a lot of ground, although I'm uncertain how having its genetics mucked about with alters that. What did you say you have again?"

"Have what?"

"Have here? Animals, the predators?"

"Cave lion, cave bear, three brown bears, a pack of wolves, a couple of lynxes, and then we have foxes, badgers... the usual for here."

Steph turned to look at Davey who was busy looking down the length of his gun.

"Well," she said, "that is quite the hotpot, isn't it? No wonder the animals are bloody skittish."

Davey wasn't listening to her; he seemed to have his eyes fixed on something. There was a sudden rumbling sound coming from the ground.

Steph looked down to see hooves raining down on the ground as the herd thundered towards a far treeline towards the ben. From the other side, dark grey shapes whipped out, bounding towards the writhing mass of confusion.

"Wolves," Davey said.

"Obviously," Steph replied, shaking her head but not taking her eyes off the events.

The wolves were quick to home in on a doe that was struggling to keep pace with the others. She was desperately trying to get back to the herd but her back left leg seemed to be out of step with the rest. It was not long before the first wolf had thrown itself at the stricken deer's haunches, clinging on with clamping jaws. This lowered it further. Then another wolf was pulling down on its flank. And another. And another.

The rest of the herd continued into the treeline at the foot of the small ben, eager to leave one of their number behind in exchange for their own escape.

"Well, that was quick," Steph said, breaking the silence.

Davey wasn't listening. He was still looking down the sight of his gun.

"I suspect it's not over yet," he whispered.

"Of course, it is, look!"

Blood was already visible down the front of one of the wolves. Steph presumed this to be the alpha. It was big. They were all big. Oddly big. Not freakishly big but definitely large.

She decided that she could risk moving a little closer to get a better look at things to see if the pack behaviour of the wolves was normal. She took her first step but felt something grip her arm tightly. She looked back to see Davey looking stern, his large hand wrapped firmly around her wrist.

"Get off! You're hurting me!"

"I said," Davey whispered in a low growl, "I suspect it is not over yet!"

Steph tried to free her arm. She couldn't: Davey's grip was too strong. She was about to lash out but when she looked up, she realised he wasn't looking at her. She stopped struggling and followed his gaze. She felt the pressure on her wrist release, but a heaviness in her chest took its place.

Strolling purposefully towards the wolves and their fresh kill was the largest bear Steph had ever seen. Larger than a polar bear, the thing must have been the height of a man at the shoulders. Muscle rippled underneath the brown shaggy fur.

In unison, the wolves turned to face the newcomer, hackles raised. However, they were moving backwards, there was no doubt about that. The bear didn't even acknowledge them as it tucked its head into the carcass. Moments later, it raised it again with blood fresh on its muzzle. It was only then that it seemed to appreciate the proximity of the wolves. It let out a roar which ripped across the open land. The wolves got the picture and slunk off to the edge of the treeline. There they contented themselves with waiting in the hope there would still be something left for them at the end.

"Do they not try to defend their kills?" Steph asked, still mesmerised by what she was seeing.

"Not anymore; not against him anyway," Davey replied, also still looking.

"What do you mean by that?"

"I mean that when they lost one of their pack trying to, they stopped."

FIFTEEN

As fascinating as the cave bear was, Steph knew that she could not spend all day admiring its size and presence. She had a job to do. Two jobs, in theory. The one Kelvin had hired her for and her own (she was still shaping that one). Either way for both jobs, she felt it best to make use of Davey's knowledge of the place. She might not like the man, but she would definitely need to converse with him.

She wanted to see the beavers and discover how their handiwork had shaped the environment. They had dammed the river creating a small pond which acted as a bit of a drinking hub for some of the animals. Davey seemed pleased to point out that the original pair had successfully bred. Then he mentioned some trivia about the fur trade in the past. Steph was not sure why he felt the need to bring the fur trade up but listened anyway.

She continued to make notes and ask questions. Davey was knowledgeable about what he had seen in terms of the behaviour of the animals and of what had gone on inside the fences. However, his answers suggested that he lacked any prior academic grounding. His knowledge came from his own observations alone.

"The light is starting to fade," Davey pointed out.

"Fine," Steph sighed. "I shall have to come out tomorrow anyway. More than that is needed really, but I will do a couple of days and then regroup."

"For what?"

"What?"

"Regroup for what?" Davey said, widening his eyes and spreading his hands.

"To figure out what I need to do next to find out what is effective and what isn't, and what that might even entail considering the mishmash of animals and the territory, for that matter."

"And work out how secure the fences are?"

Steph paused for a moment.

"I saw you looking constantly into the distance whenever you assumed we were nearing the perimeter," Davey continued.

Steph paused a moment longer, opened her mouth slightly and then chose to ignore the bait. In her head, she questioned whether an animal could have escaped the fences unaided. They seemed secure.

"Like I said, you can knock yourself out on that front," Davey said, bending down to tie his laces whilst keeping a wary eye scanning the area around them. "Maybe you can ask Michael to take you around the perimeter tomorrow."

"I don't need that," Steph replied.

"Sure."

"I don't! What use would it be to me?"

"I know that the fences were all intact after what happened to that boy. Maybe that's of use to you."

Steph chose to ignore him. She wouldn't be goaded. Even so, if the animal that killed the boy – and Steph was pretty certain that it was an animal – had not come from the compound, where had it come from?

The pair walked for a little longer. Steph made mental notes of the track they were taking and the surrounding vegetation. The light was really starting to disappear now. If it was not to provide a slow acclimatisation to the light levels, Steph would have been tempted to pull out her torch.

Steph was about to ask who chipped the animals, when she noticed a light up ahead.

"What's that?"

"What's what?" replied Davey.

"That! That light up ahead?"

"Oh, that. That's one of the cabins."

"Ah, yes... the cabins," Steph said, frowning.

"Yeah, Kelvin has paid people to live in the cabins," Davey said. "Not quite sure how he advertised it exactly. Essentially you're looking for a certain type of person who is willing to give up their life for an extended period of time."

"What type?"

"Generally not the best type. They're all right though. They're just people. Roger's OK."

"And this is to help prove animals and people can learn to live amongst each other again?"

"That's what I have been told. If they can live here and not die, I suppose it's a reasonable green light for any leisure venture with the whole thing."

Steph supposed that was one way of checking safety. A risky one, but a straight-to-the-point test that was in line with what she understood of Kelvin.

"So the people just live out here in the cabins?"

"There are only four of them," Davey replied. "Occupied by single men. Well, as far as I am aware they are single."

"And are there fences around the cabins?"

"Nope."

"Is that wise?"

"In my opinion? No. However, they get paid very well to do it. It's interesting to see at what monetary figure people will start taking risks with their lives. That said, I am not sure they fully appreciate the danger they're in."

Steph stopped. Davey continued walking for a few steps before stopping himself, exhaling loudly through his nose and turning to look at her.

"They are briefed, aren't they?" Steph asked. "There are enough ethical problems as it is without Kelvin putting that on himself!"

"Oh, they're briefed all right. It's just that I doubt they fully appreciate the brief. They must last a year and in exchange, they are paid handsomely."

"How handsomely?"

"As I said, enough for them to become more liberal with their life."

"What do you mean by 'a year'?" Steph asked, deciding to walk again. Davey fell into step.

"Well, although this place has been running a while, you have to think how hush-hush things have been."

"I don't get you?" Steph replied. "You're in a giant fenced-off area in rural Scotland. It is hardly covert."

"Yes, I know that, but Kelvin is very good at keeping things reasonably quiet. Besides, when was the first time you heard about us?"

Steph thought about this. Maybe a month or so ago. That was when she'd heard of the death.

Davey took her thoughtful silence as a concession to his point.

"Exactly, and you're someone who actively looks for this kind of thing. The average person doesn't really give a shit what goes on in the wilds of Scotland. Sure, things are a little more interesting now, but who is going to believe that there is anything massively strange happening here? People tend to shy away from the strange and hard to explain. I know you make a living off it, but I imagine it is a niche living."

Steph was about to protest when they heard a long howl a few hundred yards behind them. Davey froze. Steph mirrored his concern.

"Fuck!" Davey hissed.

"What's the problem?" Steph asked. She had dealt with wolves in the wild before. It was not exactly ideal being caught out with them, but they had what they needed to keep themselves safe.

"We need to run," Davey hissed, grabbing Steph by the arm and pulling her forward before breaking into a jog.

"Run where?"

"The cabin!"

"But I don't see what the issue is; running will only encourage them!"

There were more howls now. They were coming from the surrounding trees. They were getting closer. It was as if they were surrounding them.

"You have to remember that these are not wolves in an ordinary environment!" Davey panted. "These doggies are hungry! Very hungry!"

Steph chased after Davey towards the entrance of the cabin where warm lighting flowed from the windows on either side of the door. Davey hammered on the door and then turned around. Steph looked over her shoulder. The howling was getting more excitable but there were still no shapes amongst the trees.

The door opened.

"Oh, it's you. What are you knocking fo... hey!"

Davey pushed the man back inside. Steph once again found his hand upon her arm, pulling her in. He then slammed the door behind them all.

"What's all this about?" asked a man who, to Steph's astonishment, did not look as surprised by the intrusion as she expected one would when two people barged into their home.

Davey put a finger to his lips. They listened. There was another howl. It was close. It sounded right outside the door. In the quiet, Steph was sure that she could hear the padding of numerous paws in the dirt around the house outside.

"Ah, I see," said the man, rolling his eyes. "You'd best come in then... or at least sit down seeing as you're already in. Come on!"

Davey gave the man an apologetic shrug as he followed him towards a large sofa where a book was opened face-down to keep the pages the man had been reading.

SIXTEEN

"Tea?" the man asked, heading towards a kitchen area at the side of the cabin.

"Please," replied Davey, sitting down and ushering Steph to do the same.

Steph sat down but continued to scan her surroundings. The inside of the cabin was larger than she expected. Although what she had expected, she couldn't really say. She'd had no time to anticipate entering the cabin. The furnishings had Kelvin Handle written all over them – it was clearly in keeping with his own design themes.

The place was all open plan except for two doors at the back of the cabin. Steph assumed one led to a bedroom whereas the other must have been the bathroom. There was a large flatscreen television on the wall which cut through the rustic feel of the wood. Presently it was turned off.

The man returned with three teas on a tray and a plate of biscuits. Davey introduced the man as Roger. Steph assumed it must be the same one he had mentioned earlier.

He was an older gentleman, old enough for his hair to have gone grey. Steph noticed a bookshelf in one corner that was almost overflowing. There seemed to be no one genre to the books that denoted a particular direction of interest. It was simply everything.

Outside there were still howls and movement.

"I suspect you'll be here for the night," Roger said after dipping a biscuit into a half-empty mug.

"They'll go," Davey said, waving a dismissive hand.

"No doubt," Roger said. "It is just a case of when and whether you can be bothered staying up to wait for it."

"What do you mean?" Steph asked.

Roger turned to face her.

"Well, these canines are rather determined, not easily put off – even, at times, by walls."

"So they would stay here all night? That doesn't seem normal."

"Is any of this normal?"

Steph conceded the point. Even so, it worried her. The balance of the place was completely off. Had it always been this way? Was the behaviour of the animals developing slowly into this unstable equilibrium or had it rapidly set into its current pattern as soon as they were put together? It was all rather fascinating. Too fascinating. There was something dangerous about its appeal. Steph could lose herself, indulging in her scientific interests and missing the bigger picture building around her. She could feel it. Allowing herself to get sucked in without stepping back could be a catastrophic mistake.

"What do you mean when you say 'even by walls'?" she asked suddenly.

"Nothing much," Roger replied, sipping his tea. "Only they will sometimes scratch at the walls and doors. They can't get in, so it doesn't really matter. Even so, the noise when everything else is so quiet, well, it can get the heart going a bit."

Steph nodded, sipping her tea. She had to admit to herself that constantly living with things around you that would happily eat you might eventually fray the nerves.

"Have you heard from Fergus recently?" Roger asked, turning to face Davey.

"I'm meant to check on him tomorrow," Davey replied.

"Has been a bit low-key recently. To be honest, I think he's struggling."

Roger nodded and pulled a knowing face.

"Who's Fergus?" Steph asked.

"Another individual like me who is making the most of a lucrative stay in a holiday cottage," Roger said.

Davey rolled his eyes.

"You knew what you were getting into when you agreed to it all," Davey said.

"I never said I didn't," shrugged Roger. "Although, I would not say I completely understood what I was getting into seeing as neither did any of your lot!"

"My lot?"

"Yes, your lot! You had no idea how the animals would behave; the lady in the white coat said as much when I started."

"Martina?"

"Something like that."

It was Davey's turn to shrug.

"I suppose that's fair," he said. "Not that I agree with any of it really anyway..."

"You go along with it for the wage!" Roger said, pointing a finger.

"So do you!" retorted Davey. "So you can put that finger away. Anyway, that's sort of why this one is here."

"This lovely lady?"

Steph almost choked on her tea. She couldn't remember the last time anyone had called her lovely. She was not sure whether to take it as an insult or a compliment. She settled on ignoring it.

"That's right," she said. "I've been employed to assess the relationship between the animals in the ecosystem as well as their behaviour in general."

Roger looked mildly impressed.

"She usually writes about bigfoot," Davey said, resting a lazy foot over his knee.

Steph could feel herself going red.

"I am a trained field biologist!" she snapped.

"And now you have a real job in a fake world rather than a fake job in the real world," Davey continued, smiling behind his tea.

"Oh, leave the girl alone!" Roger said, hitting Davey on the shoulder with his book. "Someone has to write about a sasquatch and make some money from it. If she doesn't, someone else will because there's a market for it! I was on holiday in Canada once and the resort did actual bigfoot walks. They were always fully booked is all I can say."

Hearing words she had used herself come from the mouth of another trying to defend her felt horrible. It was hard to ignore the taste of something when you were eating it yourself and not force-feeding it to others. She decided to change the subject. Ignorance was bliss. Better that than face herself in the mirror as her parents often suggested she do.

"Do you meet up with the others in the cabins?" Steph asked. "Only I can imagine it is quite a lonely existence for someone here."

"Not frequently, but we do from time to time," Roger replied. "We have a poker night once a month to look forward to and of course, we are allowed off-site. We aren't prisoners. We just have to be discreet with information."

"Poker nights?" Davey said with a raised eyebrow.

"You needn't worry!" Roger sighed. "We don't go walking off in the dark. We are usually far too deep into a bottle of scotch for night walking. Turns into a bit of a sleepover."

"Don't – and please forgive me if I am being too bold with

this question – don't you have family members that worry about you?" Steph asked. "Wives or children or..."

"I don't have a wife anymore," Roger sniffed.

Steph shut her eyes. Careless. Then she heard a chuckle.

"Oh, she's not dead!" Roger chuckled. "More is the pity. No, she decided to sleep with one of her students in her classical literature classes. He must have had a thing for older women. I don't know. Whatever the case, we are divorced. Probably for the best seeing as I am currently in the most lucrative employment I have ever been in my life. She might have taken half! Would have been unfair seeing as it's not her who risks being mauled by bears and extinct lions when she fancies a relaxed Sunday stroll."

They continued to talk into the evening. The wolves eventually quietened down but there was enough snuffling outside for Davey to suggest caution. Roger seemed all too pleased to have the stay of his company extended and set about making up a couple of camp beds. Steph noted him hurriedly binning a glass bottle from one of the sleeping bags he unwrapped, as well as pocketing some scraps of note paper that lay by the radio in the corner of the cabin.

SEVENTEEN

Roger woke the pair with a cooked breakfast. Steph didn't realise how hungry she was until she started eating. Bacon, eggs, sausages, hashbrowns, mushrooms; it all went. This was washed down with some orange juice and a black coffee. A proper 'wake up!' coffee. The two said their goodbyes to Roger and set off down the track. Steph noted the numerous paw marks in the dirt.

"How long will it take to get back?" Steph asked. "Because I was thinking, I might as well just begin my day from here rather than return to the house."

Davey looked her way and then forward again.

"Not long. But I can stay with you a little longer if you have anything in mind you want to observe. I have already radioed Michael to let him know why we didn't come back last night, so I'm sure he'll pick up my slack for the day. I only really needed to check a few of the cameras anyway."

Steph was in two minds about insisting there was no need to chaperone her. On the one hand, she could focus more without him there. On the other, she did feel more reassured by his presence. The previous night had shaken her somewhat. Although nothing had happened exactly, she was wary of the danger around her. Things felt broken and that wasn't good for the wildlife. Some of the behaviour felt more extreme. An extra pair of eyes would be useful.

"We have one stop to make first though," Davey added. "Well, second. The beavers are on the way."

"I have a lot I need to see to even begin formulating a theory for how things might be going and what I expect to see over the next few weeks. Will these stops take long?"

Davey gave Steph a sideways glance.

"No," he said slowly. "It won't take long. I just need to pop into one of the other cabins."

Steph knew her impatience irritated him but that couldn't be helped. She genuinely *did* have a lot to see. She had yet to see all the predators or the major prey animals. Forget the fact that there was the added element of human existence within the environment. That would add another hard-to-measure dynamic.

Steph was not sure what she expected to see when she arrived at a part of the river that had been blocked and had subsequently flooded the surrounding area. Broken stumps announced the presence of beavers as much as the small lake drowning the surrounding undergrowth.

Busy heads carved their way across the water until they reached the bank to reveal stocky bodies that would productively collect sticks to take back to the lodge. All in all, their behaviour seemed normal enough for beavers. A bear wandered by at one point and the beavers made themselves scarce, retreating to their home comforts in the lodge. The behaviour was perfectly normal. They seemed wholly unaffected by the odd mishmash of animals around them. If anything, they seemed to be thriving in their new home.

Davey seemed particularly pleased with Steph's assessment of things.

"They were my idea," he said.

"What?"

"The beavers. I suggested them to Kelvin and found a suitable place to release them."

"Oh," said Steph. "Why beavers?"

"I just think they're funny little things," he replied. "Besides, I heard they have a huge impact on their surroundings and wanted to see for myself."

"You persuaded Kelvin to get beavers so you could see how many trees they gnawed down?"

"Essentially."

Steph rolled her eyes.

"Are you not concerned that they might escape downriver?"

"Nah, it's caged underwater where it flows in and out of the grounds. Big enough to let fish through but not big enough to let the animals get through. Not the ones we are interested in keeping in."

Steph made a note of this in her notebook. They walked on.

Again, Steph could see the tell-tale signs of wild boar. She also saw in the saturated mud the distinctive outline of bear prints. The sliding of the prints suggested that the animal had been running at speed.

Birds whistled in the trees above. Steph wondered whether they were on a greater alert with the sudden influx of big animals around. Then again, none of them really affected the birds in any way.

Another noise announced the passing of a large bird of prey somewhere above the trees. Davey looked up smiling. Steph waited for him to look down and then raised an eyebrow.

"Golden Eagle!" Davey smiled. "One of ours. It's fascinating when they take down a drone."

"Drone?"

"Every so often one of the locals will try and fly one over to see things but these guys make quick work of them."

Steph supposed it was one way of doing things.

"How far to this cabin?" Steph asked, taking a drink from her flask.

"A couple of minutes," Davey replied, "Just over that little rise."

Everything about the surrounding land seemed to be about rises and falls. It was irrepressibly undulating. However, this made it exceedingly beautiful, mainly due to the higher peaks in the distance and expanses of trees, but didn't make it any less tiring to tread . Steph wiped her brow.

They reached the crest of the small rise. Sure enough, there was the cabin, just a couple of hundred yards ahead near a small clump of trees but otherwise in a more open location than Roger's.

They began descending towards the lonely dwelling. Davey looked left and right, ensuring they were not being followed or watched. Steph had already started to become accustomed to doing the same.

She was curious as to what the man in the hut would be like. What would his story be? Would he be similar to Roger? She fixed her eyes on the cabin. Davey continued to look over his left shoulder, something clearly bothering him.

Steph narrowed her eyes at the cabin, slowing her walk. Something was wrong, but she couldn't tell what from where they were. She had never even seen the cabin before – but something felt wrong. She held out an arm across Davey.

"What?" he said, reluctantly turning his head.

"I don't know," Steph replied.

"You don't know? What?"

Davey's face displayed his mild irritation at the hold-up, but he didn't move. Steph thought about her words. She didn't want to come across as overdramatic or even oversensitive.

"Does everything look right to you down there?" she asked

after a few moments.

Davey began looking intently towards the cabin, craning his neck slightly to try and spot what exactly might not be looking right.

"How so?" Davey asked, unable to spot what had made Steph uncertain.

"Is the door open?"

"Yeah, so?"

"So he is not outside."

"What's your point?"

"Is that wise, considering?"

Davey took a deep breath and then exhaled, puffing out his cheeks.

"Probably not, but I have never found Fergus the most careful of men."

"But there is a chair on the decking that has been turned over," Steph said.

"Again, Fergus is as tidy as he is careful," Davey said. "Probably knocked it over himself when getting out of it... or an animal knocked it over when snooping around and he can't be arsed to pick it up. Probably the latter."

Davey continued walking. Steph followed. Still with an uneasy feeling in her stomach, she made sure there were a few yards between herself and Davey. Her heart was beating slightly faster, and some primal voice told her to stay vigilant. Hairs stood up on her neck. Davey began to slow as he approached the cabin. Then he stopped. Steph stopped behind him.

Davey took his tranquillizer rifle from his back and stood holding it, staring at the cabin.

"I said something wasn't right," Steph whispered.

Davey waved a quieting hand in her direction. It took more self-restraint than she'd care to admit not to snap at his dismissiveness. Instead she watched him. Slowly he began to move, lowering the rifle.

The ground was soft near the cabin from the rainfall the night before. It was also scarred with prints. Large prints buried into the ground deep enough to display the power of the animal that made them.

Steph was sweating a little now, yet her mouth was dry. She edged closer to Davey who still silently stalked forward. They were nearly at the decking now. They stopped. They listened. Nothing. Davey edged forward again. Steph reluctantly followed.

As they looked at the decking, it became clear that something had moved across it. Something bleeding.

Davey put one foot on the grooved wooden planks and there was a gut-churning creak. They froze. They listened. Still nothing.

Davey lifted his other foot onto the decking and began to walk towards the open doorway, its door hanging heavily.

"Wait!" Steph breathed.

"What?" Davey mouthed in irritation.

"Are you sure it's safe?"

Davey ignored the question completely and crept inside. Steph didn't know what to do. If anything, she felt more concerned now that she was outside alone rather than inside.

A sudden voice crashed through the doorway and into the still air.

"Fucking hell!"

Steph bolted to the door. What she could do she didn't know, but her legs had recklessly carried her there all the same.

"What?" she gasped. "What happened?"

In front of her lay Davey, one hand pushing himself up from the floor. Steph wretched.

Davey lay surrounded by blood seeping into the floorboards.

"How did you end up on the floor?" Steph asked. "Didn't you see the... well, how couldn't you see the blood?"

Davey still didn't answer. Instead, he leaned against a table, lying his rifle on the top and then lifting a foot up. He examined what was on the bottom and then looked away, closing his eyes.

He then proceeded to scrape the sole of his boot on the table leg whilst saying, "Forgive me, Fergus."

"What was that?" Steph asked as she looked at the pink scum that was now stuck loosely to the table leg.

"That," Davey said, shaking his head, "is what little is left of Fergus."

"What?"

"It's why I slipped," Davey exhaled between deep breaths.

Steph grimaced.

"Anyway," Davey said quite seriously, "I think we had best close the door."

"Are you sure?" Steph replied. "I mean, the door didn't do anything for... him." She nodded at the mess on the floor.

"I don't think that his door was broken down if that's what you mean," Davey replied. "Besides, once one of these creatures has hunted somewhere successfully, they will try again. Any field biologist worth their salt would tell you that."

Steph ignored the barb and shut the door. She noticed how heavy it was and, although made to look rustic, had heavy metal parts expertly intermingled with the wood. It looked strong. She had not had a chance to examine Roger's door – why would she have done so anyway – but she found this door looked almost impenetrable. A thought suddenly occurred to her. She looked at the windows.

"How did Kelvin secure the windows?" she asked.

Davey looked taken aback for a moment. He had been

looking around the room and had not expected the question. Nor, Steph suspected, was he prepared for how calmly it was asked, given the circumstances.

"Bulletproof," Davey replied, continuing to wander around.

Steph continued to watch him for a moment. She was not sure how much longer he could walk aimlessly around pretending he knew what he was looking for. It was a form of mild shock, she supposed. Even for someone as supposedly calm as Davey, the sight of someone's limited remains was always going to have some sort of impact on a person. That was not to say that there was no impact on her. There was. She was just able to hide it better due to at least some previous acclimatisation.

"I suppose that Kelvin and the others probably already know about this?" Steph said another thought crossing her mind.

"What?"

"What happened to Fergus? I expect that people back at the house already know about it?"

"Why would they?" Davey asked, finally giving up on his nervous pacing and now looking out of the window.

"Well, I assumed there are cameras surrounding each cabin. You have enough of them around the perimeter fencing; it makes sense that you would have them watching over people for safety reasons. More sense than the fence if you had to compare the two."

"You'd think, wouldn't you?" Davey sniffed.

"What do you mean?"

"I mean nobody will know about this yet – it is unlikely at the very least. There are no cameras in here or out there watching the cabin."

"How come?" Steph asked, the pitch of her voice rising slightly. Her heart beating a little faster once more.

"Funny thing about people; they don't really like other people watching their every move."

"What do you mean?"

"I mean the people that agreed to go in the cabins all refused the cameras. Kelvin was pushing for them initially. Claimed it would make things safer – I'm not sure how exactly; most hunts are over before we can even blink. Anyway, everyone refused them, and Kelvin respected their need for privacy. Admired them for not wanting them if anything. Roger was particularly forceful on the issue."

Steph looked down at the blood again. The fact that it was still wet suggested to her that the kill had been recent enough. She looked out of the window. As she did, she heard Davey's voice on his walkie-talkie. Davey had been right; nobody had known about what happened.

EIGHTEEN

Davey contacted Michael. Michael told Kelvin what had happened. Kelvin sent Michael to pick Steph and Davey up. Michael drove back with the two of them in near-silence.

This silence was eventually broken by Davey slowly leaning over and asking Michael, "Has he... has he done what I expect him to?"

Michael risked a glance at Davey and, grimacing, said, "What do you think?"

Davey cursed softly under his breath.

"So I'm assuming it is just us three, him and Martina?"

"And Dino Dan."

"Him? Why?"

Michael shrugged.

"How long until he calls them, do you think?" Davey asked.

"Said he wants forty-eight hours," Michael replied. "In forty-eight hours, we go back and make the call. I assume some money exchanges hands between someone, but who is to say whose hands."

Steph listened carefully to all of this. At first it made little sense to her. It was not until she was back at the house and quickly ushered into a room by Kelvin himself, that she worked out what Michael and Davey had been on about.

The room looked like a small library. There were a couple of big armchairs in one corner, a hammock in another set between a free-standing post and two large bookshelves along two walls. Kelvin directed Steph and Davey into the two seats.

Michael lazily went over to the hammock and sat in the middle of it, using it as a sort of canvas chair.

"The body?" Kelvin asked, looking at Davey.

"Not there. Mostly not there."

"Fuck!"

Steph watched him carefully. His facial expressions continued to change slightly as he stared at nothing in particular. It was as if he were reacting to some sort of internal conversation in his own head.

"Right, here's what we do: we give ourselves forty-eight hours to get things in order – it was the cave lion, wasn't it?"

"Almost certainly."

"Good, that makes things easier with paperwork. Anyway, we give ourselves forty-eight hours to make sure we find what is left of Fergus, work out what the hell happened and then act as if we have only just found out. Probably say it was a bear."

"What?" Steph said, looking towards Davey and Michael for support. They ignored her and looked directly at Kelvin. "We can't do that?"

"We can and we will," Kelvin replied, putting his hands in his pockets.

"What about any family Fergus had or... or the fact someone has been killed? The police will need to conduct an investigation!"

"Exactly!" Kelvin sniffed. "They'll want to investigate my property – our property! Investigations outside are fine, but anything inside could jeopardise what we have been working on here. Remember, you've signed paperwork, so you are as much a part of this as anyone; it doesn't matter how new you are. They'll be asking you all sorts of questions – especially when they do a bit of research into who you are and what you do."

"Probably good for book sales," Davey smirked. Michael barked with laughter.

Steph glared at him.

"Someone has just died! We cannot act like it hasn't happened!"

"Only for forty-eight hours," Michael shrugged.

"Believe me, we're not going to act as if it hasn't happened," Kelvin said, frowning at Michael. "We are going to get to the bottom of this shitshow."

Steph didn't reply; she couldn't really fathom what was going on.

"As for Fergus," Kelvin continued, "I would not worry too much over his death."

"What do you mean?"

"I mean, there won't be many people who would miss him. I won't say why – one should respect the dead – but he was here for a reason and, unlike one or two of the others in the cabins, he had not fallen on hard times."

"What do we do about the others?" Michael asked leaning back slightly to see whether he could balance in his hammock chair.

Kelvin ran a hand through his hair, exhaling as he pondered the question.

"Do we need to do anything?"

"Probably," Steph sighed. She could sense that, despite her better judgement, she was going to be caught up in whatever messy whirlwind was about to tear through. Maybe she needed to be. Perhaps this was what she had been hoping for on some subconscious level, why she had taken the job.

The others looked at her.

"As you realised earlier," she began, turning to Davey, "once a predator picks up on a new technique that works, they will try again."

"Will it be hungry though?" Kelvin asked, looking between Steph and Davey.

"Probably," Michael put in. "Fergus was hardly a Thanksgiving turkey... more of a spare rib."

Steph shuddered.

"Jesus Christ!" Kelvin growled, tilting his head to the ceiling. "Fine! You two bring them in... no! No. Just go and make them aware of what is going on and tell them to stay indoors for the next forty-eight hours. I don't want people getting panicked."

"So who else knows?" Davey asked.

"Martina and Daniel," he replied. "Right, Davey, Michael, get out there and let the other cabins know. Steph, rest up as I will need you to go back out there to work out exactly what it is that the cave lion learnt that led to this mess in the first place."

Did Steph want to go back to the cabin to find out? It was the only place she could think of to go to first, other than locating the animal itself. Then again, there was chaos at the moment. It was trying to be controlled, but it was there. If there was one thing her father had taught her – he had tried to teach her many things, but she was a headstrong pupil – it was that opportunity was born in chaos.

"I will need to restock," she said.

"Not a problem!" Kelvin replied. Then he nodded and left the room.

NINETEEN

Steph took some time to gather herself in her room. She grabbed her notebook and tried to put her thoughts down on paper. It was easier to make sense of them that way. It was a struggle. With so much crashing around the walls of her mind, she had expected everything to pour out. However, after nearly twenty minutes, she had written just two things and circled them repeatedly: 'the territory is unnaturally small' and 'the project is *everything* to Kelvin'.

She wondered how this helped her. Did it help her? She got up and looked out of the window. She could see trees and not much else.

She sat back on the bed. Her aims, she supposed, had become somewhat multi-faceted. Her book research *had* been padded out with discovering what was going on in an insanely rich man's ecological experiment asking how rewilded animals cope in Scotland, finding out how extinct hybrids mix with present-day species and whether humans could cope with it all? Some of those areas felt like they had obvious conclusions. Yet it was when scientists felt overconfident, that they generally made their biggest mistakes.

After a few hours of lying on the bed and letting her thoughts simmer until they were reduced to their strongest essence, Steph left the room. She was taken aback when she opened the door and saw Daniel. His fist was clenched and raised in a knocking motion. Steph stared at him. He stood frozen for a moment, then smiled.

"I was just coming to get you," he said.

"So I can see," Steph replied. "Why?"

"Well, I know you need to try and work out what happened to Fergus, and I would like to come with you... rather than wait for Michael and Davey to get back..."

"Ah, I see," Steph said, allowing herself a small smile.

"Yeah, I just feel that maybe a bit of time without them to really look at things might be useful... you know."

Steph suspected she did know. Daniel was playing with the bottom of his t-shirt, rolling it between his finger and thumb. She held out an ushering arm. Daniel smiled and led the way.

It was not long before the pair were in a buggy heading towards Fergus's cabin. For the first time in a while, Steph had a tranquillizer rifle across her lap. She had used one a few years ago when working with a park ranger and a vet. It had been an odd experience then. She felt like a fraud holding one. It was the type of tool an individual who was actively engaged on the frontline of animal welfare might use, not some conspiracy theory flame feeder from Sheffield who was yet to really start the career her university degree suggested she should. She still considered herself a fraud now if she was honest. Even so, she was glad she was holding the tranquillizer rifle and not Daniel. As they drove, however, a thought suddenly struck her.

"How long will it take to develop another cave lion?" she asked.

Daniel bit his bottom lip. For a moment Steph thought he was going to pretend he hadn't heard but he eventually said,

"It is more a case of how far along the next specimen is."

"What do you mean?"

"Well, this might be where the environmental experiment takes place, so to speak – it is even where the first scientific steps take place in terms of embryos and all that stuff Martina does – but it's not where the animals were raised."

"No?"

"No. Kelvin has a private manor further north. To an outsider it might just seem like the private zoo of someone with too much money, but really it is a nursery for this. I went there once. Cool place. Of course, I went when the current crop of specimens was there: the bear and the lion – the other animals can generally be imported. I think they are working on backups. They were not really sure how they would all act once out together so needed spares."

Steph grimaced.

"The idea is, of course, to do away with the nursery and eventually have mating pairs living out in the experimental enclosure."

Steph nodded, allowing her head to process everything. It was interesting that nobody really used any consistent label for the fenced-off area where the animals ran wild. What was the real aim of the whole thing? Did Kelvin genuinely believe in rewilding and a drop in the human population? Did the others really share his vision?

"I suppose they will need that second cave lion soon," Steph said.

"Not too soon. She's still a bit young to be out here."

"Yes, but it will mean having to do without a cave lion here for a while and then reintroducing one which will upset the balance again... not that anything actually is balanced."

Steph could see Daniel opening and closing his mouth in tiny movements, his eyes skittered around the road in front of him as if he were considering many different lines of conversation at once. In the end, he settled on one.

"Why would we be without one?"

"Because I assume the other will have to be put down; it

has killed someone!" Steph shrugged, holding the gun up, pointing it at a tree and then trying to keep the trunk at the end of the sight as the buggy drove past.

"I think you might underestimate the sway Martina might have over that decision," Daniel replied.

"What do you mean?"

"I mean it took her a while to get to where she is with her genetic experiments – as that's what they are to her – so I'm not sure she will want to take backward steps."

"But the police will demand that it's destroyed!" Steph said, bringing the tranquillizer rifle back in.

"They might, but don't be too surprised if money finds its way into pockets and there is not a genetic sleight of hand... or some sleight of hand anyway."

"But it will likely kill again!"

"It will try, I'm sure. We just need to take steps to prevent it having the opportunity. That is how Martina will lay it out to Kelvin... has laid it out to Kelvin. She has a lot of sway there."

Daniel risked looking away from the path to give Steph a knowing look. She acknowledged there was a whole line of questioning there, but for now she was focused on one thing only.

"You cannot control nature!" she said, shaking her head. "We can take steps to direct it somewhat, but never control it. It is not how things work. People know that. All scientists know that! Like you said that lion will find a way to kill again. Especially if it thinks it has found a prey animal there is little competition for, namely, us."

"So you're saying we should kill it because it has killed someone?"

"Yes! To prevent further death!"

"Does your logic apply to people?" Daniel asked.

"What?"

"Should a person be killed if they have killed once before? What about a person who kills animals? They usually kill again – hunters and such."

"What's your point? People and animals are completely different!"

"Seems like an odd thing for a biologist to say," Daniel shrugged; he was staying irritatingly calm.

Steph tried to say something but could only make a growling sound. Did he have a point? Was it odd that she had, as a default, elevated human life above animal life?

"But do you think it is right to risk the danger?" Steph asked, trying to calm her voice.

"I dunno," Daniel replied quite honestly. "I don't pretend to know either. I think this whole thing raises all sorts of philosophical questions. Most people will pretend they know the answer and that their view is completely right. But I personally don't know. In fact, I think nobody really knows because it isn't black and white. As such, I just try and enjoy the opportunity that I have been given to be part of it. That is not to say that I want anyone harmed, only that things happen in life and, as *you* said, we cannot control everything."

Steph wanted to reply, to say something insightful and highlight an angle that had been invisible to Daniel. She didn't have one. She stayed quiet and pondered. She started trying to add a few more pieces to the puzzle in her head, building the picture of the place. However, she still had no idea what she thought about the little boy and his death. Was that where she drew the line? Was it the death of children because they hadn't had a chance to make any decisions? Was the line children?

TWENTY

Steph and Daniel pulled up to Fergus's cabin. For a moment they stayed in the buggy surveying the nearby area. Satisfied it was safe enough, they disembarked.

Once inside, Steph was again greeted by the carnal mess that littered the floor. It wasn't so bad this time. She was more ready for it, even the smell. Unfortunately for Daniel, he had no prior experience with the mess and was, or so it looked to Steph, working hard to hold down what was in his throat.

"So what are your thoughts?" Daniel asked. "Surely you have come across animal attacks in your line of work before?"

Steph glanced sideways at the man. She wondered what he knew of *her line of work* and quite where he'd got his information from. Maybe he'd meant nothing by it.

"I have," Steph conceded, looking around.

"What causes it? Just a rogue animal looking for an easy meal?"

Steph looked at the floor. For the first time, she really took in the pattern of footprints and smears of red. The lion's prints did not go deep into the cabin although whatever area the struggle – and Steph assumed it must have been brief – had taken place in was a mess. There were objects on the floor, claw marks and shreds of flesh. Had it started eating straight away?

"Sometimes," Steph finally replied, not looking up. "Although it is hard to consider humans as an easy meal; animals aren't stupid. There is an understanding among most that humans often lead to their death. Years of being on the wrong end of a pointy stick or a bullet will usually instil that. Or the parent does."

"Nature versus nurture in the animal kingdom?"

"I suppose so," Steph replied, slowly walking back out the door. "How would this animal have learnt to fear humans and how far back would genetics be able to reach in terms of knowledge, if they play any part at all?"

"Which was why it attacked?"

"Possibly."

Steph stood on the porch decking and looked around. It was open. Too open. She then looked down as a board creaked underfoot. It was loose. A couple were loose in the same spot. She looked up.

"Often something causes an animal to go after humans. It could be an injury, which makes them unable to hunt faster, more aggressive prey. It could be a territorial thing. It could be a lack of learning opportunities from species' elders. There was a load of delinquent teenage elephants in Asia once. Males. All the older males had been killed and the younger ones never learnt how to behave. They went around raping and murdering like pissed-up pirates. You wouldn't think it of an elephant."

"So you think our cave lion might be a delinquent?"

"It's possible," Steph replied. She then went inside and fetched a chair which she put on the decking just slightly away from the small overhang of the roof. She climbed up.

"My personal worry is the idea of territory."

"What do you mean?" Daniel asked.

"Well, you have an awful lot of large predators in here that usually have large territories. Territories for most of them, each larger than the one area of land you have provided them, despite your generosity."

"I didn't decide on the land size!" Daniel replied holding

his hands up. "I am just the palaeontologist!"

"My point is," Steph continued. "There will be fierce competition. Adaptations will have to be made. Otherwise, at least one of your species of animal won't survive."

"So?"

"So I suspect that you have a bunch of apex and near-apex predators who are acutely aware that they might just have to become desperate... except maybe the cave bear."

"You saw it?" Daniel asked, his face lighting up.

"I did," Steph replied, studying the roof.

She found what she was looking for. There were scuff marks on the roof felt. Along the sides, where the roof was edged with wood, there were clean-looking grooves consistent with claws.

"It seems this was an ambush," Steph replied, getting down and surveying the area once more. The word ambush caused Daniel to look around too, craning his neck this way and that in rapid sweeping motions.

"What do you mean?"

"I mean the cave lion was waiting on the roof. Seemingly, it waited until Fergus went to open the door, dropped down and hammered its surprised victim in through their own doorway. There was a brief struggle in which Fergus was killed and the lion began eating. Quickly."

"Why quickly? Ah, don't answer. You already have."

"I get that the animal needed to eat quickly but it cannot have eaten the whole body. Not in a short space of time. That's the part I don't get."

"Well, I might have an answer to that," Daniel replied. "We have seen the odd carcass that has been dragged halfway up trees."

"You mean, it hides its kills?" Steph asked. "Like a leopard? Did cave lions do that?"

Daniel shrugged.

"There is no evidence I know to suggest they used trees, but it is possible they hid their kills. That's not uncommon for any predator to do, right?"

"If they can't eat quickly enough or defend a kill."

"Right."

"So if that is the case, I assume that the lion is trying to outmanoeuvre the bears," Steph said, running a hand through her hair.

"Well," Daniel said, puffing out his cheeks momentarily. "Even a full-sized brown bear is a match for the lion... the cave bear is something else but..."

"But I get the picture," Steph replied.

There was silence for a moment.

"Does the lion have a preferred tree?" Steph asked.

"For what?"

"For hiding kills. I mean was it the same tree you have seen these carcasses in each time?"

"Not me but Davey and Michael observed where," Daniel replied. "They just said it was not far from where the beavers were."

Steph nodded. She had too many things to consider now. Things were exciting – danger was excitement's shadier partner – but a lot to handle, nonetheless.

"I suppose that's where we should head then," Steph replied.

TWENTY-ONE

Upon nearing the beaver lodge, Steph and Daniel came upon the wolf pack again. They had taken down one of the wild boar and were ripping at the flesh and snapping at each other. Daniel stopped the buggy.

"Why've you stopped?" Steph asked.

"Because of that," Daniel replied, pointing over Steph's left shoulder.

She turned her head to see a large brown bear lumbering forward. It stopped to survey the scene before it. The wolves seemed not to have noticed it. Deciding to make the most of this drop in focus, the bear accelerated, charging at the writhing mass of grey fur. At the last moment, it let out a yell that sent the startled wolves skittering away. Steph expected she would now see this large creature fend off the wolves and claim the kill as its own. She was wrong.

The bear, without breaking stride, ran straight at the bloody carcass and began ripping flesh from bone. The wolves gathered themselves and turned to face the creature. This all took no more than a few seconds.

"This should be interesting," Daniel breathed.

It was. The bear, noticing the wolves rallying, began to rip ever more hungrily into the shreds of boar. Steph could not be sure, but the bear seemed to change its stance as well. Ever so subtly. It looked braced for something. Then Steph found out why.

The whole pack launched themselves simultaneously at

the bear in one ferocious tsunami of fur and teeth. The bear reared up and swung out, sending one wolf flying. To Steph's surprise, the bear returned to the kill whilst still being snapped at by the pack. It put its large front paws upon the carcass, clamped its jaws around a leg and snapped its head back. The leg ripped off. The bear turned tail and ran back from where it came, wolves falling from its flanks. At first, the wolves looked like they would try to retrieve part of their lost prize, but then turned, writing the leg off as a minor loss. They returned to their feeding as if nothing had occurred.

The wolf which had been flung so effortlessly by the bear limped over to join the rest of the pack.

Steph gripped the tranquillizer rifle a little tighter.

"There is a desperation," she said.

"What do you mean?" Daniel asked.

"There is desperation in the animals. It's not good. It will lead to behaviours that are generally chaotic and not completely in character. Usually, when animals act like this, there is an external pressure. It could be a drought, whatever. But it typically passes. It is expected to pass. But this..."

"There is no drought and there's enough food as the population of deer and boar are often topped up. And there are the bison."

"And yet some of the behaviour is frenzied."

Daniel shrugged and started driving the buggy onwards once more. Steph watched the wolves over her shoulder as they left. They currently seemed completely uninterested in the vehicle. She then looked at Daniel. He may have shrugged at her concerns, but his brow was furrowed in a way she had never seen from him before except when Michael was around.

They passed the beaver lodge. The beavers were still going about their business collecting sticks for their dam. Upon hearing the buggy, they swam for the safety of the lodge. Steph wondered how much protection the lodge would really give them if the cave bear found itself determined to get in. Had been an issue yet? Also, what was the cave bear's territory like and what were its usual routes?

A thought then occurred to her. How *had* the territories been shaped? Was there data on it? There had to be! The predators were chipped. Surely there was information on where they spent their time and where they roamed. Could they really afford to shrink their natural square milage of roaming ground to suit what was available? She had her thoughts on this.

Daniel slowed his speed to a crawl.

"Right, keep your eyes open," he said.

Steph scanned the trees around them. Nothing. It did occur to her that the likelihood of them stumbling across a tree that potentially housed Fergus's remains was somewhat slim. It might be that they would have to get out and walk to have any luck.

The radio kicked in. It was Davey.

"Daniel, you there?"

The voice didn't seem panicked which was a positive.

"Daniel?"

Steph looked at Daniel who was continuing to scan the trees as he trundled slowly forwards.

"You going to answer that?" Steph asked.

Daniel sighed.

"I suppose so."

He picked up the radio and clicked the button on the side. "Yep?"

"Where're you two? You find anything that we didn't find the first time?"

"Yeah, some scratch marks. Seems the cave lion had waited

on the roof to ambush Fergus."

"Fucker!"

"Poor bastard!" came a voice in the background.

"Who's that?" Daniel asked.

"It's Roger," Davey replied. "I just picked him up to take him to the main house whilst this is all sorted. Where're you now?"

"Just past the beavers. Looking for that tree you mentioned where you had seen kills being hidden."

"But you don't know where that is!"

"I know it's around here somewhere!"

"I'll come and meet you!"

Steph watched Daniel mouth a curse before replying, "No need!"

"Don't be stupid! I know where it is. You think some of Fergus is there?"

"You have to get Roger back though, don't you?"

"I don't mind popping along," came Roger's voice in the background. Steph found herself suppressing a smile.

"Stay where you are; we'll see you in ten or so."

The radio went quiet. Daniel sighed loudly.

Steph kept quiet and studied Daniel's face in profile. He refused to turn.

"Why didn't you want him here?" Steph asked finally, keeping her voice soft.

"Who said I didn't? I just thought it made sense for him to focus on Roger and for us to focus here."

"Really?" Steph raised her eyebrows.

Daniel turned to look at her. She stared at him, unblinking. For a moment he tried to hold her stare but then his shoulders sagged.

"I dunno," he said. "I mean it is better than Michael I

suppose, but it's... It's stupid really."

Steph thought she would rather it was Michael but that was neither here nor there.

"Try me," Steph said.

"I just feel that – and nothing has really been said as such – but I feel I am just the young enthusiastic dinosaur lover. I'm a fun novelty to have around. But I'm not really trusted with any big jobs. I'm nearly thirty. It's degrading!"

"But there aren't dinosaurs here?" Steph said.

"Yeah, I know!" Daniel replied, looking at the trees. "I was using it as an example. Like that kid in the family who knows all the dinosaurs and has all this intelligence in one area, and everyone nods along humouring them as they reel off fact after fact. And then the adult says, 'that's nice' and sends them off to wash their hands before dinner."

Steph considered this.

"So you don't want to wash your hands before dinner?" she said, keeping her face straight.

"What?" Daniel gasped turning around to face her. "No, that's not what I meant! I meant... ah, forget it!"

"I'm winding you up!" Steph said, putting a hand on his shoulder. "I get it. You just want to feel like you are being taken seriously for *everything* you can contribute. Not just the things people think you are."

"Exactly," Daniel replied, sighing and relaxing a little into his seat.

Steph thought about her own family in this, what they thought of her work and what they considered as *real* long-term careers. She sniffed and looked away into the trees.

TWENTY-TWO

Steph and Daniel sat in relative silence waiting for the others to arrive. After Daniel opened up a little and Steph reflected on her own life, both were not in the best place for conversation. There was little in terms of animal sightings as a distraction either, as Steph had yet to see any moose. There were birds. There were squirrels. Relative to what Steph knew she could potentially see, they seemed hardly noteworthy.

Davey and Roger pulled their buggy up alongside Daniel and Steph's. Davey looked serious. Roger was smiling sadly.

"I wish we were meeting again under better circumstances," Roger said to both Steph and Daniel, his eyes flicking between the two. "Poor old Fergus."

Steph couldn't help but smile. She was not even sure why. Perhaps it was the way in which Fergus's death was almost made out as a mildly unfortunate accident rather than his life being ripped violently from him. Maybe it was the pained look on Roger's face. Pained on the surface but with a definite giggle lying underneath. It reminded Steph of being at school and how the other boys would laugh at each other if one fell over. They knew it hurt. They knew the shouts of 'stack' would draw attention and embarrassment with it. Perhaps there was a part of Roger that wanted to laugh. What was the other option? Despair?

"From what I remember, you're in the right vicinity," Davey said looking around, ignoring Roger's greetings to the others. "I take it you haven't seen anything?"

"Not yet," Daniel replied.

"Well, that's because, if I remember rightly, it was slightly off the track – in that direction."

The others turned their heads in the direction of Davey's extended finger. He started to clamber out of the buggy, a tranquillizer rifle in hand. Steph noticed for the first time (as his shirt lifted away from his trousers slightly) that he had a handgun holstered to his side as well.

"Careful!" Daniel said, standing in his seat and looking around. "The wolf pack is nearby and there was a bear not far from them."

Davey continued to clamber down. Steph looked at the expression he gave Daniel. She could see where Daniel had been coming from earlier. The look was somehow pitying and patronising all at once even though Daniel's point was legitimate. If he had directed it at her, she might have rammed her fist down his throat.

"I think I'll be all right," Davey said. "Besides, we have little option if we are going to see whether Fergus is there or not – some of him at least."

"Well, *we* aren't staying here either!" Steph snapped.

Davey turned to look at her. He kept his face impassive, but Steph was pretty sure she heard a low growl.

"You will need extra eyes anyway!" Steph finished, starting to clamber out with her own tranquillizer rifle.

"I suspect he probably has enough eyes," Roger said, leaning back in his chair.

"I had best come too," Daniel piped up, having watched Steph get out.

"What? Why?"

"Because I have a theory I want to test – a hypothesis on the cave lion's behaviour," Daniel replied, his eyes flicking constantly past Davey's face to wherever they felt safe.

Davey sighed.

"Fine!"

"Well, hold on a minute!" Roger said, standing up. "I'm not going to stay here if he is going!"

"But you were happy enough to stay before?"

"Yes, but that was before I realised everyone else was going. We all know what happens to those who are left alone when things go wrong."

"What?" Davey asked, checking his rifle.

"They die! Just look at Fergus!"

Davey rolled his eyes as Roger leapt out of the buggy, punctuating his point.

Steph frowned. 'When things go wrong.' She had never really thought of it like that. Or had she? She considered the whole enterprise that Kelvin was trying to execute to be a complete mess. It was skewing natural behaviour. She couldn't see how it could *work*. But was it going wrong? It was designed – albeit unintentionally – to go wrong. Could something already failing, go wrong again? Her stomach churned slightly.

They set off into the trees, Davey leading from the front with Daniel not far behind and Steph bringing up the rear with Roger. To Steph's eye, Davey seemed far more nervous than his earlier bravado had suggested. He flinched at insignificant noises and constantly wanted to stop and cock his ear. Roger, on the other hand, seemed surprisingly untroubled for someone who hadn't wanted to come in the first place.

"You seem quite calm," Steph whispered.

"Well, I must admit I am somewhat concerned but I have spent a long time practising focusing my mind."

Steph frowned.

"I mean I am scared, obviously, but I can quickly add layers of context which make things easier to handle. For example, I have done enough in life already – more than most anyway – I am getting paid well for this, and, most comforting, I suspect I could probably outrun poor Daniel."

Daniel must have heard the whisper as he turned around and shot Roger a pitying look.

"I might be older than you, Daniel, but I used to represent my county in athletics before I went to university," Roger said with a wink.

Daniel turned back around, shaking his head. Steph couldn't help but laugh which gained her a reproachful look from Davey. They continued in silence. There was little evidence of any large animals. Nothing larger than a squirrel at least. Not even the common sight of churned mud that denoted the movements of wild boar was to be seen. Then Davey began to slow down.

"It was around here somewhere," he whispered, looking in all directions.

"You do realise the cave lion could be here if this is where it hides food," Steph replied. She regretted stating the obvious as soon as it left her mouth. It made her feel stupid. Panicky. Of course, they had known that. Davey didn't even bother looking at her.

They continued moving slowly, examining branches. They were further off the path than she expected to be. It was a quiet, secluded little area. No wonder the lion had thought this a place worth hiding kills in. However, it was quite far from Fergus's cabin. Too far, surely. They were wasting their time. She knew it then. She should have known it before. Why had she not realised it before? Why would the cave lion drag a kill so far? It wouldn't, surely?

Birds sang in the trees. This put Steph a little more at ease.

Squirrels then jumped overhead, chasing each other down trees. Steph's finger moved slightly further away from the trigger of her rifle.

With the fear subsiding, in herself at least, Steph noted that the area was quite beautiful in a way. The seclusion gave it a feeling of separateness from what was going on around it. A haven in the chaos. Then a thought crossed Steph's mind. She opened her mouth. However, the same thought must have simultaneously crossed Daniel's mind.

"Why were you here, exactly?" Daniel asked Davey.

Davey, who had been turning his head this way and that, stood up a little straighter but did not turn around.

"What do you mean?"

"I mean when you were with Michael when you saw the kill up the tree. Why would you have needed to come here to this point exactly?"

Davey turned around. He didn't look annoyed, as Steph had expected. Instead, his brow was a little furrowed. Still, he kept his eyes scanning the surroundings.

"Michael wanted to come here," Davey replied. "Said he had seen the cave lion slink off in this direction before and wanted to know why. He didn't want to do it when he was by himself and waited until we were both out together."

Daniel was frowning. Steph could see that Davey, for the first time she had seen in Daniel's presence, looked uneasy.

"Doesn't that seem a little odd to you?" Daniel asked, folding his arms.

"In what way?" Davey replied, his voice a pitch too high.

"Surely, you have seen animals go off in all sorts of directions and never thought to follow them before?" Daniel said.

Davey licked his lips but said nothing. Instead, he turned and continued his search. Daniel unfolded his arms and strode after him.

"Well?"

"Well, what?"

"Well, is it not odd that you went off in this direction?"

Davey sighed and turned around.

"In all honesty? Yes. It was odd we went off this way."

This had clearly not been the answer Daniel was expecting. He'd been assuming a disagreement to the point or Davey being defensive. He was lost about what his next move should be having received an admission so easily. Or was it a confirmation rather than an admission? Steph decided now might be the time to voice her own concerns.

"There's no point us being here anyway," she said.

The others turned to look at her.

"No?" asked Roger.

"No," agreed Davey.

Steph turned to look at him. He was looking at her.

"Sorry?"

"That's the tree; empty!" Davey replied, pointing to a tree to their left with a couple of lower-hanging branches.

"It was never going to be there," Steph said. "There is no way the cave lion would have dragged a kill so far from where the hunt took place."

"Maybe not," Davey conceded.

"Maybe?"

"You'd be surprised by some of what you see here; you must remember that you have only just arrived, relatively speaking. You are just scratching the surface of the place."

"Maybe, but I think I have a better idea of what lies underneath the surface than you do."

"Oh, I doubt that," Davey snorted. "I believe Daniel and I probably know the goings on behind the scenes a little better than you."

The expression on Daniel's face softened a little at this inclusion onto Davey's platform.

"I meant with the animals," Steph replied. "I couldn't give a crap about what's going on in the house or how deep into Martina Kelvin has gone."

Roger barked with loud laughter. Daniel and Davey simply looked at one another.

Steph then opened her mouth to explain what she was going on about in her *professional* opinion when something interrupted her.

A large squealing hog shot from the undergrowth. It seemed startled to be met by the four of them but had set its path and was not stopping. The only issue was that Daniel seemed to be standing on that set path. He tried to step sideways, but the move was clearly not enough for the ninety-kilogram pig who flicked its head sideways, knocking Daniel to the ground whilst simultaneously goring its tusk down his thigh.

Daniel screamed. The pig ignored him and carried on into the trees.

Steph ran towards Daniel whose leg was bleeding badly below his hands clutching at the wound. She put the rifle down, whipped off her bag and began rummaging for her first aid kit. A sudden sound, like an explosion of air, made her whip around.

Standing where the boar had just emerged from was a bear rearing on two feet, a dart protruding from its neck. It groaned slightly and fell back down on all fours. It made to move forwards again but something about its movements suggested it was uncertain. The head began to lull, its steps seemed laboured.

Already, Davey was loading up another dart.

He needn't have bothered. The bear sank to the ground with a defeated moan.

"Christ!" said Roger. "What's in those things that they work so fast?"

"Martina came up with the concoction so that it could deal with the cave bear; just means the other animals get a somewhat heavier hit. It'll be fine though."

"Will it?" Roger asked, walking up to the animal and prodding the thing with his foot.

"We need to get Daniel back," Steph said. The other two turned to look at Daniel. It was as if they had forgotten anything had happened to him. "It's quite nasty. He's going to need stitches and for the wound to be properly cleaned."

Davey nodded. He handed a somewhat surprised Roger the tranquillizer rifle as he walked past, and then helped Steph pick Daniel up from the ground.

"We'd best get back then," he said. "We'll just have to tell Kelvin that whatever is left of Fergus is likely to soon be in the digestive tract of... well, could be anything depending on how careless the lion was."

TWENTY-THREE

Davey drove with Daniel; Steph followed behind with Roger. She had never driven a vehicle quite like it. It was like driving an oversized go-kart. At the house, they were met by Kelvin and Martina. It was Martina and Roger who helped Daniel inside, who was moaning quietly as he hopped on one leg using the other two as crutches.

Davey wanted to know how Michael was getting on. Kelvin waved a hand dismissively that he was doing something or other but had delivered Thomas and Calum (the other cabin dwellers) safely to the house.

A little while later, Kelvin was sitting in the lounge area with a newly returned Michael, Davey, Martina and Steph. Daniel was up in his room recovering having been treated by Martina. Her father had been a vet, so she said she knew how to stitch well enough. Daniel didn't question her ability. Although, it could have been the gulps of whiskey Roger had encouraged him to have that held his tongue.

Steph looked at Kelvin. He was staring straight-ahead at a picture of three bear cubs on the wall. Eventually, he spoke.

"So what did you find?"

"Well as you know, we didn't find the rest of Fergus," Davey said. "We did look but... Roger seems in reasonable spirits though, given the circumstances."

"Money will do that," Kelvin replied, still looking at the bear cubs. "What about yours, Michael?"

"My what?"

"Your two whom you picked up. What did you tell them? How much do they know?"

"Well," Michael said, turning out his palms. "They know that Fergus was killed by one of the animals although they don't know which. They are a little shaken I suppose but coping."

"Coping?" Kelvin turned his head around at Michael.

"At the loss of a friend. No. *Acquaintance* is how they put it."

"But no calls to drop out of the study?" Kelvin asked.

"We're calling it a study now? Nope. If anything, they seem reassured by being moved into the house so quickly and that you're looking for the delinquent animal. Again, their words, not mine."

Kelvin nodded to himself.

"Yes," he said slowly. "Yes, tell them we found the animal. Maybe hunt one of the bears. It might not be such a bad thing for them to see it coming into the compound."

Michael nodded. Steph was not sure what she was hearing.

"Why would you need to lie to them?" Steph asked. "Surely, they have a right to know the truth. Besides, we can't carry on with the cave lion running loose."

Martina snorted and rolled her eyes.

Kelvin turned slowly to Steph, studying her. Steph was not sure whether to continue talking. A part of her told her it would weaken her position, whatever that was.

"I have heard from Daniel," Kelvin said slowly, "About what happened. However, I would like to hear from you what you believe happened. As well as your thoughts on what is going on out there thus far."

He pressed his fingers together and leaned back, his eyes not wavering from Steph's face with his unnerving gaze.

Steph looked momentarily away and then turned her head back, and trying to match his tone said,

"I believe that the lion had been studying Fergus and his movements for a while before it made its move. Maybe days."

Martina laughed.

"It is an animal. Yes, it probably knows how to hunt but it is reactive, not proactive!"

Steph ignored her. It gave her great satisfaction to see Kelvin do the same.

"The attack was too well-timed and too perfectly executed for the lion not to have done some learning before. It waited on the roof and must have got Fergus as he came back in through his doorway."

Steph then had a thought.

"Did Fergus ever say anything about noises on his roof recently?"

Kelvin shook his head but Davey suddenly piped in.

"Yes."

"Yes?" Kelvin asked, his head cracking in its new direction.

"Well, sort of. He mentioned a few days ago that his roof tiles might need seeing to, as he thought he heard them banging slightly the other night when it was windy. He assumed they might have come loose. That was all."

"That doesn't prove something was on his roof!" Martina sneered. "Fergus might have been right. It was windy, so who is to say it wasn't roof tiles?"

"Look," Steph snapped. "All I'm saying is what I think. If you think differently then I don't really give a shit!"

Martina laughed.

"And what about the other animals... from what you have seen?" Kelvin asked, still very calm.

"From early observations, I think it's a mess," Steph said.

"There seem to be too many big predators out there, territories are overlapping horribly, the behaviour of the animals appears verging on desperate – probably what encouraged the cave lion – and there will be more trouble before there is a balance. I would assume there will be killing between the animals until an equilibrium is found."

"Just give them more food, then there's no issue," Martina said, looking out the window.

Steph watched Kelvin closely. His eyes turned to the ceiling slightly. He took a deep inhale through his nose, held it, then noisily released it.

"I do believe you are right, Steph," Kelvin said, quite deliberately.

Steph had not expected this. From the reactions of the others, neither had they. Martina silently seethed.

"We cannot leave the cave lion out there," Kelvin continued.

"What do you mean?" Martina snapped. "That animal took ages to create! It is far too valuable to be just wiped out!"

"A man has lost his life!" Steph snapped back.

"A stupid man who did not take enough care of himself and who knew the risks anyway; he signed the papers. He knew!"

"Enough," said Kelvin, barely raising his voice. "We move the cave lion to the nursery facility before the police come. As for Fergus... any animal could have got him. In this case, I think it was a bear."

There was silence. Martina allowed her shoulders to sag slightly as she sat back. Her scowl eased.

"You can't do that!" Steph said. She was looking around at the others. They appeared impassive. "It's not right! The lion killed Fergus. It can't be trusted!"

"Correct," Kelvin said, taking Steph by surprise once more in his agreement. "Then again, it could never be trusted. It is a hybrid between a top predator of our age and one from the past. To assume it could ever be trusted would be folly and Fergus knew this. It was explained to him when he signed the paperwork, which he was happy to sign for the arranged financial compensation for him committing to a given time period. Martina is correct on this front."

Steph looked at Kelvin. For once she really didn't know what to say. He looked at her almost pityingly. Like a parent would at a child who just doesn't understand due to overwhelming naivety.

"Look," he continued. "Killing the lion will not bring Fergus back. In fact, it would deny us the opportunity to study it to prevent something like this from ever happening again. If one of the bears takes the heat, then so be it."

"Surely," Steph whispered, "The cave lion is a failed experiment? You can't keep going with it knowing what it will do?"

"Ah, but is it a failed experiment, or are its environmental factors failing it? You said it yourself: things are out of balance out there!"

"But it will kill again!"

"Do you crush a car when it has accidentally run someone over because there is the risk it could do it again? Do you, knowing there are road accidents all the time, refuse to drive?"

Steph folded her arms. Was she wrong to think the way she did? No. Surely not. In any other walk of life, the animal in question would be put down to prevent the loss of other human life.

Human life? Something about her own line of thought didn't sit comfortably with her. She was putting human life above animal, and in her line of work it felt wrong. Yet, she couldn't shake the feeling that it was the right thing to do.

"I can't say I agree with it," Steph said.

"Noted," dismissed Martina, flicking her hand. "So what's the plan?"

TWENTY-FOUR

The plan sounded simple enough. Get the cave lion. Sedate the cave lion. Transport the cave lion to the nursey further north until the police were satisfied that it was not the lion who had killed Fergus. Michael was keen to take the lead in transporting the animal. There was a discussion on whether the cave bear should also be transported away; there was a concern over whether it could catch the eye and draw attention away from speculation. In the end, it was decided that it stayed.

Martina had, at the last minute, suggested not reporting Fergus's death at all. This was instantly dismissed by Kelvin, who thought that would only lead to bigger problems down the line – money could only protect you so much. Steph didn't pretend to like the reasoning but was at least satisfied with the result.

The problem with the plan, however, was that it was to be carried out at night. Kelvin wanted it all done and dusted during darkness, with the police to be called in the morning. Kelvin would take control from the monitoring room, letting the other teams know where the cave lion was based on its chip. Unfortunately, the chip was only accurate to within a couple of hundred square metres. This was why it was decided that a couple of teams were needed.

Davey and Michael had initially assumed they would go by themselves, but Steph refused to be left at the house. She felt she might learn more by staying behind, but her instinct said more important matters lay elsewhere. Besides, she needed to make sure she was in the right place to do the right thing when it was needed. If and when it was needed. So she partnered with Davey.

Michael was happy to go alone in another buggy, only to have his plans scuppered by Daniel. Steph had told him of the plan, and he had limped from his room to insist he joined. He could barely walk and looked pale. Kelvin insisted he stay behind but Daniel seemed adamant. He was then backed up by Martina who claimed that Daniel would have the animals' best interests at heart, as he knew of the hard work that had gone into their creation. Kelvin had then relented, much to Michael's disgust.

Martina needlessly pointed out that Daniel could barely walk so he could hardly get in Michael's way.

Concerned by his lack of colour, Steph tried to suggest that he gave it a miss, but still, Daniel remained unbending in his determination not to miss out.

Everyone having eaten and prepared what they needed, they set out. Davey and Michael had stocked up on the equipment necessary for the night with Davey handing Steph some night-vision goggles.

"Do I not get a tranquillizer gun?" Steph asked as the gates to the compound opened and the two buggies drove through.

Davey shook his head. "You're going to sight for me, and I'll take the shot... or Michael will."

"I would feel better if I had something," Steph replied, looking around at the darkness that was swallowing them as the lights of the house faded behind the trees.

Taking one hand off the wheel, Davey leant down, pulled his trouser leg up a little and revealed a sheathed knife strapped to his calf. He unstrapped it and dumped it on Steph's lap.

"There."

Steph bit her lip. "I'd rather have something I could shoot with."

"Throw it then. Same thing."

Steph shook her head but remained silent. They drove on.

They knew the direction they were meant to head in and the rough area where the cave lion was when they had left. The large cat was somewhere to the northwest, completely the other side of the compound to the house. However, they were only halfway there when the radio kicked in and Kelvin's voice crackled through.

"How are you getting on?" came the question.

"About halfway," came the reply. It was Michael. Steph noted that Davey seemed quite happy to sit and listen.

"Well, you might want to alter your course. He seems to be moving east."

"Probably found a meal to chase. Fergus wasn't the largest of men."

Steph clicked her tongue.

"Maybe. I will keep you updated anyway. Might be best to get close and then I can tell you how far it's moved."

"Where do you think we should aim?" asked Michael.

"A couple of miles northeast of our small ben, seems like it might work."

"Small ben! It's a glorified hillock is what it is!"

"Fine, a couple of miles northeast of the glorified hillock!"

The radio quietened and they continued onwards. Every so often, the radio would kick in again and there would be a short update from Kelvin. It would be greeted by a short acknowledgement from Michael but no one else. This lasted until Davey finally communicated his own thoughts.

He picked up the radio transmitter and pressed a button on the side. "We have to be close now, surely?"

Michael must have agreed as he stopped his buggy not far ahead of them. His red brake lights on the attached trailer indicated to Davey to follow suit. Davey pulled up alongside him. They were no longer amongst trees but in another open area. Well, Steph assumed it was open. In the faint waxing moonlight she could just about see a treeline in the distance, but their position seemed to offer no shelter from the cool night wind which flicked at her hair.

Both Davey and Michael turned their lights off. Steph could make out the shadowy figure of Daniel holding up what looked like a pair of binoculars to scan the area.

Before Michael and Davey could exchange words, the radio kicked in again. "Based on where you are, the cave lion is anywhere between two to four hundred metres from you."

"In which direction?" Davey asked.

"East... roughly."

Steph could see Michael instantly scan his own shadowy outline in the supposed direction of the animal. The scope of his tranquillizer rifle came up to his eye.

"Bison," Daniel said.

"They seem pretty quiet," Michael exhaled.

Steph strained her eyes into the darkness but could neither see nor hear a thing. That was until she heard an exasperated noise to the side of her as Davey muttered something and then thrust something heavy into her hands.

"The switch is on the side," he whispered.

Steph recognised that it was the night-vision goggles. She felt along the side of them until her fingers touched something small but pronounced which easily moved. She raised the goggles to her eyes. Instantly, things became far clearer.

Like Daniel, she scanned the area whilst Michael and Davey readied themselves and went through their little rituals. The bison were clear to see. Michael was right, they all seemed quite relaxed. Maybe they had no idea they were being targeted. They were quite content, heads down chewing on the grass save for the odd raised head. Steph found this interesting, not just because she was aware of something they were not, but also because their calmness felt at odds with what she had witnessed from the predators. It was almost as if the relationship between predator and prey was not yet in sync. The prey did not seem to realise the gravity of their situation. That, or numbers kept being boosted without social learning filtering through cleanly enough.

A small gleam of light momentarily distracted Steph. Davey had turned on a heat sensor. He was directing it at the bison to check it was working. Sure enough, red figures tinged with a yellow/green outline graced his screen.

"Right, you two, stay in the vehicles whilst Davey and I go and find this thing," Michael said. "We'll radio you once we have it and you can drive the buggy with the..."

Michael stopped as he realised who was in the buggy with the trailer.

"Maybe swap over and then Steph can bring the buggy with the trailer attached."

"Why do we need to stay here?" Steph asked.

"Because," Davey butted in, "Daniel can't walk and you don't know what you're doing – you're a liability we could do without."

"Of course, I know what I am doing!" Steph spat, struggling to keep her voice low. "Part of my job entails the ability to track animals. And anyway, I thought you said I was going to be your spotter?"

"I didn't mean you are a liability in that you can't be trusted!"

"Oh."

"I meant that you would be another person at risk. It just doesn't seem necessary to me. I only said the spotter thing to keep you from kicking off in the house."

"Right."

Steph thought for a moment. She couldn't leave it there.

"But wouldn't an extra pair of eyes be safer?"

"In this case, she might be right," Michael said.

Steph heard Davey trying to subdue one of his growls in his throat.

"Who would bring the trailer over then?"

"I can!" Daniel whispered excitedly.

"Don't be stupid!" Davey moaned. "You have a gaping wound in your leg and less blood inside you than an anorexic mosquito!"

"It hurts, sure, but I can do it!"

There was quiet whilst Michael and Davey considered their situation.

"Fine!" hissed Michael, causing Davey to click his tongue in irritation. "But if you can't bring it over, let me know and I'll come to you whilst the other two stay with the lion."

Michael and Davey then leapt out of the buggies. Steph followed. It felt odd when her feet hit the grass. She suddenly realised just how open the surrounding grassland was. It was incredibly exposed. She supposed for the bison there was less chance of an ambush, but even so, had they known what she knew she doubted they would be quite so relaxed.

Michael and Davey walked a couple of steps before Davey turned to Steph.

"Listen. Michael and I will find and tranquillize the lion. Your job is to be the lookout behind us. Essentially, be the eyes in the back of our heads – keep the night-vision goggles handy.

Right?"

"Right," Steph whispered.

Davey turned to continue walking but stopped instantly to prevent himself from bumping into a still-static Michael.

"What's the problem?" Davey asked.

"The wind is blowing to the east."

"So?"

"The deer are right in front of us."

Steph decided to use the night-vision goggles to watch this exchange lest she miss any subtle facial expressions. Michael was waiting for what he said to sink in. Davey was still frowning. Then he looked behind. Then he looked forward and sighed.

"Right," said Davey.

"What?" whispered Steph. What had she missed that was so obvious?

"Basically, we have been under the impression that... put those down for a moment!" Davey pushed the goggles down from Steph's face. They scraped her nose on the way down. She decided not to complain. "We have been under the impression that the cave lion was tracking the bison from west to east."

"Right?"

"But the wind is blowing eastwards!"

"Right?"

Davey said no more. Steph wrinkled her nose. Then it sank in.

"Ah, he isn't here, is he? He is the other side of the herd!"

"Exactly!" whispered Michael from somewhere to her left. "We're going to have to go around them. The little furry bastard probably has our scent too."

"If we start going around, won't he lose our scent and focus on the bison?" Steph asked.

"Maybe," replied Michael. "But it also means dipping

141

closer to the tree line, which is a danger in itself. It will also add more time to the whole thing, which will make our chance of success that little bit slimmer. Still, we have little choice!"

They headed further south towards the shadowy tree line. Every so often the cloud above would clear to let slivers of moonlight through. At such times Michael would hold his hand up and crouch. For all of Davey's comfort in the outdoors, it was clear to Steph that Michael was the more experienced tracker with the traits of a hunter. Davey must have learnt what he knew from Michael. Steph was still unsure what Davey's experiences had been leading up to his current employment,. He was a difficult character to pin down.

The bison remained calm as they reached the trees, keeping a wide-enough distance between themselves and the animals. Spooking them would blow their chance. It was only now that Steph started to appreciate what a delicate operation they were undertaking. She had known it was not a simple one, but appreciating it was something else. The risks were high: other predators being attracted to the bison, the cave lion bolting early, or the bison fleeing causing the lion to escape. It was all problematic.

"How's it going?"

The sharp sound of the radio coming from Michael's hip made Steph's heart almost leap from her throat.

"Shut that damned thing off!" hissed Davey.

Michael fumbled angrily at his waist. He didn't even answer the voice. He just switched it off.

Steph couldn't tell whether it had been Daniel or Kelvin whose voice had pierced the quiet. She suspected Kelvin. He would want control.

Steph raised her goggles to watch the bison. It seemed Davey was doing similarly with his heat-signal detector. A few of the bison nearest to them had trotted further away. Most were settled down to eating again just a hundred yards or so from where they were hidden. A few kept raised heads in the direction of Steph and the others, but deciding there was little threat settled down to periodically taking mouthfuls from the ground.

The group kept moving. Steph kept her eyes behind them, constantly looking over her shoulder and occasionally walking backwards. She kept this up until bumping into something solid. It was Michael. He was staring out from the edge of the tree line across the open land that – now that Steph looked carefully – was open heathland.

She felt a hand on her shoulder pushing her down slightly into a crouch.

"Keep an eye on the trees behind us," Davey breathed. "If anything seems odd, tell us!"

Steph nodded. She was not sure whether the lion had been seen in the darkness. She settled down against the tree they were crouched behind and looked deep into the darkness at their back.

Apart from the sound of an owl there was nothing of interest for Steph to be wary of. She thought this would have relaxed her. If anything, it heightened her senses. It was as if something bad *was* going to happen and it was a question of when and not if. The anticipation she was building in herself twisted her insides.

Minutes passed. Nothing. She risked the odd glance back at Davey and Michael. Michael was crouched looking through the scope of his rifle. Davey was scanning the area with the heat detector.

Still nothing.

"This isn't right," Davey whispered.

"I know," sighed Michael.

A loud snap suddenly cracked through the silence of the trees.

TWENTY-FIVE

A wild boar shuffled into view, its head down, snuffling through the dirt. Michael hissed and the animal turned tail and threaded itself back through the trees.

Steph was aware that she could hear her heart beating. She wondered whether the others could hear it too. They seemed not to. They didn't say anything.

"What are your thoughts?" Davey asked.

"Well, there are a few possibilities and options," Michael replied.

The whispering of the pair seemed to calm Steph a little as she controlled her breathing. If they were happy to whisper, they must have felt they were not within earshot of anything to concern themselves about. That was her thinking anyway.

Michael continued to scan the area through his night-vision scope. "Either the lion has not yet found a target – this seems unlikely, it might have moved on and found something else – we know the boar are about, it was never tracking the bison at all, or we are just in the wrong position and it is out there but can't see it. Even so, I would have expected it to have attacked by now – the bison are there for the taking. Some at least."

"And options?"

"We stay here and wait for it to make a move it might never make, we radio Kelvin to get an update and risk giving away our position or we spook the bison in the hope it forces him out of cover."

In the moment Davey took to consider the options and give his opinion, a thought surfaced in Steph's head. She looked back in the general direction she thought they had left Daniel and the buggies.

"Spooking them might draw attention to us," Davey whispered. "He has already started to see us as an easy meal. Not sure I'd trust the bugger knowing our whereabouts in the dark."

"Not a filling meal though," Michael exhaled. "Otherwise he wouldn't be here."

"In fairness, he didn't manage to get as much of Fergus in his mouth. Bit of a messy eater what with smearing him all over the floor."

"So... radio Kelvin?"

"I think it might be safer."

Steph turned to see Michael lowering his rifle whilst reaching to his side. Then all plans changed.

A distant scream carved its way through the night sky, from across the field. All three heads whipped around. Steph's stomach knotted. The bison ran. There was silence for a moment save for the heavy thudding of hooves. Then another scream, higher, more desperate.

"Radio Daniel!" Davey said, not bothering to whisper.

"Daniel?" Michael said. Nothing. "Daniel! Pick up, you jackass!"

Still nothing.

"Damn it!" Davey grunted, rising from his crouch.

There was no need for debate; the three started making their way across the heath-strewn field in the direction of the electric buggies. As they ran, the radio kicked in.

"What's going on?"

It was Kelvin.

"Have you heard from Daniel?" Michael panted, stumbling over some unseen pothole.

"Not for the last five minutes," Kelvin's voice responded. "He said he had lost contact with you just like I had. Is he all right? Also, listen, you need to..."

Whatever it was they needed to do, they never heard. Steph was appreciative that Michael had at least had the decency to switch the radio off and focus on what was important.

They neared the buggies. Sweat trickled down Steph's back as she ran. Her breath burned as it flowed back out through her throat.

A hand stopped her running. She wouldn't have seen it if it were not for the night-vision goggles she had begun to bring up periodically to her face as she anticipated the buggies. It had been Davey who had put his hand across – yet again – but it was not only him who had decided to suddenly cut the urgency.

"What are you doing?" Steph hissed. She could see they were still a couple of hundred yards away from the vehicles. Where the cave lion was, she could not tell.

"Listen!" whispered Davey, crouching down again.

Ahead of him, Michael was already looking down the sight of his scope.

Steph listened. Nothing. No. Not nothing. Just less than expected. Every so often there was a soft guttural growl in the direction of the buggies.

"It's the lion!" Steph replied, her tone purposely saying a thousand other urgent things all at once. But then it sank in. Davey needn't have continued explaining.

"Only the lion," he sighed.

Steph swallowed. It didn't seem real. It didn't seem real that she could be in such a situation. One of substantial danger.

Sure, she had seen what had happened to Fergus, but she had never met the man. There was a detachment, not just from him, but from the reality of the danger posed by what killed him. By what was everywhere. Knowing that she was surrounded by large predators – even genetically modified ones – had not made her appreciate the danger. She knew there was danger – she was not an idiot – but she had never *appreciated* it properly until that point.

"Clever fucking pussy cat," Michael sighed.

There was an audible click and Steph turned in the direction of Davey. Michael had apparently done the same.

"Put that thing away," Michael whispered. "We aren't in need of it yet. Besides, I think for every hole you put in Martina's prized possession, she would put ten in you... and then probably fill them with some extinct flesh-eating worm or something equally unpleasant. Come on."

Michael guided them closer. Davey lowered his revolver but didn't put it away.

Steph could see through the goggles that the buggies were now only a hundred yards away. Less probably.

"He's behind the buggy," Michael whispered, his voice so light that it almost blew away in the breeze.

They edged further around to one side. Sure enough, there was the lion. There was also Daniel. It almost seemed as if there was life in him still, but this was just an illusion. Each small convulsive movement was nothing more than the lion ripping at the contents of his stomach.

Through the goggles, Steph could see his throat was a crushed, bloody mess. The lion, who was now gorging itself blind to the world around, had not made quite the same mess he had with Fergus. Even so, it was upsetting.

"Why is the door open?" whispered Davey.

Both Steph and Michael trained their respective lenses on the buggy. He was right. The side door was open.

"Who knows," grumbled Michael, training the tranquillizer on the lion. "Who fucking knows..."

Steph watched him for a few seconds through the goggles. His whole focus was directed at the lion. At that moment, it was all he saw. He slowed his breathing. His chest seemed to almost cease to move. Considering the rate at which Steph's own heart was beating, she found this quite impressive. Then his finger twitched slightly over the trigger, positioning itself, getting comfortable. Steph spun the goggles back to the lion.

A large, conceited roar broke the night once more. Steph's stomach didn't so much as clench as almost fall out of itself. It appeared that neither Davey nor Michael had noticed the sudden appearance of the cave bear amongst the heath. Nor had the lion. It instinctively placed itself over its kill, roaring back. Steph felt horrifically exposed.

She began to crouch closer to the ground, backing off slightly. Davey did the same, but Michael remained where he was, his tranquillizer rifle scanning back and forth between the two large predators.

Due to the position of the bear, Steph was still not certain whether it intended to head to the lion's kill or them – not that the lion was aware of their presence.

"You have your cowboy gun handy?" Michael asked very quietly. "Might be best to have it close."

Steph watched Davey unholster the revolver that he kept at his side. He brought it up and gently pulled back the hammer.

They watched as the bear lumbered closer. The lion, sensing it wasn't going to stop, now desperately tried to drag Daniel's carcass to some sort of safety. Steph was surprised at the speed with which it was able to move with the body. She supposed she had only seen leopards trying to perform such a manoeuvre before and their prey was probably a fair bit heavier than the delicate, broken frame of Daniel. Besides, no leopard Steph had seen had ever had muscles bulging out quite like the lion. In fact, now that Steph considered it, there was something off. Or was there? Was that just how a cave lion was meant to look?

As impressive as the lion was, it had nothing on the bear. The creature was gargantuan. It started to walk with more purpose – to Steph's relief – in the direction of the lion. Again though, there was something odd about the bear as with the cave lion. It was as if its muscle was too pronounced. It was hard to tell through the shaggy fur and night-vision goggles. Also, as Steph had already admitted to herself, she had no reference as to what was normal, but she felt something which seemed slightly off. Exaggerated. Certainly, a noticeable difference compared to other bears or lions she had seen before. She'd have to talk to Martina.

"Fuck!"

Steph turned to look at Michael.

"What?" she whispered.

"What do you mean 'what'? We're going to lose the goddamn lion... and have lost Daniel for our troubles."

Steph watched as Michael pinched the bridge of his nose and crumpled his eyes for a moment before returning to the scope of his rifle.

"Why?"

"Because the bear will see him off. They might rumble, but in the end the lion will choose self-preservation. Shooting the bear will bring the attention of the lion to us and there is no way I can reload in time. Davey is likely to want to put some holes in it which would be hard to explain to Martina."

"I would," Davey whispered.

"So... yeah... *fuck*!"

"What if you tranquillize the lion now though?" Steph asked.

Michael paused a moment. Then he shook his head. "The bear would likely kill it for not moving out its way."

Steph supposed this was true. She had witnessed grizzlies coming to blows with each other when one did not give ground. The results could be hard to stomach. She doubted the cave bear would fully grasp that the lion wasn't moving because it had sedative coursing through its blood vessels.

The bear started to trot towards the lion. The lion continued to try and make off with Daniel's body – limply hanging like a lifeless puppet. It had made it a good fifty feet or so from the buggies. Unfortunately for the lion, the bear was gaining. The lion, sensing it was futile, waited until the last possible moment and then leapt aside. The bear grunted for a few moments, made a sharp movement towards the lion to test its resolve, and then buried its muzzle into Daniel's open neck.

Steph instantly became concerned as to which way the lion was going to slink off. She needn't have worried.

Seemingly going against the tide of events, the lion, who had been so comfortable in its resignation of dinner without a fight, leapt at the bear's head whilst it was preoccupied.

"Oh, shit!" Davey choked.

The bear, stunned, reared up as the lion clung to its face. Then, in one powerful thrust, the bear flung its full weight down towards the ground. The lion, sensing danger, let go just in time to avoid cushioning the bear's giant skull as it fell. It tumbled to the side, regained its footing, and edged back as the bear shook its head.

"Right, let's go!" Davey said, pulling both Michael and Steph up by the shoulder.

"What?"

"Now!" Davey said, dragging them a few feet before releasing them and bolting for the buggies.

Adrenaline took over and Steph ran. Then she began to sprint. She started to edge past Davey who was flicking glances into the darkness in the direction of where the lion and bear were fighting. Michael was slightly slower behind the others.

Steph wrenched open the door of the buggy without the trailer and leapt in. It was the driver's seat. Davey was at the open door in a heartbeat.

"Move over!" he demanded.

Steph obliged. He knew the place better than she did.

"What about Michael?" Steph asked.

"I'm sure he's fine!" panted Davey as he turned on the engine and switched on the lights.

A second beam of light, widening the radius of the first, signalled that Michael had made it to his buggy.

"Let's get the hell out of here!" Davey spat as he floored the accelerator.

And with that, they were out of harm's way. No chase from the cave lion. No giant cave bear hammering down on the front of one of the large buggies. It was odd. It was as if they could have simply walked to the vehicles rather than all the panic. They couldn't have, Steph knew that, but even so, the contrast was stark. Then Steph remembered Daniel. The person. Not the distracting piece of meat being fought over. She began to sob.

TWENTY-SIX

"What happened?" Kelvin asked.

Steph found herself back in the lounge, a whiskey in her hand. Davey had poured one each for himself, Michael and Steph. They sat together on one sofa whilst Kelvin paced up and down the room. Martina was with him, of course, spinning a pen in her fingers.

"What happened was that Daniel got eaten and the big fucking bear got in the way of us bringing in the lion," Davey replied.

Kelvin stopped pacing and stared out of the window into the darkness.

"How did he get Daniel?"

"Dunno," Davey shrugged, knocking back his drink.

"He could smell him," Steph said.

The others all turned to look at her. She didn't look up. She just stared into the bottom of her glass.

"When we first arrived, it must have picked up our scent. Probably changed its plan right there and then."

Martina laughed. Even Michael frowned.

"I'm sorry, what exactly do you think you were dealing with?" Martina said. "It is an oversized cat – a primitive cat at that – and not some neurologically superior super killer!"

Steph still did not look up.

"I am not saying that. I am saying that it knew enough. There was enough in the memory to trigger a change in choice. It can make choices. Even the more simple-minded of creatures can make choices. It scented a target it recognised, calculated based on previous experience that it was an easier meal, and went for it."

"But then how did you miss it?" Kelvin asked, turning to look at her. "How is it that you didn't see it first?"

It was Michael who answered.

"We went one way around the bison to try and change the fact we were upwind of it, and it must have gone the other way because it was already downwind."

Steph raised her eyebrows and nodded. It was that moment she chose to take a sip of the whisky. She shuddered. It was quite revolting. She took another sip before continuing.

"What is less clear is why Daniel was outside of the buggy. Had he stayed inside, he might have survived due to the protective bars. It doesn't make sense that he stepped out."

Martina shifted in her seat slightly. Kelvin flicked his eyes to her briefly. It was enough. Steph might have missed it with her eyes down, but she suddenly heard Davey pipe up.

"What? What do you know?"

Steph looked up. Davey was staring at Martina.

Matina looked at Kelvin. Kelvin looked back out the window, his hands clasped behind his back. She sighed, almost growled.

"I asked Daniel what was going on. You guys were not picking up."

"Right. We were using common sense there; it's hard to sneak up on a creature when you're shooting the breeze with someone over the radio!" Davey replied.

Martina ignored his tone. "We were worried as it had been a while and had heard nothing."

Kelvin shifted slightly but did not look around.

"It started to feel as if it wasn't going to plan."

"You can say that again!" Michael whispered, getting up to pour himself another drink before topping up Steph's and Davey's.

"Daniel said he would go and find you."

"What?" Steph spat.

"You should have told him not to!" Davey snapped.

"I did... at first."

"What do you mean 'at first'?" Davey asked, his voice lowering to a dangerous level.

"He insisted," Martina said. "How was I meant to stop him? Besides, both he and I had concerns over the lion."

"What do you mean by that?"

"I mean we were both concerned what would be used to subdue the specimen: the tranquillizers or your revolver!"

Davey choked a little on the words he was about to say.

"Yes, everyone knows about your revolver," Kelvin said, turning around. "However," he looked at Martina here, his voice becoming stern. "Nobody really thought you *would* use that. I know you are not one to give way to panic. We really were concerned for your safety – rightly so as it happened."

Davey paused for a moment before puffing out his cheeks, shrugging and letting himself collapse back onto the sofa.

"Well, there you go then," Steph said, sipping her drink and grimacing. "The lion was probably waiting for him to get out and got him as soon as he did. I doubt Daniel even considered it was close by, what with us having gone looking for it."

"What do you mean by 'waiting'" Kelvin asked.

Steph considered her next words.

"I have no definitive evidence, save for Fergus, but I suspect that the lion has not learnt this overnight."

"Go on..."

"I mean I suspect that the lion has stalked individual people and started to learn patterns. I don't think it would learn the patterns of individuals exactly – although that is not out of the question – but more general patterns of human behaviour in its environment. Once it had decided that we were a prey animal, it then set about testing what it had learnt. In very simple terms, once we are out in the open, we are an easy target. It would not have known Daniel would step out of the buggy, but once he did, he was easy prey. More so because of his leg."

Steph knocked back her drink. Did she really think that? Probably. It was just that she had not thought about it until she said it. She had essentially given voice to it at the same time the others had. It made sense. Certain pressures pushed animals to hunt humans, and there were certainly pressures for the animals in this place.

"Well, maybe this is all something to keep in mind," Kelvin said. "Whatever the case, we need a new plan."

A new plan. Steph knew that this would include not involving the police. Not just yet. Kelvin would want more time to regain the illusion of control, tightening it under his fist.

"We can discuss it in the morning," Kelvin continued. "For now, let's just get to bed. We all need some sleep. No sensible decisions are to be made now, and we owe it to Daniel to ensure his legacy is not in vain."

Steph smiled to herself and shut her eyes. Legacy. A word consolidating, potentially, what Kelvin thought was important in all of this.

TWENTY-SEVEN

Steph was awakened the next day by the light slanting through her curtains. For a brief moment she had forgotten why she felt so tired. But then her head began to whir into life. She swung her legs out of bed and sat for a while, simply contemplating. She had no idea what the day would hold for her, nor what the decisions of others would be. What she did know was that she needed to take hold of some sort of direction for herself. She was quite aware that she was allowing herself to be buffeted around by circumstance. She needed her own direction again. She needed clarity.

Why was she here in the first place? Because of the death of the boy. Why had she taken a job with Kelvin? Because of the boy? Partly. But if she was honest with herself, it was also because she had a chance to be part of something that had the potential to be big. Even if unsuccessful it would be big, and that might be enough to soothe that spiky feeling that her parents weren't impressed with her.

She rubbed her eyes. They were still sore with the longing for a bit more sleep. She shook her head and tried to think. No direction came. She was nothing more than an undercover journalist. She was no field biologist. Just another person looking for a story to tell about others because she couldn't write her own. She put a pin in finding clarity for the time being and left the room.

There was a quiet in the house downstairs. Steph had something to eat but saw nobody else. In the circumstances it was unnerving. With little or no idea what to do with herself and all plans of studying the surrounding man-manufactured ecosystem having been thrown out the window, she went looking for people. Even Martina would do. Her first thought was to take herself to the small warren of concrete corridors below the house, but upon walking past a window she heard raised voices. She looked outside. Davey was sitting on an upturned crate, his back hunched. To the side of him stood Roger. In front of him – one with his arms crossed and the other gesticulating angrily – were two more men that Steph had yet to meet. The one with his arms crossed was tall and thin – he reminded Steph of an old maths teacher she had once had. The other was slightly shorter and stockier, his face ruddy. Out of curiosity, Steph went to investigate.

She was worried she might be too late to hear anything of interest by the time she had navigated her way outside, but the firm, elevated voice that met her as she rounded the corner of the house said otherwise.

"What exactly have you been doing?"

"Nothing that you don't already know; we've been through this!" came Davey's tired response. This sounded like a different Davey. A tired and deflated Davey.

"Well, what does Kelvin intend to do about it?"

"I told you! I don't know! I'm not his spokesperson."

"Aye, well, you're close enough to him to know his mind though, aren't you!"

"Oh, hello dear!"

Sensing an opportunity to take some of the tension out of the situation, Roger turned and drew attention to Steph's arrival.

"Come and take a seat; up you get, Davey."

"No, it's all right," Steph replied. Davey was already up.

Steph, to her surprise, had already begun to sit before she had even finished suggesting she wanted to stand.

"Davey has just told us what happened last night," Roger explained, gesturing to the two other men who nodded with single short jerks of the head and poor attempts at smiles. "These are the other two cabin dwellers. The tall one who looks like an accountant is Calum, whilst the one who looks like he has been chewing on a wasp is Thomas. Both are good poker players when you get to know them. Too good. I suspect Thomas marks his cards somehow."

The two men tried a little harder to smile and mutter greetings this time, with the stockier one briefly shooting Roger a reproachful look, which seemed much to his delight, at least to Steph.

"Where is everyone else?" Steph asked.

"Michael has gone out to find the lion again," Davey replied.

"By himself?"

"Set out in the early hours this morning. Left a message saying he would clean up the mess. Kelvin and Martina are busy keeping an eye on the trackers for him."

Steph nodded, although she thought it stupid.

"And you?"

"Me?"

"What are you doing?"

Davey shot a look at Thomas.

"PR work."

"You could do with more training," Thomas replied, putting his hands in his pockets.

There was silence, save for the birds in the trees.

"Thomas and Calum here are a little concerned about what's going on," Roger explained to Steph.

"Concerned would be an understatement," Calum said. His voice came out deeper than Steph had expected.

"Worried then," Roger said, rolling his eyes.

"Two people have died!" Thomas snapped. "Does that mean nothing to you people?"

"Of course, it does!" Davey shouted. His sudden vehemence silences the others. He took a deep breath. "Of course, it does! Which is why we are trying to sort things out."

"You said you were sorting things out last night, and all that happened was another person died!"

Davey shrugged, shaking his head. Thomas spat in disgust at this response whilst Roger gave Steph a sheepish look. There was a glint in his eye that suggested he was thoroughly enjoying himself. It was as if his straight face was doing little to suppress the grin underneath.

"Did you know we were in this level of danger when you put us in those twig huts?" Thomas continued.

Roger decided to step in.

"I hardly think that's fair; they are a bit more luxurious than a twig hut. Besides, nobody made you stay here. I rather think you, like me, Fergus and Calum," Calum blinked at the mention of his name, "Were more than happy to take part in this and not just for the money."

"What's that supposed to mean?"

"It means that this is a very convenient place to get away from things for a stretch and not be disturbed..."

"I am not escaping anything!"

"We are all escaping something If it is not someone else, then it is ourselves."

Thomas shut his mouth and put his hands in his pockets.

"Michael will find the cave lion and that will likely solve the issue," Steph said, tying her hair back into a ponytail. "It might solve a few issues."

Davey raised an eyebrow but said nothing. Steph wondered whether she had spoken the truth.

TWENTY-EIGHT

The morning wore on and there was still no word of success from Michael. Davey considered heading out himself but sat down and fell asleep instead. Steph watched him go from nodding slightly to collapsing sideways into a snore whilst they were sitting together in the lounge area. She had intended to jot her thoughts down in her notebook. She hoped that if she began to put things down on paper she could formulate a plan. She chewed the end of her pen and stared at the page. It was blank. She closed her notebook and got up, with Davey now snoring loudly.

There was something on Steph's mind that was stopping her from thinking clearly. She was uncertain whether she would get an answer, but it was worth a shot.

Just like a few days before, Steph found herself walking around the small varnished concrete warren underneath the house. She stopped at a door and knocked. It opened. Martina's confused face blinked at her.

"Yes?"

"Do you mind if I come in?"

"A little; I'm in the middle of something. What do you want?"

"I just have a few questions about the lion and the bear," she replied.

Martina looked at her watch. And bit her lip.

"Fine! I can give you five minutes, but I am very busy!"

She swept inside. Steph followed her.

"I thought you were with Kelvin monitoring the screens?" Steph said.

"It doesn't take two of us."

Martina guided Steph towards her office and sat down without offering a seat to Steph. Steph sat down anyway. The pair sized each other up.

"Well?" hissed Martina. "What is it you want to know? Or are you going to ask whether I have used superhuman brain cells to make the lion so intelligent that it is running a background check on us all so it knows where we might be at different points of the day based on our television preferences?"

Steph ignored the poorly-constructed barb.

"I do want to ask about the lion, just to help me better understand things for my job here."

"Your job here? I think you know as well as I do that your job is on hiatus for the time being. Besides, how can I give you any information that can help you do your job? As I understand it, all you do is walk around the place and see whether things fit in with what you'd expect to see. You just sort of observe other people's work and then pass yourself off as a scientist."

Steph cracked her knuckles under the table but kept her voice level. "I just noticed that both the lion and the bear looked... large."

"No shit."

"Is that what you and Daniel expected to see?"

Martina leaned back a little in her chair and folded her arms. "What are you getting at?"

"Well, the animals out there are not true representations of their ancestors. They are genetic hybrids. I know they are meant to resemble their extinct counterparts, but they can never be perfect."

"They can be close to perfect. They *are* close to perfect. I'd know."

"Yes, but not exactly perfect. I just wondered, given that situation, whether you decided to add anything else to spice things up. Whether Kelvin wanted anything extra adding?"

Martina raised the left of her top lip. "Extra?"

"Something... muscular?"

Martina smiled. It was not a friendly smile. Nor was it a dangerous smile. It was almost a pitying smile. Steph found it unnerving.

"Look. We are not running some sort of amusement park here. That is not what Kelvin is about. If that was his aim, he would open a zoo. He would not have risked," here she paused to think of the right word, "*Accidents* for the sake of a petting zoo. He genuinely believes in finding a way to integrate people and animals. He wants a better understanding between the two."

"Then why bring back two top predators?"

Martina sighed.

"I did suggest trying other things. Animals that are far less distantly extinct. However, Kelvin had two trains of thought and they were both going down the same tunnel."

"What do you mean?"

"I mean Kelvin is not easily swayed when he gets an idea into his head," Martina replied, half smiling to herself. "He wanted to prove that if we could live with something such as a cave bear or lion, then, in people's minds, living with existing wildlife would be more acceptable. I know it's already normal for some, but for those in more urban areas he thought it would sway them more. He makes a habit of reading the behavioural patterns of others. It has helped him become rich in some ways, so who am I to argue?"

Steph inhaled and exhaled through her nose in one long

action. "And his other intent?"

"Other intent?"

"You said he had *two* trains of thought."

Martina shrugged. "Well, I think, to see if he could. He wanted to be the first."

"The first?"

"To bring one back. You know how men like to swing their dicks about and compare sizes. He wants to break it to the rest of the world once he has them living in harmony with their surroundings. It is all part of the dick-swinging performance."

"So he didn't get you to beef the animals up a bit?"

"No!" Martina replied. "However, we found low levels of myostatin in the genetic makeup. I might have repressed it a bit more to make up for the state of the frozen specimens: I did not have complete faith in their condition despite appearances and Daniel's excitement." Steph looked blankly at Martina who snorted and rolled her eyes. "Myostatin inhibits muscle growth; it gives the body the signal of when to stop. Without it muscle growth can run a little wild."

Martina punctuated her reply with her palms facing upward and a shrug. Then she fell silent, looking Steph in the eye. Steph looked away. She kept her thoughts to herself as she stared at more polished concrete.

"Now, if you're done with your questions that make you feel important I have work to do!"

Martina got up and left the office. Steph stayed where she was. She looked at the desk. It was tidy. Just an expanse of polished wood and an open computer. Should she look? No. She wouldn't even know what she was looking for. Besides, Martina had been surprisingly honest. She had even satisfied her interest regarding the size of the prehistoric animals. The question was: what could she do with the information? Was it even of any use or interest?

Davey was not where Steph had left him. She supposed that was to be expected as Kelvin would likely have work for him. Did he have work for her? Or had Martina been right about her job?

Steph sat down where Davey had been lying. She tapped her fingers together. She stood up. So Martina had proved interesting and useless to her at the same time. But what had she really expected? Steph paced the room.

The hunch had been well-placed; the animals were meant to be on the stronger side. But so what? That didn't tell her how the boy had died, it didn't help her regarding how to tackle the cave lion – if she even still needed to concern herself with helping – and it didn't help her understand the balance of the ecosystem any better. In fact, with events as they were, she was not even sure what her role was within Kelvin's plans.

She stopped to look out of the window. She was aware she was standing exactly where Kelvin had been the night before. She mirrored his pose from last night. What would he be thinking? What kind of person was he below the surface?

Control. He'd be wanting control. Even if he didn't have it he would be shaping things to give the illusion of it. However, would it be as a show to others or more to fool himself? Himself. Steph was pretty sure it would be for him. A man did not spend so much time away from the public eye and simultaneously feel the need to show power to them.

The trees were moving in the wind outside which was pushing at the branches with increasing force. Steph sighed. She felt suddenly caged. She needed to be outside. Predators or no predators she needed to be outside. No. Restraint. She needed some modicum of restraint.

She shut her eyes for a moment, gathered herself and went

outside anyway.

It surprised Steph to find Kelvin standing outside staring at the fencing and the gateway to the rest of his experiment. On hearing Steph he turned his head but kept his body facing forward and his hands firmly in the pockets of his black jacket.

"I would have liked you to have been able to experience things under... better circumstances."

Then he turned back to look at the fencing and what lay beyond it.

Although feeling a little unbalanced by the way Kelvin dived midway into a conversation that he seemed to have been having without her being present for the beginning half, Steph decided to seize on the opportunity.

"Could things be much worse? Even just Fergus dying would count as better circumstances, so what does that say?"

Kelvin snorted but continued to look forward as Steph walked to stand next to him and turned her eyes in the same direction as his.

"I suppose so," he said. "Although I would never discount things getting worse. You know how people say to expect the worst but hope for the best? I am not sure they know what the worst is."

Steph turned to look at him. This time he did turn and give her a look too. It was almost pitying and yet simultaneously pitiful in itself.

"Speaking from experience?"

"More than you'd like to know. More than I would like to know, for that matter."

The only noise for a minute was from the wind. Steph wondered whether to ask Kelvin exactly what he meant. She suspected there would be little point; he was unlikely to give anything up.

"What exactly are you trying to achieve here?" she asked before clarifying with a general wave of her arm at what lay beyond. "With all this?"

"The future," he replied, quite gently.

"The future?"

"The future. The world is changing at a pace unseen in human history. Socially, politically, environmentally – well, that is perhaps not moving at an unseen pace but certainly one long gone from our consciousness – even in terms of our own evolution. I just intend to try to be near the forefront of it. One can never hope to be at the very front."

"That's quite the statement," Steph said, walking closer to the fencing and noting again how wild boar had been here too.

"Perhaps. However, I am reasonably certain that is the case. I would not be the first person to suggest it. I am no revolutionary thinker. It is just that the majority like to hide from it or not truly appreciate it even when they know it to be true."

"And you think what you're doing here is the answer to it all?" Steph asked, turning around.

Kelvin shrugged. Steph turned back around. The exchange was cryptic enough but at least she had got something. However, just like with Martina, what was she meant to do with it?

In the mud, something caught her eye. A paw print. That of a big cat. Steph had no idea how old it was. Not from where she stood, but it proved that her theory from last night might have some legs to it.

"Where's Davey?" she asked.

"Trying to locate Daniel's remains. Unlike Fergus, he deserved better; the least we can do is try and bury some of him."

Steph frowned. She was sure Kelvin's eyes flicked her way, but when she checked they just stared stoically forward. She was about to push the subject when a noise in the distance made them both turn their heads slightly.

"Ah, good," Kelvin said, not smiling.

TWENTY-NINE

Michael leapt out of the buggy, with a smile on his face. His entrance had sparked the arrival of Thomas and Calum around the corner. Attached to the buggy was the trailer and in the trailer was the cave lion.

The three waiting men both edged around to inspect the animal who lay unconscious, taking slow, long breaths.

"How the hell did you manage to get that thing in the trailer by yourself?" Calum asked.

Michael flicked an eye towards Kelvin before laughing slightly and saying, "With great difficulty. I could have done with waiting for Davey really. I had to use a blanket and manoeuvre the winch around a tree and all sorts of nonsense. Took longer than I expected. He's all right though."

Steph could see by Kelvin's positioning that he was somewhat irritated by Thomas and Calum's presence. He tried ever so subtly to have part of his back to them.

"We had best let Martina know," Kelvin said. "Is he OK?"

"Like I said, he's fine," Michael responded. "Full belly and look..." Michael pulled at the lips of the lion to expose large white fangs. "His teeth are in good condition, which is a reasonable indication of health."

"Looks like he has had to fight for his slice of *health* though," Kelvin said, eying the scaring along the animal's flank. "Hopefully his ribs are in as good order too after the winching."

"Yes, well, we have told you that this one likes a scrap."

"True," Kelvin said. "Even so, Martina will be eager to see him before we transport the animal."

"Transport where?" Thomas asked, prodding the animal in the stomach. "The thing needs to be shot!"

Kelvin ignored him.

"Steph, would you be so kind as to go and notify Martina that..."

"I said, transport it where?"

Kelvin turned to face Thomas.

"That is none of your concern. In fact, I would rather you go and wait inside the house as you are interfering with matters."

Kelvin tried to turn back to Steph again, but Thomas's hand pulled him around by the shoulder.

"That thing is completely my concern!" Thomas snapped, his voice raising a couple of decibels. "We have been out there living amongst the animals and this thing and that oversized monster that you call a bear! Now, I want to know why you'd risk our safety over its life?"

Steph caught Michael's eye. He raised his eyebrows and shook his head.

"I think you will find," Kelvin said, his voice gaining a steely edge, "That if you check your contract, it is none of your business once inside this fencing!"

Kelvin swept an arm around the fencing that marked the house boundary.

"I don't give a damn about your contract!" Thomas shouted. Steph noticed that Calum, on the other hand, still did, as he edged towards the front door of the house.

"Oh, but you should!" Kelvin sneered. "For you see, if you do not adhere to what we contractually agreed, not only will you be out of pocket, but I shall ensure my lawyers do to you what Charles II had done to the men who killed his father – in a legal sense... obviously."

Calum was at the door now. Steph got it. She was not sure what a court equivalent to being hung, drawn and quartered was, but she doubted either Thomas or Calum could afford the lawyers to prevent it.

Thomas, all sense having floated off with the breeze, pushed Kelvin hard in the chest. Somewhat surprised, Kelvin stumbled back. Michael moved forward to catch him, but Kelvin steadied himself and then thrust an arm out to stop any potential aid from Michael. He then inhaled deeply through his nose and rolled up his sleeves on the exhale.

"What the fuck do you think you can do to me?" sneered Thomas, moving forward once more. "You jumped-up tech-nerd prick! Having lots of money doesn't make you any less of a slithering piece of shit who..."

Thomas bent double as Kelvin's fist buried itself deep within his stomach. Steph winced. In the background, she noted how Calum had the door open. He clearly wanted to distance himself from his associate. Perhaps his need for the money was more desperate.

Kelvin stood back to let Thomas gain his breath and stand up.

"Sorry, I interrupted you..."

Thomas's face contorted. It was clear that this was going to get out of hand. He tried to gather himself to his full height. It shamed Steph to admit part of her was somewhat curious as to who would win out of the two men. Even so, a larger part of her felt she should do what was morally right.

As Thomas stepped forward, Steph made to get in the way. However, something stopped her. It not only stopped her, it yanked her back. She turned to see Michael's outstretched arm. She was becoming sick of this. It was not the eighteen-hundreds. She could not be manhandled every two seconds.

She looked Michael in the face ready to give him a piece of her mind. His expression stopped her.

His pulling of her arm turned into a dragging, his eyes fixed firmly over her shoulder. She allowed herself to be dragged, moving her feet to match the direction of Michael's desperation. She turned her head over her shoulder which very nearly threw her balance. Her stomach fell.

Kelvin was just turning himself as Steph looked over. His expression was one of panic. Thomas's was clear enough too. One of scorn. One of disgust. One of petty triumph as his foe ran off.

Why hadn't the lion been tied down? Why was it free to move?

Steph didn't think she would ever forget that moment. It etched itself on her memory more like a photograph than a moving picture. Time slowed down to an almost still image. And yet, there was movement. The way Thomas's glare contrasted with the danger behind him with muscles silently screaming to be allowed to snap. The speed at which Thomas's expression changed as heavy paws caressed his shoulders and lethal jaws fitted themselves around the back of his neck. That was all Steph saw. She had the sense to turn and run after that. The rest of the memory was all noise. Low focused growls intermingled with high-pitched guttural screams. In the middle of it, Steph was sure that she heard the slamming of a door.

More happened in the moments that followed. They must have done. However, the next thing Steph was conscious of was that she was no longer in the vicinity of the house. Both she and Michael were very much outside the fencing, in amongst the trees and running. There were footsteps behind her. She dared not look back, but Michael did.

"Come on!"

They ran. Steph's muscles clawed at her for mercy but she would not rest. She could not. She didn't know how. It was as if her brain had got itself stuck in a single command loop. The message 'run' was all that was getting through. It was only when Michael finally shouted at her to stop that awareness kicked in.

She turned around. She had not really noticed that she had put any distance between herself and Michael, but there it was. A figure running out from behind a tree just ahead of Michael made her start, but it was only Kelvin who came to a stumbling stop and put his hands on his knees, panting loudly, matching Michael.

Steph controlled her breathing and put a finger to her lips as she stared back in the direction of the house. At least, she thought it was the direction of the house. Through the trees and the preceding chaos it was hard to tell.

The other two kept their hands on their knees but turned their heads in the same direction, working harder to keep their own breathing quiet. They all listened. Nothing. There was only silence. That was a dangerous sign in itself.

Steph turned slowly on the spot, scanning their surroundings. It seemed that Michael had gained enough air back in his lungs to similarly do what he thought prudent. Steph put her hands on her hips and looked at the other two.

"So what do we do now?" she asked. "Calum and Martina are still back there."

Michael looked at Kelvin. Kelvin looked at the branches above him. Steph could see his mind whirring as he looked at nothing in particular. You could see up to the sky through the leaves above but it was merely a grey canvas. Nothing worth distracting oneself about. She assumed that was the point. With nothing to look at, Kelvin could focus on his thoughts. He lowered his head and looked at them both.

"We get to safety."

"What?" Steph spat. "What about the others?"

"They're both in the house. I'm sure Calum will have told Martina by now and they are both taking the necessary precautions. Roger seems to know how to look after himself. Besides, objectively speaking, they are in a better position to try and ensure our safety than we can help them. We have no weapons," Kelvin looked across to Michael who nodded ruefully. "We also have no radio and no idea where exactly the lion is. On the other hand, Martina has access to the tranquillizers, has video surveillance and only has to worry about the lion."

"What do you mean by 'only has to worry about the lion'? That thing is killing people!"

"Yes, but we are currently out in the enclosure with all the other animals that, if my memory serves me correctly, are also capable of killing and are – as you made very clear – not behaving in a normal way as we have not quite got the balance of the place right yet!"

He had a point. Steph knew it. It didn't sit right with her, but she knew what he said was all true and that, despite her gut feeling that they should be doing something to help the others, the evidence suggested they were the ones in more immediate danger.

"Look," Kelvin continued, his voice softening now he had more breath back in his lungs, "If we can get to a cabin, at least we will have four walls around us, some food and there will be a radio transmitter so we can get in contact with Davey or

Martina to make sure things are all right."

"Fine," Steph sighed. "So which direction?"

Michael pulled a small battered-looking plastic compass from his pocket. He must have clocked the look Steph gave him because he smiled wistfully and said,

"My dad gave it to me when I joined the Scouts as a kid."

He went back to studying it, turning himself slightly to his right.

"I would suggest that we go this way," he said pointing. "There's not much in it between Thomas's place and Roger's. However, this way tends to keep us further away from the cave bear's territory."

"Isn't it all his territory?" Steph snorted.

"Well, yeah, but there is less going on for him in that direction, generally speaking."

"Oh good, so it is just all the other big animals that will be there trying to stay out of its way."

Michael shrugged and began walking. Kelvin, without looking at Steph or even acknowledging her points, walked after Michael in the way one would a paid guide.

Steph looked down at the ground, swore and followed the other two.

THIRTY

The ground was wet still from the previous night's rain. Steph was glad to be wearing her hiking boots and not caught short in trainers. It was a minor victory in the circumstances but at least her feet were dry. Kelvin seemed to have a harder time avoiding slipping and every so often would have to grab a tree trunk to steady himself. He was more at ease when they walked through stretches in the open through long grass, although he did little to mask his mutterings as he looked down at his sodden brown leather loafers.

Some wild boar briefly crossed their path at one point, but other than that, Steph was surprised they had not come across anything else. Maybe it was the displacement of the lion; news spreading around the animals in the area to make themselves scarce. It didn't lessen Steph's unease.

They were all visibly relieved when Thomas's cabin came into view, their shoulders relaxing. The door was shut, and for the first time, Steph considered the question 'what if it was locked?'

Michael went up to the door handle and pulled it down. The door clicked open.

"Sums Thomas up," Kelvin sighed. "All panic and no thought!"

Steph wondered what had been said to him when he left his cabin, but it must have been enough to inhibit his usual habit loops.

Both Kelvin and Steph were about to walk inside when

Michael held out a hand and turned a silencing finger towards them. Steph instantly felt her heartbeat increase. What had he heard? She took an instinctive step back and glanced over her shoulder. There was nothing there. Nothing but distant trees, bushes and overgrown grass.

Michael went inside. Steph let him go. Kelvin did the same. Neither felt it necessary to risk themselves. Once again, Steph felt a small pang of shame in her chest.

They needn't have worried; a minute later a light flicked on, contrasting with the dimming afternoon light under a sky which had dropped to a darker shade of grey.

"It's clear," Michael said as he came to the doorway. "I just wasn't sure whether anything had got in seeing as he'd left the door unlocked."

"And shut the door behind it?" Kelvin asked, raising an eyebrow as he stepped through the threshold.

"A bear could," Michael said, almost defensively. "Besides, this door swings inwards so it could easily have knocked it shut and trapped itself inside."

"And couldn't let itself out the same way it got in? By using the handle?"

"It probably would have pushed and not pulled," Michael said, quite seriously.

Kelvin gave Michael a piercing look. Michael shifted his feet uncomfortably for a second before turning away to busy himself with picking through a half-eaten packet of crisps.

Steph thought about what he said as she shut the door behind them – she was careful to turn the lock and slide the bolt across. Would a bear know how to get in? It was possible; it could stumble across it by accident. Bears were becoming pests in many areas in North America due to the ever-encroaching urban expansion. It was common for them to raid bins. Besides, despite what people would like to think, most mammals have a reasonable level of intelligence. It was part of their evolutionary heritage. Steph often imagined how dangerous orcas would be if they had opposable thumbs and fingers to manipulate things. Then again, humans were showing already how dangerous an animal could be with the manipulative digits.

Thomas's cabin was quite different to Roger's. Whether it was massively different to Fergus's was hard to say seeing as Steph's eyes had been more drawn to that cabin's red aesthetics rather than the overall arrangement of things. Thomas seemed much more minimalist. There was a small shelf with a few select books – most of them seemed to revolve around maths and card games – as well as a closed laptop on the coffee table and a half-drunk mug of coffee on a coaster. That was really all of note, apart from the crisps Michael had committed himself to. Everything else seemed to be original fittings. There was little really to say what type of person Thomas was… had been. Steph noted there were packets of Frosties and Coco Pops on his shelf, although she was not sure that a grown man who ate children's cereal suggested anything – everyone knew that children's cereal was tastier. It was only the need to eat healthily that put bland porridge and granola in her bowl.

"So what's the plan?" Steph asked.

"We radio the others, like I said," Kelvin replied, already heading towards the back of the cabin.

Steph stayed where she was, letting her eyes follow Kelvin. He reached a small side table at the back of the room between the doors leading to the bedroom and the bathroom respectively. The radio was on the side table. Even this looked like it had been tidily placed so as not to draw too much attention to itself. He began twisting the dials, a white noise beginning to fill the cabin.

A howl sounded somewhere in the distance. Steph looked outside as the first splashes of rain began to patter onto the window. She couldn't see anything. Another howl answered the first. Again, it was a way off in the distance but had clearly come from a different direction.

"Bastards," Michael huffed, rummaging through the cupboards. Steph suddenly realised how hungry she was and was grateful when Michael offered her a cereal bar. He then pulled out a few packets of dried noodles. "Not a chef, is how one might have described Thomas."

As Michael began to rummage for a pan to fill with water, Steph turned her eyes back to Kelvin. He was frowning.

"Any luck?" she asked.

For the first time since she had met him – even taking into account the deaths going on around him – he looked concerned. There was an insecurity in the way his eyes met hers before they briefly flicked away.

"No..."

"No?"

"Nobody seems to be picking up at the house."

"Have you tried Davey?" Michael called from the kitchen around the corner.

"Of course, I tried Davey," Kelvin replied, walking through to sit on one of the plain grey sofas.

For a moment Michael stopped. He didn't turn around or say anything, but it was clear to Steph something had caught him. Then he continued pouring water into a pan.

Steph sat down next to Kelvin, contemplating. Outside, the rain intensified.

THIRTY-ONE

Michael served the noodles – a meal she had not had since university. Even so, Steph found the food comforting and was surprised at her appetite considering the turmoil unfolding around her.

She wondered how things had become so bad so quickly. Had she anticipated this happening? No. No, she had not. She had been pretty sure things weren't right and that a potential disaster was looming, but never had she imagined this. After one tragic death, she would have imagined that procedures would be put in place to prevent further slippage. In theory, things had been put into action, except that none of the decisions really allowed for chaos or even considered the worst-case scenarios. Had Kelvin realised these things might not work? Maybe. Perhaps he had put them down as worthwhile risks. However, it would clash with his need for control, so possibly he was just naïve.

"So what do we do now?" Steph asked, getting up to put her bowl in the sink.

"Try the radio again I suppose," Kelvin replied. "Although perhaps that's pointless as someone would have tried to get in contact with us if they were able to."

Somewhere in the distance clouds crashed together causing a clap of thunder to rumble over the land.

"I could go back to the house," Michael suggested. "Try and collect a few weapons and check whether the house is clear. I could lock the perimeter fence to the house again and come and pick you up."

"Perhaps," Kelvin replied, looking at the floor.

"You could keep in contact with me," Michael continued. He headed over to the radio on the small side table and detached something small and black from it, holding it up to Kelvin. "It has a full eight hours of charge. I can just turn it on if I have anything that I need to report."

"What if I need to contact you?"

"We can agree on set times," Michael suggested. There was something in his voice that reminded Steph of a teenage boy trying to persuade their parents of something. There seemed to be an overly convenient answer to everything despite the obvious perils that appeared to be wrapping themselves tighter around the situation.

Again, Kelvin said nothing, instead looking up at the ceiling. There was a part of Steph hoping that Kelvin would agree to it so that she would be alone to question him. However, her gut suggested that going with Michael – even in the face of logic – was what she needed to do. Besides, she doubted she'd get much from Kelvin. After eating and getting four walls around him, he seemed to have regained his composure and was very much the boss again – in his eyes.

"I suppose Michael could check on Martina," Steph said, risking putting a hand on Kelvin's shoulder as she came to sit down beside him once more. It was an awkward hand. She was not the most accomplished person when it came to displays of care or affection. Then again, from the twitch in Kelvin's shoulder, he was not the best at receiving them. "I could even go with him."

Kelvin turned to face Steph. "But it's not safe!"

"Was it ever safe out there?"

"True, but what is in it for you?"

Kelvin's bluntness took Steph back for a moment. Not only because of the question but also because of the lack of an answer she had for it.

"Nothing is in it for me apart from sorting things out, but two pairs of eyes will be better than one," Steph replied, looking at Michael who narrowed his eyes slightly. She turned back to Kelvin.

"I suppose, in theory, it would be safer," he replied thoughtfully. "Although shouldn't you wait until tomorrow? It's only going to get darker and waiting will allow for the storm to let up."

"The weather might play to our advantage if anything," Michael said. "Heavy rain and thunder will mask the sound of us moving."

"And what about the wolves we heard earlier?"

"Probably moved on by now," Michael replied, although he didn't sound wholly convincing.

"Fine."

"Right then," Steph said, turning to Michael. Michael gave a small shrug and then went to raid Thomas's fridge.

THIRTY-TWO

It was agreed that they should check in with Kelvin on the hour every hour unless there was a good reason not to. Kelvin was not to contact them to avoid any noise at an inconvenient time, or so Michael said. In reality, Steph could not see why Kelvin would need to have them check in every hour. It was not as if he could do anything for them if they were in trouble; it was all about control again.

Steph wiped the rain from her face as she followed Michael. Michael walked a few paces ahead using a long, sharpened stick as a staff – he had taken a carving knife from the kitchen to fashion the spear. The knife he kept tied to his waist having tied numerous socks around the blade to prevent accidents. The thing looked bizarre, but Steph understood the precaution. She thought about the knife around her lower leg, still there from when Davey had given it to her.

"You needn't have come," Michael called back over his shoulder, continuing to shine his torch close to the ground.

Steph didn't answer and they continued walking. The ground was sodden. In places, Steph would find her feet sinking an inch or two into the ground. Why anyone would want to be out in this weather was beyond her. In the beam of Michael's torch, Steph could see evidence of deer tracks. They really did get about the place; probably constantly shepherded from one potential predator to another.

"So what's your plan when you get to the house?" Steph asked after a few minutes, jogging to pull up alongside Michael.

Michael acknowledged her and said, "Find out what has gone on in the house – check on the whereabouts of Calum, Roger and Martina – go and get the damned lion."

"By yourself?"

"By myself. It works better that way. Things only seem to go wrong when other people are involved." Michael let out a forced laugh. The tone was wrong. Steph couldn't put her finger on it exactly, but it was not a genuine laugh. It didn't sound like a genuinely sarcastic laugh, nor a particularly annoyed laugh. It was a masking laugh. But masking what?

"Fair enough," Steph replied. She wondered what her own plan was exactly. Go with the flow? It was more of a torrent. She was also aware of how little the police featured in her concerns. It was funny. Twenty-four hours previously, she had been adamant they should be contacted, but now she didn't care. If anything, they should probably stay away for the time being, but surely after things were brought under control, they would have one hell of a mess to look at. A lot of unforeseen paperwork for some poor bugger. Steph suddenly laughed to herself.

"What's funny?" Michael asked.

"Nothing... just that it's odd, isn't it? That we always assume we can be in control and that control is just around the corner with the next decision."

"What do you mean? Why's that funny?"

"Well, it's not funny really, just that I caught myself thinking that things would come under control soon because that's what we are setting out to accomplish."

"Why wouldn't they?"

"Well, why should they?"

"Because everything finds balance in the end."

Steph raised an eyebrow. Michael smiled slightly avoiding

her eyes despite the dark.

"I don't mean in any sort of hippy-trippy sort of way. I just mean that things always find a new status quo, even if it is not the balance that we wanted. In this case, I assume that if left unattended, some of the predators will die, the others will settle territories or at least behaviour patterns and the prey will grow and shrink in numbers accordingly. Or everything dies because the predators eat all the prey and have nothing left to eat... except for the bears I suppose. Being an omnivore has its perks."

In fairness, Steph assumed a similar thing.

"However," Michael continued, "in this case, that won't happen as I will take the lion out of the equation. Control of the house will be regained, and we will likely force the balance before it occurs *naturally* – although I use that term loosely."

He looked at Steph, holding his torch to illuminate them both. His facial expression held a look of self-satisfaction. Steph lowered the corners of her mouth and nodded in mild recognition of the logic. Even so, deep down despite seeing the reasoning, she held the unease that much was built on assumption and hopeful prediction. If there was one thing that she had learnt over her time looking into strange goings on – indeed, even in her studies at university – it was that people were generally poor at foreseeing anything. People assumed some individuals were great at guessing because their notable successes had such a large spotlight shone on them while ignoring the numerous errors hidden in the background.

They carried on. Every so often a sound would penetrate the wall of noise caused by the rain and Michael would crouch low, signalling for Steph to do the same. Sheet lightning illuminated the landscape every so often, but eventually that passed too. The first hour passed and Kelvin was informed of their progress. The exchange was short and to the point.

As the rain began to seep through the coat she had taken from Thomas's closet, she began to wonder why she had chosen to come. Her gut had definitely told her it was the right decision, although it was not clear why yet. Or was it the right decision? Maybe she'd just been hungry still.

"When you get the lion – if you get the lion – will you drive the lion to... to wherever this other place is? The breeding facility or whatever Kelvin calls it?"

"Yep," Michael replied.

"And do you think we should do the same with the cave bear?"

There was a moment's hesitation before Michael answered – it was short but it was there.

"It could be the thing to do. I haven't really thought about it but maybe one animal at a time. The bear hasn't been the one killing people."

"Yet."

"I don't think it will."

"Why not?"

"It doesn't have to! It can take the kill of any animal it wants. It doesn't even have to ambush its own prey!"

"Yet."

"What?"

"As you said, things will find a way of *balancing out*, whether that's through changing of territories or the death of other animals. At the end of it, the bear might find it needs to change its behaviour to survive."

"I suppose," Michael allowed.

There was a lull in conversation until Steph asked, surprising even herself with the topic, "How exactly does one navigate the black market?"

"What do you mean?" Michael asked, stopping momentarily before deciding that it was too wet to stand still.

"I mean, did Kelvin acquire what he needed to start breeding what he has from sources he shouldn't have touched... in a legal sense? To an outsider, it just seems that the whole thing is a bit niche if you get what I mean. A black market is underground, right? So how the hell would you find it? How would Kelvin know anyone?"

She could see that Michael was not wholly comfortable and was clearly choosing his words carefully before he spoke.

"I suppose, that money talks in all areas," he replied thoughtfully.

"Meaning?"

"Meaning, that I don't know for sure, but I suspect he knew people who knew other people who knew of people in a certain area."

"Right?"

"Essentially, he can cast a bigger net in the hope of finding something than the average man can. He probably didn't even need to use his name, just numbers. Large numbers attract people and there are a lot of large numbers going around in this game."

"What game?"

Another small pause.

"This, general... extinct animals game."

Even through the torrential rain, there was a palpable new atmosphere. It is the atmosphere someone feels when something is said by mistake. Steph was just not sure what it was exactly she had said. But the slight hunch in Michael's back suggested he had a stronger connection to the statement than he publicly acknowledge.

THIRTY-THREE

Eventually, they came across one of the dirt tracks created by the electric buggies as they navigated their favourite routes over the terrain. Michael stopped.

"What is it?" Steph asked, reaching down her leg to feel the top of the knife under her trousers.

"I don't know," Michael said, crouching lower. Steph walked up beside him to see what he was looking at. It was tracks. Tyre tracks. They were fresh. Fresh enough anyway. The buggy had clearly sunk deep into the mud as it drove along suggesting that it had been driven when it started to belt it down.

"You think it could be Martina and the others?" Steph asked.

"It could be. But I'm not really sure where it was going. I suppose there is another gate out that way. It's not used much but..."

Steph watched as he got up. He seemed to hesitate for a moment as to which way to go. Then he turned to follow the tracks in the direction of the tread.

"Not used much but what?" Steph asked. He didn't answer. He was a little further ahead and maybe he hadn't heard her. She suspected that wasn't the case.

They walked with their heads down. At one point, a lone deer crossed their path but that was all they saw. Everything else seemed to be seeking shelter from the rain. Then Michael stopped again. Steph saw why. His small circle of light from the torch still shone on the tyre tracks, but they began to lose definition now. They were becoming one long streak that started to vary in width.

"They lost control!" Michael said. "But why?"

Steph shadowed him as he followed the tracks more slowly, periodically looking up and shining his torch at random spots. Then they saw it. Steph noticed it first and let out a gasp. She didn't mean to; it escaped her before she'd registered her feelings.

New tracks met the tyre tracks which were curving completely off their usual route. These tracks seemed to slide slightly too. However, one part of them was unmistakable. That of a paw. It was huge. Steph watched Michael instinctively flick the torch in the direction the tyre tracks had gone.

"Ah, shit!" he muttered. In front of them was one of the buggies, its bonnet hugging a tree, its doors wide open and its seats empty.

Steph had to fight her instinct to shout out names. Instead she reached down and pulled the knife from its sheath. Her heart felt as if it would explode. The darkness around them now seemed somehow gloomier than it had before. She was sure there had been some light before, but now she realised she could not see a thing beyond the torchlight.

At this point, for reasons Steph could not understand at the time, Michael then shone the torch back down to the ground again, crouching low.

"What are you doing?" Steph hissed, spinning her head around in wide circles and seeing nothing beyond her nose. She turned back to look at Michael. He waved a quieting hand.

"The bear didn't chase them," he said slowly, standing up.

"What do you mean?"

"Look!"

Steph looked down at the ground as Michael slowly followed the tracks. They were spaced evenly and reasonably close together. There was nothing to indicate a running gait. The tracks meandered towards the stranded buggy for a few paces before veering off and carrying on their way.

Michael snorted as he looked at the tracks swerving off into the mud, already somewhat full of water where the animal had sunk deepest. Then he carried on towards the buggy. Steph followed.

There was nothing in the buggy of note. What was more interesting were the three sets of footprints that headed in the direction away from the path and the buggy. These did have an exaggerated gait suggesting they'd tried to move at speed. Steph thought it only suggested their intention because one set of tracks seemed to be a little streakier on the left leg as if they were dragging their leg slightly until the other pair of tracks joined them and the speed increased a little.

"It looks like they all got out," Steph said.

Michael grunted.

"We should go after them; make sure they're all right," Steph said, heading out in the direction of the beam of light that illuminated the tracks. Then the light disappeared. Steph turned around. Michael was walking back towards the pathway.

"What are you doing!" Steph hissed, trotting after him and trying not to slip on unforeseen patches beneath her.

"Heading back to the house like we planned."

"What about the others?"

"They got away; us going after them won't make a difference. We'd be playing catch-up."

"But... they could be in trouble!"

"Then getting to the house, retrieving the necessary

equipment and bringing a degree of control to the situation would likely be a big help to them."

"One of them is clearly hurt!"

Michael didn't answer straightaway. He stopped and turned before striding towards her. Steph instinctively squeezed the hilt of the knife tighter. He was marching towards her with purpose. She was almost certain he was going to hit her. But why?

Michael stopped right in front of Steph. She winced slightly. Then she felt something thrust into her hand. She looked down. It was the radio.

"If you're so concerned, you go after them!" he said. He turned around, walked a few paces and then came back, rummaging in his pocket. "Here!" He thrust something else into her hand. It was a torch.

"You had a spare this whole time?" she snapped.

"I might have needed it," he replied, then he turned and walked off into the sodden darkness.

For a moment, Steph thought she was going to follow him. He was probably right; what could they do? They would probably be playing catch-up and there was no guarantee they would find the others before they encountered something less friendly. The fact the giant cave bear was meandering about didn't fill her with reassurance. Then again, perhaps that was why they had not encountered any of the other predators.

Steph turned on the torch. She shone it briefly in the direction of Michael, his own light already starting to become engulfed in the distant night. She shook her head and turned towards the buggy. She shone her torch down, found the tracks and began to follow.

THIRTY-FOUR

As soon as she was out of Michael's sight, Steph radioed Kelvin. It was not on the hour mark, but she was sure current circumstances trumped that.

"And he just left?" Kelvin asked, his voice rising slightly.

"He said it made more sense to get to the house to try and bring everything under control."

"I suppose I can see the logic," he said, his voice calming a little. That reply did not surprise Steph. "Are any of the tracks... Martina's?... Hello?"

Steph looked down. One of the sets of shoes was definitely smaller than the others. She had no idea what Martina had on her feet, but the size alone suggested these were likely women's prints.

"Hello?"

Steph stood up and counted to six. She enjoyed listening to the slight panic in Kelvin's voice on the other end. Something she controlled and not him. She had no intention of trying to play with him as a means of being vindictive, it was more to test him. She had not known any of these people long, and given the current circumstances, she thought it was likely important she knew what kind of people she was dealing with. A little forced openness was always useful. How strong was the bond between Martina and Kelvin? Besides, if she got out of all this it would likely make an interesting side-story. One she could sell well beyond her usual market of conspiracy theorists and dreamers. This was real drama. Screw being worried about earning respect in her professional field. She would gain the respect of her parents by demonstrating financial achievement.

"Hello!"

"Sorry, I was just looking at the prints. I think so."

"You think so?"

"I think Martina was here. One set of prints is smaller than the others. One of the people is injured though. Martina and one other seem to be helping them."

"Right."

Right? Was that all he could respond with?

"Well, let me know when you find them!"

With that the exchange was over. A curtain opening and closing almost in the same movement. Steph slowly stored the radio away in an inside pocket and zipped up Thomas's jacket. She wasn't even sure whether she would find the others. She wasn't certain what she was doing. Her training had only been in following and documenting animals at her own pace, not tracking other people whilst desperation raged in both parties. Even so, she walked on.

At first Steph found it easier than expected. The small group had left numerous footprints in the saturated mud between the trees. Things got a little harder when the trees gave way to open space where long grass lessened the indentations in the ground. She paused for a while. The grass seemed to be broken in a couple of places; shallow grassy trenches where someone or something had been. The problem was, there were quite a few. Animals definitely passed through and some clearly had their preferred routes.

As she stood there, she suddenly realised how cold she was. She was uncomfortable. Water was finding ways to seep into crevasses in the jacket and she felt sweat cooling on her body.

She shone her torch at the grass again. Two of the routes

seemed to have grass which curled over at the top slightly. She huffed rain away from her lips, dipped her head and took the route which seemed larger.

This proved to be, at the very least, not a disastrous choice. She was able to make it through the open space without encountering anything unsavoury. Even the rain felt like it was easing slightly – a good omen. She wasn't sure she actually believed in omens, but in her current situation she was willing to use whatever placebo was necessary.

She climbed a small ridge leading to another treeline. She stopped. She shone her torch left and right. Nothing! She cursed under her breath. She walked along the tree line looking desperately for any sign of the footprints. The soil was soft and more exposed, no longer protected by grass and heath vegetation. Even so, she could see no prints. Well, no human prints. There were prints of two other animals: wild boar and, if she was not mistaken, badger.

Why had she come this way? Had she really thought that she would track them down? Did she really think that she was that skilled? No. No, that was unfair on herself. She had made her decision based on the assumption that she was doing what was right, not necessarily what was easy. Besides, she had presumed they wouldn't have gotten very far, not with an injured person.

She shook her head and ploughed into the trees. Better onwards than static indecision.

The trees intensified the darkness once more. Out of curiosity she turned off her light and tried to continue walking. Something to shake things up. Her world became pitch darkness. People said that if you lost one sense, your others became heightened. She decided to test this idea and took a few tentative steps, felt her foot catch under a tree root and stumbled forward, barely preventing herself from falling. For a moment she just stood and listened into the night. Once again, she became acutely aware of how heavy her own breathing was. There were a lot of other noises. Were they all caused by the rain? It was logical to suggest the majority were. But all of them?

She decided that the only sense that was being heightened was her sense of fear. She turned the torch on again. No sooner had she turned it on, than she heard a stick's snapping echo ring through the trees towards her.

She jerked the beam of light in the direction of the noise. Movement. The torch was not powerful enough to discern with any clarity the shape of the movement, but there was definitely something large advancing towards her. She stood still, becoming aware of the movement's deep guttural breaths. Why *was* she stood still? Why weren't her feet moving?

As if her limbs had finally caught up with the lag in her head, she turned and ran. It was difficult as she had to look down at where the torch shone in case she tripped over an errant root. She could hear leaves being brushed aside behind her, twigs snapping and the wet ground being pounded by something heavy. Running wasn't even sensible, was it? There was nothing that she could outrun. Yet, what else could she do?

She leapt over a fallen tree, miraculously kept her footing and took a sharp left hoping agility might save her. Foolish. On the wet ground, her feet went completely from underneath her, and she fell with a sickening slap. Her hands glided through the soft forest floor. Cold wetness instantly breaching her khaki trousers.

Thousands of thoughts crossed her mind in the brief seconds that followed. Was she going to die? How *would* she die, exactly? Could she grab the knife and fight off the creature? What was chasing her?

All these thoughts, each equally short and therefore almost incoherent in her mind, flashed through. There was a flash of light and a loud bang. Before she had time to reach for the knife and at least roll over to face her attacker, it was on her. She felt its warm weight on her legs. One giant mass, crushing her limbs, its hot breath contrasting with the cold damp air. Another loud bang. Another. The breathing stopped.

THIRTY-FIVE

Steph tried to roll over. She couldn't; her legs were trapped. The best she could do was turn her torso and try to look over her shoulder. Her torch had spilled from her hand when she fell so there was precious little light shining in her direction. Even so, she was sure she'd been right, it was a bear. It had to be, being that size.

Rushed footsteps came towards Steph. Two rough hands grabbed her under her arms, a torch hanging from the belt of the person so that all Steph could see were legs and boots. She was dragged out from underneath the dead weight atop her.

"Where the hell did you come from?"

She recognised the voice.

"I was following you! Where are the others?"

"Just over there," Davey replied. Steph had no idea where he was pointing in the dark. She got to her feet and shone the torch on the bear. It was, now that she could see it up close, a huge grizzly. Blood dripped down its flank, matting the fur underneath.

"We were trying to keep ahead of this thing," Davey said, brushing Steph off. "Anyway, we need to go. Goodness knows how the other animals will react to the gunshots."

"Wouldn't it scare them away?"

"You'd think! Who knows for how long though! I've never used my revolver before so it's an unfamiliar sound to them."

Davey turned and ushered for Steph to follow. She took one last look at the bear, ignored how close she'd come to death and pushed on.

They had not gone more than thirty or forty feet when Davey started coaxing two figures from their hiding place. In the torchlight Steph could see the tall frame of Calum being supported by the determined figure of Martina.

"Where's Roger?" Steph asked.

"Dunno," Davey replied. "Not with you?"

"No."

Davey shrugged.

The news worried Steph. She had liked Roger, what little she knew of him. Of course, 'dunno' was not a guarantee of a fatal ending, but in the current circumstances not being accounted for was not a good sign. She shook her head. Now was not the time for emotions.

Wanting to feel that her catching up with the others had at least some use, she went to support the other side of Calum.

Davey looked at her for a moment, hesitated and then said, "This way."

Contrary to Davey's fears, the gunshots brought them some space, or so it appeared. For half an hour they encountered nothing. Completely unmolested, they meandered through trees and eventually onto a track. Davey shone his torch – one that Steph noticed was considerably more powerful than her own – into the distance, illuminating the back of a cabin.

"There!" Davey hissed.

They limped on. Calum was whimpering quietly with every step, his right knee failing to bend as it should. Considering his size he was surprisingly light, his frame beneath his clothing clearly thinner than it appeared.

Steph put her head down and ground out the last few steps. It was only on reaching the porch of the cabin that Steph realised where she was.

"Isn't this Roger's cabin?" she asked.

"Yeah," Davey replied, taking over from Martina who was moaning about her shoulders dislocating.

"But why are the lights on?"

Davey stopped trying to move Calum forward for a moment and looked at the cabin again. They had all seen the cabin in the distance, but nothing had clicked. The situation seemed to have robbed them of rationality.

"Maybe he left the lights on when he left?" Davey suggested, still not moving.

A figure suddenly passed by the window. Steph's heart stopped. Calum tried to make a step backwards, cursed and then clung a little tighter to his supports. The door opened.

"Are you coming in or are you planning on continuing your nighttime stroll?"

It was Roger.

"Oh, so you did make it out then?" Davey said, helping Calum over the porch.

"So it would seem. Thanks for your deep concern. What happened to him? Are you all right, Calum?"

"Splendid!" Calum grimaced as he passed by. Roger raised his eyebrows.

Martina didn't say anything to Roger. She didn't even look at him. She did give him a one-handed, single pat on the chest as she walked past but that was about it.

"What happened?" Steph asked, approaching Roger.

"Oh, there will be time for all that in a moment. I think for now however, we should get inside, don't you?"

Steph looked over her shoulder, bit her lip and walked in past Roger, who shut the door behind them both, locking it.

Roger handed out towels and made tea. Davey was quite at ease stripping off his wet clothes and putting them on radiators in the few rooms that made up Roger's cabin. Steph supposed, from a practical standpoint, he had the right idea, although was surprised at how comfortable he was displaying his sodden Batman underwear. Martina, frowning at Davey, sat and shivered in her wet clothes under her towel. Steph was surprised to find that Thomas's borrowed coat had actually done a good job keeping most of the wet out. Unfortunately, it had done an equally good job at keeping sweaty moisture in. She wrinkled her nose a little. She had been sure that water was dripping in; to find out that she was, in fact, just incredibly sweaty was an unwanted revelation. Pale-faced, Calum was lying on the sofa with his trouser leg cut open to reveal his knee was a swollen blackish-purple mess with a red graze running down the outside.

Despite the situation, Steph had just enough wits about her to contact Kelvin. He began by asking whether Michael had been in touch. Steph confirmed he had not. Before Steph could relay what information she actually did have, Martina took the radio from her and walked into Roger's bedroom shutting the door. For a minute or two, everyone looked in the direction of the shut door, from where Martina's fast-paced angry buzz could be heard. When it began to settle – Steph assumed she had either gotten off her chest what she wanted to or Kelvin had managed to placate her – everyone began to relay their own stories of what happened after the lion had ripped Thomas from the face of the earth.

"So Michael just went off to the house and Kelvin was fine with that?" Davey asked, leaning forward.

"Well, if he wasn't, he didn't say," Steph shrugged.

Davey frowned and looked at the floor. Steph was not sure whether he was moving his lips, but he definitely seemed to be going through some sort of internal monologue. Deciding to leave him to it, Steph turned to Calum who seemed to have gained a little colour back in his face.

"What happened with you and Martina?"

Calum turned his head towards her, looking at her as if he was just noticing her for the first time. Then he turned his head back to look at the ceiling.

"An interesting story," he said before stopping. Steph waited for him to continue. When he didn't, she began to ask why, but she had no sooner uttered the first syllable when he cut her off saying, "Martina is not best pleased with me about it all, truth be told. She said that if it wasn't for me, this wouldn't have happened. A bit rich if you ask me."

Roger came over from the kitchen area with a bag of frozen peas and some ibuprofen which he handed over. Calum gingerly placed the peas on the puffy knee and swallowed the tablets without water, making Steph wince.

"I thought I'd be safe inside," Calum began again – Steph noted how he flicked his eyes guiltily towards her for a moment. "I cannot say I'm proud, but I panicked and shut the door on the others."

"Calum!" Roger gasped.

"I said I'm not proud!" Calum retorted, reddening. "If I could go back, I wouldn't have shut the door so quickly."

"Quickly? At all! Until you knew that you had done all you could have done!"

"That's what I was insinuating! Besides, it isn't you who should be annoyed, it should be her!"

Calum jerked his head towards Steph. The other two looked at her. To her surprise she was not annoyed. The looks of the others suggested she should be, but she wasn't. Maybe the anger would come later. She suspected not though.

"And are you going to apologise?" Davey asked quietly.

"I will!" Calum snapped, testily. "But properly. Not some forced thing now in front of you all otherwise it won't mean anything."

In a strange way there was a logic to what he said. However, Steph felt it was also the type of answer a politician might give; difficult to say it was definitely wrong even though it certainly felt that way.

"So what happened when you shut the door?" Steph asked. "Inside the house. Obviously, I know what went on outside the house."

Calum gave her a sideways look before turning to the ceiling once more. "I wasn't especially sure what to do, to be honest. I can't claim to know the house very well, so I sort of stood by the door for a moment... I wish I hadn't."

Steph grimaced, remembering the sound of Thomas's scream slowly choked off by blood and teeth.

"Anyway, I knew there was meant to be some underground bit somewhere (not that Kelvin ever showed me), so that sounded safest. I had half thought to lock myself in a toilet somewhere but then I would never have known when to come out – strange how your mind thinks in a panic. So I looked for the underground bit."

"You mean the labs and things?" Davey asked.

"If you say so. But I couldn't find them. You would have thought it would be obvious for signs or something to have been erected, but instead, the house just looks like... well... a house!"

"There's a lift though," Roger pointed out. "We had literally been in it the day before! It doesn't just go to the top floor you know."

"But what if it had got stuck? All these images were going through my head of getting trapped halfway down and then some giant lion thing jumping on the top and gnawing its way in. Like opening a can of tuna!"

"But the lion was outside, not in the house?" Steph said.

"Yes, it *was* outside, but at that point, Calum's stupid brain had at least been partly right to panic!"

Everyone turned their heads. Martina had opened Roger's bedroom door without anyone noticing.

"I had seen on the monitor what was happening. I had planned to go and get a tranquillizer – the right dosage – but then I saw this idiot milling about whilst the lion leapt in through an open window. I assumed Kelvin had had one of his moments again about ventilation."

Steph turned to Davey who mouthed the word *later*.

"Anyway, I didn't have long to get Calum from what I saw, so I parked the tranquillizer idea for a moment and went up in the lift to get him."

"Yes, but when the lift opened and you had beckoned me towards it, the lion was already behind me and there would have been no time for the lift door to shut before we were turned into cat food," Calum said, folding his arms where he lay.

"True," Martina said, walking over and sitting on an arm of the sofa and looking at the others. "So we ran through the house, slamming doors behind us and then locking ourselves in a bathroom." Calum turned his head a moment to give everyone a look of satisfaction at the word *bathroom*. "Goodness knows how long we were in there for. You could hear the thing outside the door. It knew we were in there but never tried to break the door down. At one point we thought it had gone as it was so quiet. I chanced opening the door and the fucker came leaping round a corner as if it had been waiting the whole time. Eventually it really did go but we waited a long time. Not knowing where it was, we didn't risk going through the house with all its hidden corners. We jumped out the nearest window instead. Then we went to get a buggy, saw they were both gone, went to get a quad bike and that is basically when Davey met us."

Steph could see that Davey was about to pick up the thread of the story, but she had a question first.

"One thing I don't quite get is why would the lion bother getting into the house if it had already made a kill?"

"Already hidden it," Davey said. "Well, half-hidden it, I assume. Sort of a rushed job probably. I arrived back – I didn't find any more of poor Daniel – to what looked like an abandoned buggy with a trailer. It was dark by the time I got there and there were no lights on in the house which I thought odd. I turned them on and saw the blood on the floor and the drag marks."

"So you followed where you thought the lion had gone?" Steph asked.

"Of course, I bloody didn't! I went the opposite way around the house. I wasn't going anywhere near that thing – not that I knew it was there. I was looking for a way in on the other side thinking I could get down to the basement where all the equipment was. Best place to get a handle on things."

Calum made a noise of agreement in his throat. Martina shot him a filthy look that missed its mark as he continued to stare at the ceiling.

Davey continued, "Next thing I know, these two are tumbling out of a window telling me to turn around... so I did."

Roger then made a noise suggesting he couldn't keep quiet any longer. "But why didn't the lion just eat Thomas? Why bother going into the house? I don't think Steph's question has been answered."

A moment's silence. It was Steph who broke the brief pause in the story by slowly answering her own question. She suspected a narcissistic part of her subconscious wanted to be the one to answer it in the first place.

"Competition."

"Competition?" Roger frowned. Martina rolled her eyes and got up, heading for the kitchen area.

"Well, there is competition with the other animals due to the overlapping territory."

"Surely the cave lion doesn't really have anything to worry about?" said Roger.

"Well, one of the grizzlies can definitely hold its own against him. But more obvious would be the cave bear," said Davey.

"Exactly," Steph shrugged. "The other night when that lion killed Daniel, it lost its kill almost immediately. The wolves too. They lost a kill to the cave bear. I suppose it could mean that one kill does not always feel enough. Usually, a predator won't make more than one kill at a time. The prey is too fast, too agile or too strong. But us..."

"You're basically saying that you think the animals are panicking into making numerous kills because they're worried they won't get to eat what they kill?" Davey asked.

"Sort of... more that if an opportunity is there, why not take it?"

"Well, I can't say I've seen any of these double kills."

"No! That's not what I am saying! I don't mean animals are roaming around like crazed mass murderers. I mean that if the opportunity arose..."

"They'd become mass murderers," Martina sniggered.

Steph sighed and sank into her seat. She could tell she wasn't going to win. She wasn't even sure what point she was really trying to prove anyway. She decided to go back to Davey.

"So what happened next then? After you stumbled into Martina and Calum?"

"Well, they were screaming and shouting, acting like the cave lion was hot on their tail!"

"It could have been for all we knew," Calum squeaked.

"Whatever the case, we bolted for the buggy and tried to put some distance between us and the house. Just a bit of breathing space. It was then I found out they had no idea where the lion actually was and that it could have been long gone."

"Or still there," Calum added.

"However, they also said they had no idea where you were."

"So what did you do?" Steph asked.

"Well, they said Michael was with you so I assumed that his first call would be to get you and Kelvin to safety... especially Kelvin."

"Why Kelvin?"

"He is where the money comes from," Davey smiled, ignoring Martina shuffling on the sofa arm and looking away momentarily. "I guessed that he was heading to Thomas's cabin or possibly out to a fence exit judging from some footprints we stumbled across."

"Well, they were in Thomas's cabin so good deduction on your part I suppose," Roger said.

"Thanks. However, then things went a little wrong. We came around a corner and straight into the cave bear, which was like driving towards a large furry brick wall."

"Should have run the bloody thing over!" Calum said, taking a sharp inhale of breath and clutching his knee.

"Idiot!" Martina spat. "It would have caused too much damage to the bear!"

"Precisely!"

"Less damage than you think," Davey said. "Those buggies are ridiculously light. Economical, but not built for crashing."

Martina ignored him; she was still glaring at the top of Calum's head as he stared at the ceiling. Davey gave Roger and Steph a tired look.

"Anyway, I swerved and, cutting a long story short, crashed and overturned the buggy."

"Fucking my knee in the process," Calum added.

"Yes, *fucking* his knee in the process."

Steph waited. Roger was leaning in, clearly also expecting more.

"Well, I have gathered that you got away, but how?" Steph asked. "Surely it doesn't make sense that the bear just let you go, but that's what the tracks suggested!"

"You read the tracks in the dark?" Davey asked, his tone betraying mild admiration.

"Despite my current forms of revenue, I am actually trained for field work – including tracking!" Steph replied, flicking her hair back and realising that half of it stuck to her damp cheek. She thought it best not to say it was Michael who had made the assessment on the bear and not her.

Davey smiled slightly and continued, "It surprised *us* if truth be told. We didn't really hang about to find out why we weren't followed. Maybe the bear was startled. Maybe it couldn't be arsed to chase us despite us having to help hop-along over there. I don't know. Maybe it just wasn't hungry."

Steph had not really considered the cave bear before and what made it tick. It was certainly the apex of the whole sorry project. How that impacted its actions was unclear – everything underneath it was desperate. Maybe it didn't need to worry about chasing every food source yet. It could, for now, let the peasants fight for scraps whilst taxing them on their kills.

"Of course, it didn't matter that the big bastard left us alone," Calum said.

"It's not a bastard," Martina sniffed.

Calum ignored her. "It wasn't long before we started being followed by another bear."

"The one you shot?" Steph asked, turning to Davey.

"Yeah. It started trailing us as we left some trees. We weren't going to get away because we needed to help Calum, that much was clear, so I hid us. I sort of hoped that, given the weather, the bear might lumber past us. But then you came along and stuffed that plan right up."

"How was I meant to know? I was trying to find you to help you. Michael would have left you to die! In fact, he basically did!"

"And what a help you were," Davey said rolling his eyes.

"Oh, come on now," Roger tutted. "You can't fault someone for trying to help others... even if they do end up becoming the one in need of help instead."

Steph turned to Roger who was smiling at her behind his mug of tea as he lifted it to his mouth.

"What about you?" she asked.

"What about me?"

"What's your story in all this? You're the one enigma nobody can account for."

Everyone turned to Roger who shrugged. "I'm afraid my story is not actually that interesting. I saw Michael arrive back with the thing whilst looking out of the window. I assumed that was that and everything was taken care of so got my bag and started walking back to my cabin."

"What?" Davey spluttered. "You thought that you would just walk back to your cabin?"

"Yes," Roger replied, raising his eyebrows in surprise to the question. "Why wouldn't I?"

"You don't just go for casual walks in the woods here!" Davey continued, clearly agitated by Roger's calm demeanour. "It's not safe! You know it's not safe! You were clearly concerned by the wolves when Steph and I came around the other night, so it is not like you're blind to the danger!"

"Yes," Roger grimaced, "I must admit I don't trust the wolves. There are too many of them and they are rather incorrigible."

"And what about the other animals?" Davey continued.

"I treat them with a bit of respect and I seem to do OK," Roger replied, as if it was the simplest thing in the world. "Besides, the cave lion had been detained as far as I was aware, so I was even safer. I would ordinarily take a few more precautions..."

"Precautions like what?" Martina asked, her eyes narrowing.

"Ah, you see, Davey! This is why I kept my forest jaunts to myself!"

"Forest jaunts?" Davey spat.

"What precautions?"

"Well, I usually make sure I carry a deterrent with me when I walk," Roger replied.

"Like?"

Roger sighed and walked over to a free-standing wardrobe by the front door that Steph assumed was used for coats and shoes. He opened it, reached inside and came out brandishing his deterrent.

"It is just a little machete," Roger said.

"That thing is more than a machete," Davey said, puffing out his cheeks. "It's basically a Scottish claymore!"

"Well, yes, it is a little larger than a machete, but then so are some of the animals here."

Before Martina could voice her objections, Steph said, "But would that really put off some of the larger animals? I mean, you might get a swipe or two in, but it is a lot tougher to kill something than one would imagine."

"Ah yes well, I did think about that," Roger said, suddenly smiling. "Really the machete is a last resort. My first line of attack is a concoction of mine. I came up with my own bear mace. I made it from a few everyday sources; incredibly easy to make, very natural ingredients. And then, just to be sure, I also lace the machete in it when I go out."

Roger began to chuckle to himself as he looked past everyone to the opposite wall. "The one time I did have to use it, it certainly gave the lion something to think about."

"What?" Martina snapped.

"Oh, calm down," Roger said. "It was just a bit of a bloody scratch on the arm to go with some of his other scars. Honestly, you wouldn't know I'd done anything. He did, obviously. The mace saw to that. The surprise on his face was something else. Not that I think it would work again – surprise is a powerful weapon, but it is hard to garner the same response using the same method."

Ignoring an indignant-looking Martina and a speechless Davey, Steph asked, "What was in the mace, exactly?"

"Oh, like I said. Basic things one might find in a kitchen or somewhere. Chilli sauce from those really hot chillies you see on television. Ghost chillies, I think they are called... and a bit of watered-down sulphuric acid."

"Sulphuric acid!" Martina squealed, standing up. "You have been attacking my work with sulphuric acid? You said it was natural ingredients!"

"Watered down," Roger reminded her holding his hands up. "And remember, it was him who attacked me! Hasn't done it since though. Besides, sulphuric acid is natural. Read a book!"

Lost for words, Martina sat down again. Davey also looked like he still needed time to digest what he'd heard. It was not a particularly life-changing revelation that had any real consequences, it was more that it broke a preconceived notion of who Roger was.

"Anyway, do you want me to finish my story or not?" Roger asked.

"Yes, go on," Steph said, suppressing a smile at the twinkle in Roger's eye.

"Right, well, as I said, I saw Michael was back, left the house and headed out – bear mace in my pocket but no walking machete. Nobody seemed to notice me leave as Thomas was busy running his mouth again." Calum jerked his head in Roger's direction and narrowed his eyes. Roger ignored him. "I hadn't gone more than fifty yards when I heard a commotion. I turned and saw the lion had become a little more animated than was ideal. You know, no longer lying down. So I scarpered and came back here. And that, I suppose, is that."

Martina continued to scowl at Roger who appeared to be enjoying the attention from her. Davey sat quietly staring at his empty mug and muttering to himself about machetes and lions.

Steph looked down at her own mug to find that she had drained hers as well. It was interesting filling in the blanks of what happened. But did it help? Did it help direct any future plans? Probably not, or so Steph thought. Then again, with a little more reflection, maybe there was a nugget buried there somewhere. Either way, what to do now?

THIRTY-SIX

Martina later conveyed details about her radio call with Kelvin. He had still not heard from Michael. He was torn between two plans of action – as if his ideas were the only ones necessary and it was inconceivable that anybody else should have one. His first suggestion was that they sit tight and wait until Michael makes contact. His second suggestion was that they all go back to the house, take stock of the situation, secure the house boundaries again and then come and get him.

The way Martina relayed the information clearly showed that she also assumed these would be the only options and no discussion was needed for anything more than deciding on either the former or the latter.

"I suppose it makes sense to some extent," Roger said. "As long as the lion is out of the house it will be easy enough to secure everything and go from there. Then again, if the lion is out of the house, goodness knows where it could be."

"What if other animals have breached the fence?" Steph said, running through a series of possibilities in her head. "What then? I mean, Roger only has one machete laced with mace."

Roger bit his lip as he caught Steph's eye and then swiftly tried to look in the opposite direction of Martina.

"I dunno," Davey sighed. "Depends on the animal I guess."

"Should anyone really be walking around out there with that lion going around killing at will?" Calum asked.

"It is not killing at will!" Martina spat.

"Well, it is not exactly killing against its will, is it?"

Martina ignored him. "Besides, Davey and Michael have walked around the place plenty of times before. Just the other day you went out with Steph." She looked imploringly at Davey and then at Steph.

Steph felt it odd to suddenly have Martina looking at her for support. She was right, of course, but Steph felt less easy about the prospect of a walk in the current circumstances. There was a calculated intelligence in this lion that she had not been exposed to then. She was naïve to the plight of the rest of the animals too. More importantly, the lion had killed people since she last went *walking*. It had opened Pandora's box and thrown away the lid.

"Look, whatever the case, let's decide in the morning," Steph said. "We all need some rest as we won't make any sensible decisions right now. Kelvin can wait."

Martina protested for a bit, but she could see that she wasn't going to turn any heads away from the allure of sleep. Everyone was too tired and damp to contemplate heading out in the dark again. As if to cement the decision, a wolf howled not far from the cabin.

Morning came which brought with it a breakfast of bacon and eggs, but no agreement over a plan of action. There was disagreement. Disagreement over who should go, what to do once they were at the house, whether or not Calum needed to go to a hospital for his knee (which seemed to have worsened during what had been left of the night) and what should be done about the lion if they caught it.

In the end, it was agreed that Steph and Davey would go to the house before coming back for the others. Then they'd secure Kelvin who, it was agreed by all but one, was in no real danger. Roger and Martina would stay and care for Calum.

"Is Martina not worried about you shooting the lion?" Steph asked as the two of them walked through the trees."

"Probably," Davey shrugged. "It's not my intention though. She's probably just as concerned about you disfiguring it with the sword."

Steph looked down at the machete in its mace-soaking sheath on the right side of her hip. On her ankle, she still had the dagger. She was surprised that Davey hadn't asked for it back.

"I would have thought the stuff on this is so potent that it would deliver a clean wound," Steph said, tapping the hilt of the machete.

"Are you sure that's how it works?"

Steph shrugged.

The two proceeded cautiously. As there were obvious potential dangers, Davey decided it was best if they walked the perimeter fence to the house. He seemed to feel they would pass an exit on their way so that if things were looking particularly sticky for them, they at least knew where their out was. He also seemed to think there was less chance of bumping into anything. Steph was not completely convinced that a passed exit was much of a safety blanket, but the idea of being nearer the outside and in sight of guaranteed safety appealed to her.

The day was a clear one. The sun added a bit of warmth to the morning as they trudged over damp ground. It seemed that the sky had emptied itself of all it could hold and was now spent.

As they walked, Steph noticed the footprints of wolves in the mud. She looked up to tell Davey, but he was already looking at her. He looked down briefly at the prints himself and then back at her, grimacing and then flicking his head onwards. She gripped the handle of the machete.

Seeking the reassurance of a blade was becoming an uncomfortable habit for her. She had never understood youths carrying knives before as she felt it raised the chances of danger rather than lessening them. Now she was doing the same thing. She supposed growing up in a residential cul-de-sac in Sheffield with parents who both worked and encouraged extra-curricular activities was a safe environment. Now she wasn't in one, she appreciated that maybe they weren't either.

"What are you thinking about?" Davey asked.

Steph jerked her head in his direction. "What?"

"I said what were you thinking about?"

"Why do you ask that?"

"You were frowning, and your lips were twitching as if you were having a conversation with yourself."

Did she really do that? Steph made a mental note to ask her parents whether they thought she did. If she did, she supposed she should find a way to tame it.

"I was wondering how this all ends."

"What do you mean?"

"This whole thing." Steph flicked her hands behind her. "I mean, it's now such a mess that I am not sure it is a problem that can be solved."

"I still don't get what you mean?"

"Look, if someone wanted to build a house but they put the roof on the bottom and had sideways walls or whatever, what would you suggest?"

"That someone smashes it down and starts again whilst the original person is never let loose near bricks and mortar again."

"Exactly."

Davey puffed out his cheeks. "So you're saying that we should do the same here? What would that even look like?"

"Well, as precious as that lion is to Martina and Kelvin, it *must* be put down, *surely*? Possibly the cave bear too – it is just not naturally sustainable here. Imagine what it would be doing if there was not an abundance of food. Even as it is, it's meant to eat berries and such as much as it eats meat but right now it appears more carnivorous than omnivorous."

"It would be a shame though, wouldn't it?" Davey said, pushing back a branch and watching it flick behind him as he passed. "I mean, these creatures haven't been seen for thousands of years."

"The technology that created them isn't going anywhere. Now that it has been proven to work, it can be replicated. It's not as if Martina is going to forget everything she's done."

"Maybe. But there is also a lot of money in those animals. Money talks."

Steph supposed that Davey was probably right. Even so, she still believed the animal in question – no matter how much money it was worth – had to go. Once an animal had killed a person it was hard to train it out of them. In fact, it was impossible as far as she was aware.

Walking around the perimeter fence proved a good move. They managed to reach the house – taking a little longer than they would have done directly – without any interference. There was one moment that worried Steph when a herd of deer passed nearby. If there were deer, she believed there was a chance there was something behind the deer. Fortunately, they passed on without much concern. If anyone was going to pick up on impending danger first, it would be them. If they weren't concerned, then she felt neither should she be.

They slowed as they reached the house. The gate was closed. Steph asked whether there was some sort of timer that triggered it to close automatically but Davey shook his head. He claimed that people had been against this in case it had shut them out at an unfortunate moment. Steph sniffed in response.

"I suspect Michael has been here," Davey said, looking around and putting a card to a reader which opened the gate. Steph couldn't see why people would be worried about the gate shutting on them if they could just open the gate again to get in. The timing for something to go wrong would have to be perfect. Then again, mathematically speaking, things happened. Look at the current mess.

Steph was surprised not to hear the gate closing after she walked through. She turned to see Davey hesitating after walking through himself. He looked around. Then he looked back through the gate. He repeated this a few times before finally growling to himself and tapping his card against the reader to shut it.

"What was that about?" Steph asked.

"I'm not sure whether it would have been better to keep the gate open. We don't know if anything... fast is in here."

"You mean you're worried that the gate being shut could prevent a quick escape from something that may or may not be in here?"

"You saw how long the gate took to open!" Davey hissed defensively. "One second in the wrong place and you're done for. Look at Fergus or Daniel!"

Steph folded her arms. "You're getting a bit panicky, aren't you?"

"I'm sensible! There's a difference."

"Sure."

Davey tutted and pushed past her. He insisted they did a loop of the house before they went in. Steph noted that all the windows had been shut. Whether Kelvin had been able to get through to Michael and relay what Martina had told him, or whether Michael had just taken precautions, Steph was unsure.

She suspected the latter.

Both quad bikes were still there hooked up to their chargers, but the electric buggy with the trailer was gone.

"Michael definitely must have been here," Davey whispered.

Satisfied that there was nothing inside the fence now that it was shut, Davey allowed Steph to open the door to the house. Steph's pulse quickened as the large door swung open. She half expected something to jump at her. Nothing did.

Steph felt Davey push past her and watched him raise his revolver as he began to walk further in.

"I don't think anything is here," Steph whispered. "The windows are all shut – not sure someone would shut themselves in with something."

"Unless they didn't realise it was there."

Steph rolled her eyes and strode past him. She headed for the lift. She could not help but notice the sound of Davey's footsteps behind her, matching her pace. She rolled her eyes again.

The two of them headed down to the room where Steph had seen the monitors for tracking the movement of the animals. It was strange seeing it empty yet with all the systems working, lights flickering on maps. Life continued without anyone to witness it. The animals were seemingly unaware of the turmoil that had descended on the area.

Davey peered at the screen, muttering to himself. He clearly had a better understanding than Steph of what all the lights meant and which one represented which creature. He flicked his head slightly from one direction to the next as he studied the screens.

"This seems odd," Davey said, not taking his eyes off a screen whilst aiming a lazy beckoning hand in Steph's direction. "That light there is the lion."

Steph looked at where he was pointing. "It's heading north."

"Right. But it is the speed at which it is heading north."

Steph studied the screen again. It did seem as if the dot was covering ground quickly. Was it running? The problem she had was that she didn't really know the scale of the map. That, and she had always struggled with ratio and proportion in maths. Her parents had got her a tutor but to little avail.

After another thirty seconds of silent study, Steph finally said, "It couldn't sustain that speed chasing something for that long."

"Right."

"So... Michael has it?"

"That's what I'm assuming, but why is he heading north?"

"Is there another gate there?"

"Yes, but it doesn't lead to any main road and he's still in the buggy. The whole idea was that the lion was transferred to something more secure and roadworthy in the house compound. Kelvin was going to call someone in."

Steph frowned.

"So what are you saying?"

"I don't know," he replied, slowly stepping back from the monitor. "I don't know."

THIRTY-SEVEN

A quick sweep of Martina's lab showed that Davey's hunch was probably correct as a large amount of sedative was missing from the store cupboard. Davey took what was left before marching down the corridor with Steph trotting behind him, then opened a door she had not really noticed before. The door opened to a small, well-lit room with rows of tranquillizer rifles on one side (with gaps where some were missing) and real rifles on the other. There was one real rifle missing. Steph saw Davey momentarily frown at the gap before taking a rifle and handing it to Steph. He paused. Steph saw his eyebrows furrow and was then surprised to feel him wrench it from her grip and place it back on the rack. He filled the gap in her arms with a tranquillizer rifle whilst pouring a couple of darts into her pocket.

"Two darts?"

"Well, I need more as I'm going to do any shooting, and Michael has taken the rest!"

Steph had her retort ready, but Davey was seemingly in no mood to listen to it. She had not really seen this side of him before. There was a cold efficiency about what he was doing. It was as if he was bothered by something for reasons he had not explained to Steph. Yes, it seemed that Michael was up to something, but it was still not apparent what exactly – not to her anyway. Also, even if he was causing mischief, there was nothing in the way Davey had behaved in the short time she had known him that suggested he should care quite so deeply about how Michael chose to act. He wasn't responsible for the man, Kelvin was.

At some level, Davey must have felt the same as his next act was to lead Steph back to the tracking room. There he took control of a radio and proceeded to contact Kelvin; previous plans out the window.

"He's doing what?"

"Heading north."

"In the same buggy he'd used originally?"

"Yes."

"But the thing won't be fully charged unless he managed to charge it last night and move damned quickly about his business. Even then it won't get all the way to..."

Steph saw Davey raise his eyebrows in the silence. The type of look you give someone when they realise something slower than they should. Steph was embarrassed to admit she still had no idea what that was.

"Oh! Oh, Michael you fucking idiot!"

"Yeah," Davey replied, tapping his foot and looking at the screen. The dot that represented Michael and his quarry was almost at the fence.

"Come and get me!" Kelvin snapped.

"But that makes no sense!"

"You won't get to him in time anyway! Come and get me. I will sort out a car to meet us there. We can still cut him off somewhere else."

"But..."

"Do it!"

Davey growled as he flicked the switch on the radio.

"Fuck!" he barked. Then he turned to Steph. For a moment she assumed he was going to tell her to stay where she was, but to her surprise, he said, "Let's go!"

They took a quad bike each, with their tranq rifles hung diagonally across their backs. If it wasn't for the seriousness of the situation, Steph would have labelled that moment one of the coolest in her life. How she actually looked was irrelevant; for once, she was acting purely in the moment, without concern for how her actions reflected on her.

"He's clearly going to meet someone!" Davey called to Steph as they weaved over the mildly undulating terrain, avoiding trees and scattered ferns.

"What do you mean?" Steph called.

"He's been paid off!"

Michael had said that money talked. He'd also made Steph aware that there was a black market willing to pay a pretty penny for things. Now, she supposed she better understood why he said so much.

The two of them carried on to the cabin where Kelvin waited behind a closed door. He didn't open the door until both bikes had been stationary for a few seconds. Steph assumed this was a reasonable precaution in the circumstances. When he did leave the cabin, there was a cold fury etched across his face.

He marched up to Davey's quad bike, swung a leg over and said, "Let's get going."

They went. Steph had half assumed that she would be forced to give up her quad bike, but either from a need for haste or simply an unconscious expectation to be served, Kelvin chose to be driven.

They headed northwards, passing the small ben. At one point, they ploughed right through the middle of one of the herds of deer, scattering them. Movement in her peripheral vision made Steph look around to see the pack of wolves careering over the heathland towards the panicked deer. She looked long enough to see the first set of jaws clamp onto the rump of one of the animals unlucky enough to have run directly towards them. Then she swung her head back around. To not look and thus crash, could be a death sentence. Besides, she got the idea that Kelvin would not be the most willing to stop if she did tumble.

Their going was quick despite Davey's speed being hampered by his quad bike having to take double the weight. They were soon in trees once more. Davey began to slow.

"What's the issue?" Kelvin asked as Davey brought his bike to an almost walking pace.

"I'm trying to remember which way to go."

"What?" Kelvin hissed. "How the hell can you not know where to go? I literally pay you to know these things!"

Steph saw Davey let the anger wash over his head, ignoring Kelvin's spite as he replied, "I know, but usually we take the track. I've gone a more direct route so... it's this way."

"You're sure?"

"Yeah, I recognise that tree by the fencing."

Steph had managed to miss the fact that they were at the fence already. Now that she looked, she couldn't help but notice bits of mesh in the near distance between the trees. They sped off again.

Steph was not exactly sure what she expected to find when she reached the gate, but she supposed it would just be open. Michael must be long gone by now and, she assumed, so would the lion and its new owner.

They reached a tunnel in the forest floor, the entrance of which had been left wide open. Davey took a sharp right to enter it, popping up on the other side of the inner fence. Steph followed. From there they made the short journey to the next fence. Steph wondered whether Kelvin would have people waiting for them like he suggested he could. Would they have to reach a main road first? How much would these people know, or would they simply provide a car? Steph supposed that having enough money paid for whatever service you needed. You didn't look for a service provider, you created it.

The quad bikes trundled forward, weaving between trees. Caution descended. Davey and Kelvin went ahead of Steph, and it was clear from the way Davey was half stood up on straightened legs that he was uneasy. That was understandable; it was quiet.

As they rounded a large oak, the outer fencing came into sight. Steph felt odd being on the current side of it. Seeing the world outside it – despite it looking just like the trees and heath inside the fence – made her acutely aware of what a strange little universe Kelvin had managed to create in this relatively remote part of Britain.

There was an open space in the fencing which was where Davey headed. He stopped in the gap. Two wire doors were pulled all the way back to the fence, a padlock lay on the floor.

"A padlock?" Steph asked, pulling up alongside Davey.

Kelvin looked around. "One that requires card recognition. The type that breaks bolt cutters. Only to be opened by my employees or scabby little shitbags."

Steph raised her eyebrows. Kelvin had already turned away from her.

Davey had ignored the brief interaction. Instead, he spent a few fleeting moments studying the ground around him and then stared out towards the trees beyond.

"What's wrong?" Kelvin asked. "We need to get going!"

Davey held up a hand to quieten him. At first, Steph thought Kelvin would explode, his whole body going rigid at the instruction. However, a small noise in the brief silence that followed the hand was enough to make him alter his focus. He turned his head in the same direction as Davey's.

Steph was not exactly sure what she was hearing. Nor could she work out whether it was coming from quite a distance away or close by. It was a pitiful sound. A moan more than anything.

She watched Davey unsling his rifle and instinctively she did the same. Davey swung his leg from the quadbike. So did she. Kelvin hesitated for a moment but then followed suit.

Steph pulled up alongside Davey who pointed to an area on the floor. She looked down. There were tyre tracks intermingled with footprints. It almost didn't make sense. Everything Steph expected to see was there, but not in the right order exactly. Or the right creature. There were tyre marks going out, but there were also some going in the opposite direction. It was these that were the most interesting as they had run over the tracks left by a large animal. Then it clicked.

"Where are the lion tracks?" Steph whispered. Davey gave her a concerned look but didn't answer. Instead, he began edging in the direction of the mournful noise. Although Steph's head seemed to think it a good idea to stay where she was, her legs had already begun following with Kelvin close behind.

Each step forward through the trees brought with it a heightened feeling of dread. Her heart was raging against the quiet of the still day, the sun the only resident of a crisp blue sky above the branches. Then they saw where the noise was coming from and they lowered their rifles.

Lying slumped against the side of one of the buggies with the trailer still attached was Michael. He had his hand clamped to his stomach, blood oozing between his fingers, staining his trousers. At first, he didn't look up. Then, with what appeared a monumental effort, he turned his bleary eyes towards them.

"You've been shot!" Kelvin said quite matter-of-factly.

226

Michael smiled slightly, blood starting to fill the gaps between his teeth.

"Very observant."

"No more than you deserve."

Steph winced. Michael, on the other hand, started to laugh but regretted it instantly as he began to cough up more blood. Kelvin turned away in disgust.

"Find out where my animals are!" he snapped at Davey as he wandered off to lean against a tree with his arms folded.

Steph could see that Davey was hesitant about what to do next. Steph could understand why. Kelvin was a man who was used to getting whatever he demanded, no matter who he had to flatten to get it. It was not clear quite how Kelvin expected Davey to 'find out' where the lion had got to; Steph hoped it didn't involve unnecessary violence. Michael was clearly dying as it was, and not peacefully. There was no need to add to his suffering.

Davey shuffled up to Michael and bent down. He pulled out a small hipflask from his pocket and offered it to Michael. Michael nodded almost imperceptibly but didn't take his hand from the bullet wound. Davey unscrewed the cap and poured a little of the golden liquid into Michael's mouth. Most of it dribbled down the dying man's chin but his expression softened a little at the taste.

"What happened?" Davey asked.

At first, Michael's eyes rolled to look past Davey. For a moment Steph thought he might even ignore the question. Or die before he could answer.

Then he sighed and said, "They took the lion and then paid me with this." He looked down.

Davey frowned. "So why are there tyre tracks going the other way through the gate?"

"Ah," Michael said, his voice weakening slightly at the effort of sustained talking. "Well, that was an interesting occurrence. The bear came out to investigate whilst they were packing up the lion into their truck."

"Into?"

"Into their truck," Michael nodded, ignoring Davey's confusion. "They fired some shots near it which sent it back through the gates. Then they went after it. Don't think they had their tranqs handy at the time."

"They went in there with a truck?" Davey asked, looking back at the trees.

Michael pulled a face in reply that suggested he was as confused as Davey.

"I mean," Davey continued, "I suppose they could get through, but they'd hardly be able to chase it. And even if they caught up with it, they wouldn't be able to keep both the lion and the bear in the back of the truck."

"Who said anything about the back?" Michael wheezed.

Davey looked at him.

"Where's my lion?" Kelvin called from his tree.

"Back inside," Davey called over his shoulder. "In a truck."

"Well, let's go and take it out of the truck," Kelvin replied, pushing himself away from the tree and heading back in the direction of the quad bikes.

For a moment, Davey just looked at Michael. Then he bent down and gave him another swig from the hipflask and turned to follow Kelvin. It was then that Michael's eyes settled on Steph. She hadn't moved.

Michael was clearly weak and lacked the will to initiate any talk. Steph came closer.

"Why did they shoot you?"

Michael smiled.

"Black market. Didn't trust me after the last time. Not that they let me know until after I'd delivered the animal."

"What do you mean by 'last time'?"

Michael's smile vanished and, with a groan, turned his head slightly so he didn't have to look at Steph.

"I tried to give them the lion before. Went wrong. Gave it too much sedative and looked like it was dying. Gave it something to wake it up. It woke up. Killed one of their men and ran off. Killed a boy."

Silence descended save for the singing of a few territorial birds in the trees. Steph watched as a tear rolled down Michael's cheek.

"Maybe this is what I deserve," he whispered.

"Steph!"

Steph turned her head in the direction of where her name had been called from. Then she turned back to Michael.

"But how did you get it out? It's chipped!"

"Cut it out. The lion is so cut up from scrapes with the bear, no one noticed. Then it was put it back in after."

"Steph!"

So there it was. She had the answer she had been seeking for the book she wanted to write. Now that she had it, what use was it?

Michael coughed. Somehow even more blood trickled from his mouth that was set sunken between his pale cheeks. A pang of shame shot through Steph, and she bent down meaning to inspect the wound. Michael growled pathetically, and she looked up.

"It's too late," he whispered. "Besides, there are worse places to be right now."

Steph looked around. Laying slumped against a tree beside an abandoned buggy with a bullet wound in your stomach, was not high up on her own list of ways to die. Then again, she supposed he was talking about the weather and being surrounded by nature.

"Steph! Hurry up!"

Michael moved his head slightly in the direction of the voices. Reluctantly, Steph turned and left. She tried to ignore the fact she was walking away from a dying man – let the disgust die within her. She'd never seen a person dying before. She looked up at the trees and noticed a wood pigeon sitting peacefully on a branch.

What was she doing? Why was she walking towards the quad bikes to head back into danger? She had what she came to Scotland for. What more was there? Another interesting story? Was that why she found herself heading back? Yes. And no. Yes, what was unfolding was fascinating, but no, she was not there for that. It was more than that. It was that sense of doing something worthwhile. Something that would satisfy her subconscious desire for self-credibility. What would help her gain credit more than the delusion of acting to save lives and doing *what was right*?

She reached her quad bike. Kelvin looked like he wanted nothing more than to put a bullet in her gut and have her slouch against a tree like Michael. Davey just looked troubled.

Without a word, Davey began driving off. Steph straddled her quad bike and followed. Then stopped. Davey had pulled up as soon as they went through the outer fence gate. He leapt off his quad bike, shut the gate and replaced the padlock. Then, again without acknowledging Steph, he got back on his quad bike and headed off. Steph followed, after chancing one last look over her shoulder at the closed fence.

THIRTY-EIGHT

Steph was baffled by how a truck designed to haul large animals could have navigated through the trees. It all became clear when they emerged back out from the tunnel gate and took a sharp right onto a small path. Again, Davey pulled up and ensured the tunnel gate under the inner fence was shut and locked. However, this time he did engage Steph in conversation.

"I'm not quite sure where we go from here."

"What do you mean?" Kelvin asked.

Davey looked at Steph and then at Kelvin.

"I mean, it doesn't look like they are following the bear exactly as his tracks go more through the trees, but the tyre tracks stick to the path. By the look of it at least."

"So?"

"So you're not quite sure what they're up to," Steph said, answering Kelvin for Davey.

"Exactly. There's no way they would be able to track that bear in that truck through these trees. But that's meant to be the whole reason they came in and didn't just drive off with the lion. It doesn't make sense why they've come in at all."

"Yes, it does," Kelvin cut in, his voice sombre. "It makes complete sense."

Steph turned to look at him. Kelvin slowly bent down and carefully picked up a stick which he began mindlessly inspecting.

"They sense weakness," he explained. "There is every chance that Michael has explained the mess in here and they smell an opportunity. After all, I can't call the police. Even if I did, I would think that they believe themselves above such a trivial force."

Steph opened her mouth to protest. Then she shut it. Of course, he couldn't call the police. Not now. To some extent she wondered whether he had ever planned to and whether she ever really believed it was an option to him when she had advocated for it before, or whether she was just trying to alleviate some of her own sense of guilt at her involvement in the whole sorry affair.

"Essentially, they believe they have free reign. If I was them, I would go to the house first. Although, they probably expect anything important to be protected by locks and codes, which it is. Then again, they might have taken Michael's key card. Did either of you check to see whether he had it?"

Steph shook her head and looked at Davey who was shaking his.

"No. Neither did I – careless. Either way, that's where I would head. However, they might genuinely think of going after the bear and believe they have the time not to rush it, which is why they didn't go recklessly through the trees after it and smash their vehicle up. Whatever the case, we need to stop them."

"Need?" snorted Steph, raising an eyebrow.

Kelvin turned to look at her.

"Do *we* need to? I mean, is it worth us risking our lives to protect what is, at the end of the day, your investment, your vanity project?"

Kelvin stared at Steph for a few seconds. Then he spoke.

"Because right now, the lives of the others are at risk. Not only that, but you are also banking on these people who have never seen or studied the animals before to have an understanding of them. Who is to say one wouldn't escape whilst being transported? What damage could it cause? Who could it harm? I don't think you're the type of person to take such a risk. I am not sure you would be able to sleep if you made the wrong choice and something happened. You're plagued by your life choices enough as it is, Steph. So vanity project you might think this is, the danger to others caused by these men is still very real."

It sounded odd to hear Kelvin admitting that danger could be caused by his animals. She knew it wouldn't alter his decision-making concerning them once he felt in control again, but it was nice to know that he did at least have some consciousness of their potential liability. More importantly, however, it was infuriating how accurately he had assessed her as a person.

"Fine," she said. "So what do we do?"

To Steph's surprise, Kelvin turned to Davey. Davey's eyes widened slightly.

"Oh, right. You expect me to come up with the plan, do you? Of course, you bloody do."

"You know the grounds better than us," Kelvin said, quite calmly.

Despite the expectations being placed on Davey, Steph found herself speaking first.

"Do we not go and make sure the others are safe first?"

Davey thought for a second.

"I'm not sure that's necessarily a good idea."

"Why?"

"Because there is always the risk that we lead these people to them. They may follow us."

"What do you mean 'follow us'? We are following them!"

"Right now we are, but as soon as we go off in a different

direction we open up the possibility of being spotted and tracked."

"Then we just make sure we aren't spotted," Steph shrugged.

Davey looked at Kelvin who chewed the skin on his knuckle as he pondered.

"I think Davey is right. It might not be such a good idea."

"We need to find *them* first," Davey said.

"Why?"

"Because we don't know who we're dealing with," Davey replied. "We don't know who these people are, only that they're dangerous. We don't know whether they know what they are doing in terms of the animals or whether they have been hired for... other reasons."

"Either way," Kelvin added, "if they were to kill us all, take the animals or whatever, they would get away. That we can be sure of. They'll be backed by money and will have their escape route all ready to execute at the drop of a hat."

"So we need to find these guys," Davey said. "Then once we know what we're dealing with, we might be able to go and warn the others."

Steph could see the logic in it all. Or at least she thought she could. It sounded convincing enough in the moment and she supposed that was enough.

"Right then," Steph said. "I suppose we had best get going."

She pulled back on the accelerator of the quad bike.

THIRTY-NINE

Tracking the truck was easy enough. Despite the clear day, the ground was still drenched from the night before, so the tyres left long imprints in the mud. They finally found the truck at the foot of the small ben. Davey insisted they get off the quad bikes and leave them deeper in the clump of trees from which they were emerging. They were some distance off, but Davey made sure they remained hidden. From what Steph could see, this was a sensible decision.

Although she didn't have her binoculars – they were lying on a table in her room in the house – she could see that the men had rifles suited to hitting targets over long distances. They may have been a couple of hundred metres away, but it was not so much that a good shot could not have taken a target. Steph doubted that the tranquillizer rifles would be able to offer the same back. Nor would Davey's revolver from that far away.

The truck they had been driving lay some twenty paces behind them. What was instantly noticeable about this truck was that it was clearly no run-of-the-mill transport vehicle – this was a bespoke piece of machinery. It looked more like an oversized pickup truck with the back covered over. Its paintwork was black and shiny and spattered with mud up the sides. Its windows were blacked out. Its tyres were designed for rough terrain.

"Someone has money to burn," Kelvin whispered.

Steph stifled her response about irony and continued watching the men. What were they doing? Had they spotted the cave bear?

One man had a rifle held loosely in his hand. The other had his with the butt against his shoulder, holding it lazily with one arm. Then, all of a sudden, his other arm came up and he gripped the gun far more seriously. He trained an eye down its length. Steph turned her head slightly to try and work out what exactly he had seen.

Out of the bushes trundled a bear. It wasn't the cave bear, but it was still a sizable creature. It came out slowly at first, a deep guttural growl carried on the breeze to Steph's ears. When the two men didn't back away, it went onto its hind legs. Then the shallow valley filled with a single reverberating crack, and the bear was no more. For a moment, both men stood holding their pose. Then they simply turned and got back in the vehicle, not even bothering to look back at the bear lying dead on the ground, blood dribbling from its muzzle.

"Bastards," Davey spat.

"It tells us a few things though," Steph said. "They don't know where the cave bear is, and they don't give a damn about life... as long as it doesn't belong to them."

"Also, there are only two of them," Kelvin said. Steph turned her head. "One is obviously more competent with a rifle – the heavier, chubbier of the two – and the other seems to be more wary as he kept nervously jerking his head. Their vehicle is custom-made for this job, so they are being bankrolled by someone who knew what I was doing here – I assume Michael must have been in contact for a while. Most important for us is that they can be distracted. They are not the professionals that their employer thought they had hired, which is why they took some time out for what I am sure they considered 'big game hunting'. It seems they are willing to drive around until they find what they want, but that limits their ability to actually achieve their goal. The question is: how do we use all this?"

Kelvin began to bite his lower lip in concentration, a slight snarl etching his face. Steph just blinked and looked in the direction of where the truck had gone. She was surprised that Kelvin had taken so much in. She'd not noticed the glances of the other man. Nor had she considered the callous act of killing one of the animals unnecessarily a distraction. She supposed there was a reason that Kelvin had become successful. It made her wonder why he had made such a mess of his current project. Perhaps he had simply overreached and been blinded by his own ambition. Whatever the case, she was curious to hear his plan now.

FORTY

Steph was relieved to find the first part of the new plan involved going to the cabin where Roger and the others were. There was a part of her that wondered whether it was sensible to use up the battery on two of their few resources, but that was outweighed by checking on the safety of the others.

"Well, why are we staying here if two gun-wielding maniacs are running around?" Calum snapped from the sofa.

"Calum, if you wish to leave, then you know where the door is," Kelvin replied.

"How the hell am I supposed to leave with this?" Calum gestured at his leg, which if anything looked worse than when Steph had last seen it.

"Well then, there we are," Kelvin shrugged. He then continued his speech. "We must ensure our own safety, but we must also protect others. These two cannot be trusted with the animals. Nor should their bankroller get his hands on our hard work. God knows what they'd do with them."

"Because you've done such a sterling job with them," Calum muttered.

Kelvin ignored him.

"It's simple. We need to get them where they have no choice but to leave the safety of their vehicle, and there we ambush them with superior numbers. Whoever came up with this whole operation clearly doesn't believe that I have trained enough personnel to patrol and protect the land. They're right. I am not a warlord; I'm a businessman. However, it means that the two out there will underestimate us. I also doubt that – despite their custom truck – coming in here was part of the initial plan, so I highly doubt they know what their next steps are. That being the case, we are the ones in control."

Calum muttered under his breath. Once again, he was ignored.

"So we need to track them down if we're going to lure them anywhere," Davey said.

"Yes, but first we must agree on where to lure them to."

"But what about the cave bear?" Steph asked.

Kelvin turned towards her; his eyes slightly narrowed.

"Well, what do you think? You're the field biologist."

Steph thought about it. There was no mucking about with the question. She supposed her response should be of a similar clarity.

"It's clearly the top of the food chain here, which is why we all seem to forget that the animal is actually an omnivore. It has yet to show any desperate tendencies like those under it. The cave lion has been detained, so even he is not an issue. Based on how it reacted to you guys running into it..." She swept her hand over in the direction of Martina, Davey and Calum. "I suspect we won't have any issue with it if we stay out of its way. It is the wolves that bother me the most."

"And they are manageable," Kelvin replied dismissively.

Steph suspected that, next to the cave lion, they were the least manageable aspect in a ten-mile radius, but she kept it to herself.

"Davey," Kelvin said, "where's the best place to lead them?"

Davey got up, still looking at the floor. He then walked slowly to the window accidentally catching Steph's eye briefly as he passed – he looked away as soon as he realised that she was looking at him. From there he looked out. Steph guessed that looking outside better helped him picture trouble ahead.

Eventually he turned around chewing his lip. Once more he looked at Steph, looking away quickly as she looked him in the eye. What was that about?

"I have two suggestions," he said. "Each with their ups and downs. I'm not completely sure which is best as there is danger with both of them. I suppose with those guys there is always the risk that..."

"Spit it out!" Martina snapped, tensing her hands into claws. "There is danger. We get it. Just tell us your ideas and let us assess!"

Davey looked momentarily to Kelvin who said nothing.

With his eyebrows furrowed, Davey said, "We could try and lead them just upstream from the beavers. The track deviates further away from the river at that point, and the beavers haven't cleared that area of trees which are still thick, so it will be easy for us to ambush them as they won't be able to use their truck."

"And the other idea?" Steph pushed, her voice purposely softer than Martina's.

"Well – and I know it is going to sound ridiculous – but I thought the cave that belongs to the cave bear might work."

The others stared at him.

"You want to set an ambush for these guys whilst waiting at the mouth of a cave of a six-hundred-kilogram prehistoric monster?" Calum asked slowly.

"What do you care; you won't be coming along, will you?" Martina said, gesturing at his leg.

"Why there?" Kelvin asked, chewing a knuckle.

"There's a ledge plateau leading up to it and it's surrounded by trees. They wouldn't be able to get their truck near it, so they'd have to come out on foot. The fact the bear is there would be the added incentive to get them up there – just in case trying to kill one of us isn't enough. More importantly, they'd be in the open and we would not be."

Kelvin lowered the sides of his mouth in appreciation of the idea. One thing troubled Steph, however.

"How would they know the cave bear is there? Wouldn't that rely on them chancing upon the animal or some equally stretched hope?"

Davey looked at her again. This time, however, he didn't take his eyes off her. Steph adjusted her sitting position.

"Well, that's another issue with the plan," Davey said slowly. "I mean, it is an issue to an extent – quite a risk in fact – but it is also an integral part."

"What is?" Steph asked, her voice no longer soft.

"The cave bear plan involves them catching bait."

"Right?"

"I wondered whether you'd be up for *being* the bait," Davey said before finally losing his nerve and looking at Steph's feet.

Everyone was quiet. Steph felt like she should be infuriated by the suggestion. Instead, she found herself wanting to know what being the bait entailed.

"So when you say 'bait'...?"

"I think you should allow yourself to be captured."

"Why not you?" Calum interrupted.

"Because she is a woman, so I believe – although I might be wrong – that they would be less inclined to kill her."

Steph wrinkled her nose.

"Why not Martina in that case?" Calum continued. Steph didn't understand why he insisted on being so argumentative. She supposed he was angry. Angry at his situation, thus lashing out when he had the chance. Roger, Steph noted, was being incredibly reserved on the matter.

"You can't have Martina because she is an asset," Kelvin said, not looking at Calum.

"Exactly," said Davey before turning to Steph with open palms. "Sorry, Steph, but she did all the research and has all the knowledge, so she is worth taking as much as the lion or bear. More so even. They'd take her and run."

It made sense, Steph supposed. Although was there something everyone was missing here? An angle they weren't seeing. Everyone seemed too sure of the situation and their analysis of the men they were dealing with.

"So what's the rest of the plan?" Kelvin prompted. "Why the bear's cave?"

"Like I said," Davey continued. "The geography is good there. But the idea is that Steph leads them there in exchange for them acting more favourably towards her. My concern is that they would be looking out for some sort of mischief in both my plans, and this was the best I could think of to dull their caution. By that I mean they could still wonder whether Steph is leading them into danger, but what with the ground being as it is after the rain, there should be numerous tracks leading up towards the cave which should confirm Steph's story – in their heads at least. Focusing more on whether Steph is lying about the bear which constitutes the most distracting danger, they'll then forget to worry about the danger we pose."

Steph was mildly impressed with the logic. Kelvin more so. For the first time in a long time, she saw him smiling.

"Misdirection," Kelvin said, almost to himself. "Very clever."

There was quiet for a moment as people digested the plan a little further. Then leaning against a counter in the kitchen area with tea in hand, Roger said, his eyes directed at Steph,

"And are you willing to put yourself in such danger?"

Everyone looked around. There was an unspoken feeling that she had already accepted. That was certainly Steph's impression. So much so that she hadn't even questioned it herself. But did she want to put herself in such danger?

"Of course, she does!" Martina sneered. "It will give her something to write about."

Steph snorted at Martina. She had been inclined to say yes, but Martina's comments opened a fresh window on the situation. Why should she risk her life for people who clearly didn't respect her? Why not let Martina risk herself and then let Kelvin and Davey figure out how to get their asset back? What did she care?

Kelvin seemed to read the situation and calmly said to Martina, "You cannot fault someone for seeing an opportunity. She obviously understands her market just like you understand yours." Martina folded her arms and looked away. Kelvin then turned to Steph. "Of course, any writing would have to adhere to the contracts you signed but, yes, you could write about some of this. I dare say that putting yourself in this situation *would* be good marketing."

Roger could not help but laugh and look away. Steph understood why. It was odd that, even in the current situation, Kelvin the businessman was still active. Even so, Steph knew he had a point. Which, more irritatingly, meant so did Martina.

Steph thought for a moment, clicking the lower knuckles of her right hand. What did she really have to lose? Lots, from an objective perspective. Fortunately, her attachment to those elements that were objectively measurable – a reasonable income, her own flat in San Francisco, a season ticket to the Giants – somehow didn't mean much to her at that moment. Not something she would have expected to feel just a few weeks previously.

Her fingers wouldn't click anymore. She looked up. Five faces were turned towards her.

"OK. Tell me where the cave is."

FORTY-ONE

A mist had started to roll in from the west by the time they got moving. It was not a thick mist and visibility was still good, but it was still a variable that Davey had not really accounted for.

There had been a debate over whether to keep Calum in the cabin or not and whether he should be left on his own. As the quad bikes could only take two, it was agreed that Roger would stay behind with Calum, whilst Martina shared a bike with Kelvin and Steph went with Davey. Davey was wary of the charge left on the bikes, so stressed the importance of finding the men sooner rather than later.

It was agreed that they would first go back to where they had seen the men shoot the bear as it would likely give them a reasonable starting point to track from. The tyre tracks left by the truck would be distinctive enough.

The sun had passed its mid-point by the time they reached the site. The blue sky contrasted with the light wispy blanket trying to spread in the open spaces. When they pulled out cautiously from the treeline, they quickly realised that they were not the only ones there. Some fifty yards ahead of them was the body of the bear. Its body was not going to waste as a host of short-haired creatures surrounded it, gorging themselves as if merely eating from a trough.

"I didn't realise that boar ate meat," Kelvin said, as if he were merely passing comment on the weather.

"They will if it's on offer," Steph replied.

Deciding that there was no threat, they came forward. One

or two of the boars looked up but then continued feeding – the new distraction evidently an uninteresting one.

"Greedy bastards," Davey snorted.

Steph watched the top of the body of the bear. It quivered as if there was still some life in the animal. The image was sobering knowing that it was all due to the various mouths ripping at the flesh. Upon dying, the shell that once housed everything you were could be mistreated so revoltingly. Not that Steph suspected bears really cared about all that. She wondered when in human evolution people began to care. Elephants also showed signs of caring during death. Had they always?

"Right, the tracks are pretty clear; they head this way," Davey said, pointing to the reasonably worn dirt track that carved itself through a small group of trees.

No other words were uttered. Davey's assessment was accepted, and they returned to the quad bikes to follow.

The tracking was quite straightforward. Even with the gradually increasing mist trying to smother the land, Davey could pick up the deep tyre tracks. So could Steph for that matter. Every so often they would get off the bikes and Davey would assess the ground again as if he'd lose the trail if he didn't. He wouldn't. Even Steph could see the clear turns in the mud.

They eventually caught up with the sleek black truck outside one of the huts. Having never seen it before, Steph assumed it to be Calum's. They parked the quad bikes someway off behind a couple of particularly large bushes that littered the heathland around Calum's cabin.

"They're clearly inside," Kelvin whispered as they hid behind the bushes. "They'd have seen us coming otherwise. They're distracted by something."

"So what should *I* do?" Steph asked. It had sounded straightforward when Davey had suggested the plan. She was to be caught and then bargain for safety by delivering the bear. However, now that the situation was upon her, she realised that there were numerous fine points that needed considering. For example, how would she create a fake situation in which she was caught?

"I have an idea," Kelvin said before Davey could tell Steph how he saw it. "Go in there and pretend to be all grateful that you've found them. Say how much of a mess it is out here and that you were fearing for your life."

"Well, it's easier to act out reality so I guess that is helpful," Steph said.

Kelvin ignored her.

"Say how you can deliver the cave bear to them; it's as simple as that," Kelvin said. "These men will not want a long conversation. They just need to believe you think the cave bear needs taking down for the general safety of yourself and... well, generally."

Steph nodded but didn't move, looking over the top of the bush.

"Go then!" hissed Kelvin. "Or you'll miss the window."

"You probably need to run there too," Davey added. "It won't look good if you come out of hiding and meander over. You must make it look as if you ran there as soon as you saw the truck."

Steph nodded again. But still didn't move. Instead, she analysed the cabin. She knew she needed to go. She knew by leaving it she would either get them all caught or look like a coward. She tried to imagine what she would say and how she would act. She supposed...

Whatever it was that she supposed was cut short by a hand

in her side which sent her sprawling to the ground and away from the cover of the bush. She looked sideways from where she was on the ground. It was Martina, neither smiling nor frowning.

"Go!" she hissed. "Stop wasting our time!"

Steph muttered a retort under her breath that she was sure was wasted on the breeze and began to run. She ran because it was her way of taking the plunge – and Davey had said to. There was no turning back now. She'd have to go for it. If Michael was anything to go by, she'd receive a bullet between her shoulder blades if she didn't.

To her surprise, nobody came out of the front door as she approached. Had they seen her? Like the other cabins, there was a decking area onto which she leapt with a loud thud. She involuntarily glanced up at the roof before looking back to the door. There was a sudden noise of movement inside. Steph's guts squirmed.

"Hello?" she shouted. She hoped this warning to those inside that she was a human and not some other more worrying animal would be enough to prevent anything being fired her way through the door as a precaution. They were strong but she doubted they were bulletproof.

"Hello?" she called again, pushing open the door that she noted was slightly ajar.

She was greeted by a rifle muzzle. It was the larger of the two men looking down the barrel at her, his finger caressing the trigger. The other man seemed perfectly relaxed. He was sitting on one of the chairs with his feet upon a coffee table.

"Who the fuck are you?" said the larger man, sunglasses perched over his balding head.

"Steph!" she replied. *Steph?* Why use her real name? Did it matter? Probably not. The man on the sofa barked laughter.

The rifle-wielding one did not smile.

"OK, who the fuck are you, *Steph*?" he said. There was a definite London undertone to his accent. "And don't say 'me' or I will shoot your shitting teeth out!"

"I work here but..." Steph tried to remember what Kelvin had said. He had made out that the situation was going to be straightforward with little conversation. Instead, she already felt that the line of questioning was drawing her away from the prepared script she had in her head. She was no actor. She couldn't improvise! Why did he want to know who she was instead of where the hell she'd come from?

"But everything has gone wrong!" she panted. "People are dead! The animals are... are out of control!" Would they believe this? It sounded vaguely correct. No, it sounded very accurate. But was it what someone in her situation would choose to say?

"Are they now?" said the man.

"Yes!" Steph implored. "I've lost friends! They're dead! I saw my best friend getting ripped apart by wolves whilst they were still alive!" She began to sob. At least, she was trying to sob. She cuffed at her face anyway and then turned to shut the door.

"Hey!" said the man with the gun. "Nobody said you could fucking move!"

"Didn't you hear a bloody word I said!" she suddenly screamed, whipping around. The man on the sofa sat up a bit and the man with the rifle widened his eyes. This was the encouragement she needed. "It's not safe out there!" She slumped against the door looking at the shins of the man ahead. "It's not safe out there..."

The two men looked at each other. Through her peripheral vision, Steph could see them gesturing to each other.

"Anyway." She sniffed. "Who are you?"

"Never you mind who we are!" said the larger man before his friend stood up sighing.

"Ignore him," said the smaller man, walking over and putting a hand on his friend's rifle to lower the barrel. "We are here to sort this *mess* out. I must apologise for my associate's behaviour, but his nerves seem to have got the better of him. He shouldn't have pointed a gun at you, but as I am sure you're aware, this is an interesting situation we have walked in on."

"So you work for Kelvin?" Steph asked.

"Yes," the smaller man said, bending down to offer Steph a hand. The lie rolled off his tongue with such ease that Steph was almost inclined to believe it despite knowing it not to be true.

"But we haven't been able to communicate with him since we got here. Is he still alive?"

"I think so," Steph said, allowing herself to be guided to a seat. "He escaped when the cave lion got loose. I saw him run into the woods but..."

"And Martina?"

Steph was impressed with the casual use of first names as if the man had been a regular acquaintance of these people.

"She's alive, I suspect," Steph said. "She was with me until we became separated."

The man leant forward.

"Where was that? What happened?"

"We were trying to head to one of the gates, but we were cut off by the cave bear. I went one way, she went another."

"Why did you separate?"

"Because it chased her and not me."

"Why didn't you head back towards the gate once it had gone after her? Are you sure she escaped it?"

The intensity in the voice was increasing ever so slightly.

She pretended not to notice.

"Wherever the bear is, the wolves are not far behind," Steph said, gripping her hands together and squeezing periodically. "I guess I don't know for sure whether she escaped but I didn't hear a scream, and if anyone is going to escape that bear, it's the person who created it!"

The small man gave his friend a mildly concerned look. He then slowly began to walk away from Steph, sighing.

She was not sure what it was, but at that moment, Steph's stomach clenched. She could sense danger. At least, she thought she could. There was the possibility of it. It was as if she had exhausted her use to them as far as they were concerned. She couldn't prove this was the case, but she felt it in the way they looked at each other and the way they moved around her.

"If you're here to help," Steph said, standing up. "Then we need to kill the cave lion and the cave bear!"

The two men stopped looking at each other and turned with benign interest to face Steph.

"I don't know where the lion is," Steph continued, studying the men's faces for any flicker of a tell (there was none), "but I know where we can get the bear. If the bear topples and the lion topples, the other animals will fall into place. There will be balance."

The two men looked at her.

"I'm a field biologist," she said, again hearing how pathetic it sounded only when it came out. "It's my job to know these things."

She knew that most of what she said meant nothing to the men. It intrigued her as to what lie exactly they would tell in response.

"Our instructions from Kelvin were not to hurt the bear," the smaller man said. This was completely believable.

"However, if you know where we could *subdue* the creature, then you will need to lead us there."

Steph stared at the floor. Looking anywhere but at the two men to give herself time to think. She hoped it gave the illusion of how troubling a decision it was to lead them there. Would Kelvin's plan have worked better if she simply pointed to a place on a map and then been free? She supposed it was perhaps beneficial for her that they wanted her to guide them. She dreaded to think what would happen if they didn't. Also, how could she suddenly come from nowhere wanting their help and then change her mind and walk off having pointed to a location on a map? No. She needed to feign some sort of reliance on them. A need for protection.

"Al right," she said, raising her head. "I can show you the way. You'll protect me though, right? If I lead you there?"

"Of course," said the smaller man. "We wouldn't let anything happen to you."

His facial expression reeked of deceit.

"Right, well," he said. "We'd best get going then."

"Can't I finish my coffee?" replied the larger of the two as he took a sip from a mug on the side and instantly recoiled with a grimace.

The other man rolled his eyes.

"Fine but hurry up!"

FORTY-TWO

Apart from the general sound of the engine and the wheels going over the terrain, there was not much noise in the truck. It was as sleek inside as it looked outside. Steph was pleased that she had not been put next to the cave lion, which must have been in the hold in the back; something she knew but the two men didn't know she knew. The grey leather seats were comfortable but seemed an unnecessary expense. Steph smiled. It was odd that a part of her dad's frugality had rubbed off on her and chosen such a moment to make an appearance.

"So what are your names?" Steph asked, half eying the small arsenal strapped to the ceiling of the vehicle. The larger man also kept glancing up at the weapons, periodically touching one.

There was a moment's hesitation from the smaller one before he replied, without looking back from the wheel,

"Kelvin said we are not to give names in case we get implicated in anything by mistake."

"Oh?"

"Yeah, just the line of work we're in."

The larger man sniggered drawing a scathing look from his partner.

Steph sunk deeper into the leather. She supposed it didn't matter whether she knew the men's names or not. Even if they had given her their names, she doubted they'd have been genuine.

She looked out the window. Davey had told Steph the signs

to look out for that would let her know she was getting close. A tree that had snapped in the middle in a storm was, he said, the most obvious one. From there it was suggested she get them out the car and walking, using the excuse of not wanting to alert the bear as the reason to dump the truck.

They passed a small tree that, to Steph's eyes at least, looked as if it had snapped in the wind. Was that the tree? Was that the landmark? It didn't seem as obvious as Davey had suggested it would be. It wasn't even snapped in the middle exactly. Should she suggest stopping now? But what if it was the wrong tree and they were too far out?

Steph's concerns were quickly alleviated when they trundled past a huge pine that looked as if a giant had kicked the top down. It was an odd sight. The top of what was left of the trunk was splintered horribly but the branches below it still showed some greenery.

"Stop," Steph muttered.

"What?"

"Stop!" she repeated forcibly.

"Why?" said the smaller man, slowing down but not coming to a complete standstill.

"We're there. We need to get out here or the bear will hear us!"

That sounded legitimate to Steph, but the man just clicked his tongue and sped up once more.

"We want him to hear us, so he comes out to play," said the larger man touching the weapons again.

Steph could see the logic. It was not, however, what she wanted.

"But the truck won't be able to get up the slope!" she said, her voice a little more urgent as she watched the trees pass them by; the small ben's eastern slope getting closer into view.

"This one will," said the man driving. "Anyway, if the worst comes to the worst, we just get out at the bottom of the hill."

"Yes, but you can't do that," Steph said, shutting her eyes and pinching her nose.

"Why not?"

"Because as soon as the bear hears a motorised vehicle, it will run! It is why we only use electric ones. It has associated the motorised ones with our local vet and being brought in for checks. So it runs."

Steph was impressed with herself. Both the story and the faked disbelief in having to explain so obvious an error was, in her mind, a moment of genius. Even so, had the act landed?

The smaller man slowed the car to a stop.

"What are you doing?" asked the larger one.

"You heard her! If we get too close he'll hear us and run, and then we'll have to chase the bugger!"

The larger man shrugged.

"Could be fun. I'd be up for a proper chase."

"You may well be, but we don't have the time. We need to *sort* things out sooner rather than later... people are dying, remember?"

"How could I forget?" huffed the larger man, already choosing what he wanted to take with him from above his head. Steph watched. He settled on his rifle and two handguns. He caught Steph watching.

"They're dart guns," he grinned. "Look."

He pulled back the chamber of one of the handguns and, sure enough, a sleek-looking dart was inside.

"Looks real though, doesn't it?"

"And the rifle?" Steph asked.

"Ah," the man said, "better to be safe than sorry. Things don't always go as planned."

"No, they don't!" said the smaller man helping himself to a rifle to the right of his head. "Although, it would be best if it did."

He then turned to his friend.

"You sure you don't want to use this instead of them?" he gestured at the rifle he had taken down that, Steph recognised, was a tranq gun.

"I suppose I should," the larger man sighed. "Not as fun though. You carry it for now and I can take it when I'm there."

With that, he opened his door.

"He's the better shot," the smaller man said, noticing Steph staring at him. He too got out of the cab. Steph followed.

"Hang on!"

"What?" asked the larger man, turning around.

The smaller man then chucked the keys to the truck to him. The large man caught them, looked at them, rolled his eyes and put them in a side pocket before zipping it up.

"Zip pockets." The smaller man shrugged. "I know I need them, but they never seem to be on the clothes I like."

Steph then noticed his eyes flick towards the rear of the truck before he turned to follow his partner.

FORTY-THREE

The walk was a slow one. Firstly, there was the slope to deal with. There was no man-trodden footpath worn into the ground over the years; there was only the light outline of the preferred route probably taken by the bear. A large footprint in the dirt made clear that this was the case. On top of the need to navigate the terrain, which sloped upwards at a gradient steeper than Steph expected and yet still seemingly able to anchor a healthy number of trees, there was the worry of the bear itself. In fact, there was the worry of more than the bear. There were other bears, that was true, but it was the wolves that really concerned Steph now the lion was secure – or at least was assumed to be secure. There was a reckless abandon that enveloped the wolves. They were willing to take risks in a way the bears weren't from what Steph had seen. Would they risk venturing close to the cave bear's actual cave? She wouldn't put it past them.

As they moved up the slope, Steph noticed collections of bushes here and there that seemed out of place; blackberry, raspberry. Davey's doing, she assumed. Food for a creature who was, after all, an omnivore.

As they ascended the slope, Steph kept her eyes peeled for any sign of the others. She knew the plan was to actually reach the cave before they revealed themselves, but plans changed. In the current climate, it would make more sense to expect it to change than stay the same. Perhaps it would help if the strategy altered slightly, and they ambushed early; Steph was not wholly sure she was going the right way. It was only the assumption the faint outline of an animal highway would lead them there that made her think she was even possibly going the right way.

"What do you keep looking around for?" the larger man said, jerking his balding head in the direction of the bushes Steph had just been looking at.

"Keeping an eye out for danger," she whispered.

The man looked around again. Then he said, matching Steph's whisper,

"Wouldn't the danger come down the path we're following if it's going to come from anywhere?"

"Or up it," Steph replied, using a partially exposed rock as a step to power herself upwards. "I would assume the bear wouldn't really deviate from this track, but you never know. That said, we'd hear it before we saw it in this vegetation. It's the wolves I'm more concerned with."

"Why wolves?" the smaller man whispered, stopping.

Steph turned around. The smaller man was clearly calling a break as he sat down on a naked tree root which curled into the air before plunging back underground. He took out a flask of water as he awaited a reply.

"Why not wolves?" Steph said, holding out her hand for the water. The man hesitated a moment and then passed her the flask which she greedily tipped back.

"Wolves are hardly a big issue for people these days," the man replied. "Basically, big foxes, aren't they?"

"Not these ones."

"Why? They dire wolves or something?"

Dire wolves? Were they? Nobody had ever said. Did anybody know? Steph hadn't really thought about it before. She supposed they were on the larger side of things for a grey wolf, but nothing obscene. Was it possible that they'd found a preserved specimen from which they could extract the DNA? From what Steph was experiencing, it was possible. However, as far as she was aware, it was only the lion and the bear that had been genetically modified. Popular television dramas had made dire wolves out to be gargantuan in size when really the truth was less impressive. That's certainly what she remembered one of her dates saying once. His shoe-horning dire wolves into the conversation as a way to impress her was why he was only *one* of her dates.

"As far as I'm aware, they're just wolves," Steph said. "Although they have rather unforgiving competition all around them, so I don't doubt only the largest of the pack survives. Or the most ruthless."

The smaller man shrugged and then nodded back up the slope. Steph groaned slightly but began moving once more, followed by the others.

Although the direction in which they walked filled Steph with anxiety, she was once again struck by how peaceful the place could be. Sure, the birds were singing, but apart from that you could hear nothing except the larger man's panting. A chill ran over her skin.

She stopped walking and listened. The others stopped too.

"What is it?" asked the larger one, not working too hard to keep his voice down.

Steph turned and mouthed 'shut up' before cocking her ear again.

"You've got a bit more wind in your sails since whimpering in the cabin," the larger man snarled, at least attempting to lower his voice this time.

"Well, then I only had your rifle to worry about; now your rifle is the least of my concerns." She let that hang in the air for a moment and then carried on walking, leaving the two behind her a little more wary. Perhaps that was a mistake. Would they be more alert to movement other than the bear's?

In fairness to herself, she genuinely felt as if something had been nearby. This was no place to throw any degree of caution to the wind. Yes, she could have been being watched by Davey or one of the others, but it was just as likely it was something else. Hell, she wouldn't have put it past the cave lion if it had escaped from the truck and was now stalking them. Come to think of it, the lion had been awfully subdued in the back of the truck. She wondered how much tranquillizer they had given it.

They carried on up the slope for another hundred metres or so. After that the small pathway widened slightly onto an opening on the incline where the land flattened briefly. Again Steph stopped walking. She crouched down. The other two copied her. Ahead of her, reaching into the slope that continued around the small relief from the incline, was a cave. It looked fake. It was clearly fake. In fact, even the small levelling of the land seemed unnatural.

Steph studied the rocky outline of the cave. It looked like concrete. It was definitely concrete. It was, Steph reckoned, probably housing some sort of metal support. The whole thing was artificial. She supposed it had to be. The chances of there being a perfectly habitable cave in the surrounding land were wishful thinking. Artificially you could guarantee it. She edged back down the slope. The other two, having had a look for themselves, also edged down, ensuring their heads were below the lip of the small plateau.

"Right, so what's the plan?" the larger of the two asked. He made sure not to look at Steph when he said this. However, the smaller man was not so exclusive. He moved a dark lock of sweat-pasted hair away from the corner of his eye as he looked at Steph.

"If we go in there, what's the risk?"

Steph screwed up her face in what she hoped looked like concerned thinking.

"It depends how far back in the cave he's gone." This seemed plausible. They might have built the cave to go back a way. "The further you go the darker it is and the more chance of something going wrong. You don't have night-vision goggles with you, do you? Torches?"

The men looked at each other before turning their heads back in the direction of the truck.

"So you're saying that it would be better to coax him out?"

"I'd say so."

There was a definite strangeness to organising a plan for people when you were already part of a counter plan to ambush them, despite not being privy to the finer details of the original plan.

"If he is in there, I'd suggest wolf howls."

"*If* he's in there?" the larger one said, looking down the length of his rifle at something in the distance.

"Well, I can't guarantee anything," Steph said, "but I assume he's in there."

"Why do you assume?" asked the smaller one.

"Because the most recent tracks were the ones going up the slope."

Was that true? It could have been. Steph hadn't really paid enough attention. It didn't really matter to her. Staying alive and stopping these two making off with any of the animals was what mattered. Although, thinking about it, *why*? Why should she care if they made off with the animals? Kelvin had made it seem in her best interests to care, but without him there, his reasons didn't feel nearly as compelling.

Frowning, the smaller man held out the tranquillizer rifle to the larger man. The larger one sighed and handed over his own rifle.

"He would make a great talking point in my snooker room."

"Well, that's not what we're being paid for," said the smaller man. "Anyway, you won't be able to afford a snooker room if you don't shoot your tranquillizer straight, and you can't use those damn pistols either."

"Come off it! I could hit a squirrel between the eyes at two hundred yards, I'm hardly going to miss a great fucking lump like that, am I?"

Then taking Steph a little by surprise, he got up and began walking off to their right. The smaller man had seemingly expected this and simply sat on the slope raising his eyebrows at Steph for want of nothing better to do.

"Where's he going?" Steph asked. "What about the wolf sounds?"

"When he's in position!" the smaller man said. "I can't claim to be an expert at making such sounds. You?"

Steph recalled trekking to trace a man-eating wolf in Alaska. Certainly, that was how she sold it in one of her books.

"I'm not bad. But why is he changing position? Why's he not going up the slope?"

"Good, you can do it then. As for his moving, it is so we don't put all our eggs in one basket in terms of a safe position. It also means we can confuse the bear momentarily if need be. Us, we will make the howls – you'll make the sounds – and the bear should come towards us, exposing his wide flank to... to my associate, who should be appearing over at the side by some trees..." He poked his head over the lip of the small plateau. "Any time... now!"

A balding head poked out from between two trees a mere thirty yards away. He nodded and then slipped back out of sight.

"Right then," the smaller man said, suppressing a smile, "get howling!"

FORTY-FOUR

For a moment Steph just stared back at the smaller man. Despite his smile, he was clearly serious. She clicked her tongue as she turned towards the cave. She tried to remember how she had been taught to do it. It was an old Indigenous American man who had taken her on the night walk when she'd learnt how to do it. She doubted he'd ever have imagined her having to use it in such a strange scenario.

Gathering her breath deep within her lungs she began to howl. Thankfully the man didn't laugh. Instead he raised his head a little to look eagerly at the mouth of the cave. Nothing. Steph howled again. Still nothing. They waited a further few seconds.

Steph could see that the man was about to ask questions, so Steph howled again. In the pause that followed, there was only silence, not even the sound of bird song. Perhaps they'd been scared off by the howling.

"It doesn't seem our quarry is here," the man said, an edge to his voice.

"Which could be an issue," Steph whispered.

"Obviously."

"Because if he is not here, where is he?"

"I dunno; could be anywhere. Could be miles away, couldn't he?"

"Possibly, possibly not..."

Steph hoped that the seed she planted might at least make the man slightly more concerned with his immediate surroundings rather than what to do with her and her failure to deliver the bear. It must have been on his mind. He kept flicking looks from the cave to her to where his friend was hidden. More importantly, where were Davey and the others to make her need to distract him with fear as irrelevant?

Growling slightly, the smaller man stood upright, stretched and called, "You might as well come out now! He isn't here!"

Following the man's lead Steph stood up. She looked in the direction of where the other man was meant to be hidden.

"I said you should come out!"

Still he remained hidden.

"For fuck's sake!" muttered the smaller man before hoisting the rifle onto his back and beginning to walk across the small plateau to where his friend was hidden. Steph followed.

"Why are you still crouching down there, you dozy turnip?"

The man then stopped, colour draining from his face as he looked at a spot behind a tree. Steph could not see what he was looking at. The branches of the great yew hung low. Cautiously, she took one quick glance at the cave mouth to her left before sidling up to the smaller man.

"Shit!"

Steph couldn't help the outburst. She knew there would be some sort of ambush, but she had no idea how it was going to play out. It had been silent. A quiet, efficient sweep.

The large balding man lay face down in the dirt with blood pouring from the wound at the back of his head. His tranquillizer rifle lay next to his open hand. There was no sign of what had hit him.

As the smaller man appeared frozen by shock and indecision, Steph took the opportunity to kneel down and place two fingers under the man's neck. She moved them around trying to find what she doubted was there. She was right, it wasn't there. She turned to the man looming over her and shook her head.

The man just stared down, his mouth slightly ajar. He was not looking at her as such. It was more that he was looking through her, lost in his own thoughts. Steph stood up. As she did so there was an audible snap somewhere further up the slope within the trees. Steph jerked her head upwards. So did the man, the noise seeming to shatter his trance and crystallise his thoughts.

In one swift move, Steph felt the man grab the scruff of her neck before cold metal settled itself just under her chin. It all happened in the space of a couple of seconds. Seconds, Steph thought, would be her last on the planet.

"Right, enough of this act," the man snarled.

"What act?" Steph replied, her voice rising and her heart beginning to prep itself for action.

"I said enough! You know who I am, and I know who you are, so let's stop the pretence! Now where are the others?"

"I don't know!" Steph squeaked. Did he really know who she was? Did he really think she knew who he was? Or did he just mean that she knew what he was doing? Either way, she supposed she'd given the game away by saying 'I don't know'.

"I suggest that you don't lie to me!"

Steph felt the bite of a blade nibble at her neck, something warm trickling down it.

"I really don't know!" Steph panted, trying to subdue the sobs. "I promise, I don't know. They didn't tell me!"

"But you were happy to lead us here, weren't you? Happy to bring us here for your friends to smash our heads in!"

"I didn't know the plan, I swear! I thought they were just going to knock you out or... or tranquillize you or... I swear on my life!"

"Well, your life isn't worth much right now, is it?" the man snarled.

"Put her down, Ashley!"

Both Steph and who she assumed was Ashley snapped their head in the direction of the voice. From the right of the cave, carefully edging down a sharp slope, came Kelvin followed by Martina. Ashley eased the pressure of the blade a touch but didn't remove it from Steph's neck.

Kelvin made sure to stop a short distance from the pair. Steph appreciated a ten-yard gap would allow him some sort of comfort. Even so, he had what looked like Davey's revolver held loosely in his right hand, just to be sure.

"I should have known you two might resurface at some point," Kelvin said in a bored sort of voice.

Steph could sense Ashley's body tense.

"You killed Baz!" snarled Ashley, rather pathetically.

"You killed Michael," Kelvin shrugged.

"He was going behind your back."

"Still my man though. If anyone had a right to kill him, it was me!"

There was a small pause as Ashley assessed the situation.

"In fairness, you had this coming after what you did," Ashley said, flicking his eyes left and right.

"Fairness?" Kelvin scoffed. "You and *Baz* were paid the amount agreed upon in the contract you signed. It is the definition of fair!"

"We didn't know the market value of what we were dealing with!"

"Not my fault," Kelvin shrugged again.

"Not that you seem to have been able to make use of it," Ashley replied with an undertone of satisfaction.

Kelvin's eyes flashed. He opened his mouth, but the words

snagged in his throat as a new thought crossed his mind. His expression changed and his body eased.

"Yet," he replied. Both he and Martina began to move in their direction whilst keeping their distance as if they meant to go around. This put Ashley on edge even more, spinning his head in the direction they were heading before turning the other way to look over his shoulder. Steph felt the knife ease in the distraction. She considered whether she should pull her own knife out of the sheath on her ankle. No. She wouldn't have it halfway out before she felt Ashley's blade warming her with her own blood.

Perhaps sensing Steph's thoughts, Ashley raised his knife once more and began pulling Steph in the direction of the slope.

"I guess we have no more to say to each other then, for now," he said to Kelvin, clearly disturbed by his heading towards the slope.

"Oh, I'm not completely sure about that," Kelvin said. Ashley stopped guiding Steph towards the lip of the plateau but said nothing. "For one thing, I am very interested in where you are going."

"What do you mean?"

"With Steph, I mean. Well, in general really."

"What do you mean 'in general'? I'm not an idiot. I know you'll have someone waiting for me somewhere. The moment I let her go, I'm gone. I know you never did Baz in; you don't have the stomach for it. Besides, you don't like to get your dainty hands dirty!"

Kelvin laughed, the revolver still loose in his hand. Martina, Steph noticed, was less at ease. Much like Ashley, she continued to flick her eyes in numerous directions.

"Even so, could you tell me exactly where you're taking

her?" Kelvin asked.

"Let's not play more games here than we need to. You know where I'm taking her."

Kelvin stopped grinning now. His face became steely.

"Indeed, I do know where," he said, reaching into his pocket for something. Steph felt herself being pulled tighter to Ashley's body. "I just don't get why when you can't go anywhere!"

Ashley growled a revolting profanity before Steph felt his body slacken again. Ahead of him, Kelvin dangled the keys to the truck.

Steph could hear Ashley muttering to himself under his breath, but it was so quiet that she couldn't make out a single syllable despite her close proximity. Eventually, he sighed.

"Fine," he said, pushing Steph a little further ahead of him but still gripping her collar. "The girl for the keys."

It made sense. Steph could see that he genuinely feared the risk of running down the slope without any collateral, but what choice did he really have? Kelvin basically had him in checkmate. More importantly, what plan did Kelvin have to stop him from running down the slope and reaching the truck? Was Davey down there now?

"No."

Steph blinked.

"What?" she said before even Ashley could digest what had just happened. Martina, for the first time, stopped flicking her eyes left and right and allowed herself a small smile. Kelvin ignored Steph. His eyes looked just past her.

Ashley seemed as surprised as Steph. His bargaining chip was worth nothing. Even so, Steph noticed that he had looked at her as soon as the no had come out. Despite having her at knifepoint, he understood the insult that had been delivered.

"Why 'no'?" Steph said.

Still, Kelvin ignored her. His eyes were firmly set on Ashley.

A quite sudden and explosive rage started to build within Steph. It was a rage that enveloped everything. The world around her and all its context seemed to melt to nothing in the face of the heat she felt.

Eventually Ashley asked, taking his eyes off Steph, lowering the knife a little further, "Yes, why won't you trade?"

Kelvin shifted his feet slightly.

Steph took a step forward. She meant to march right up to Kelvin. What then? Bury her knee into his bollocks? Shout at him until she got an answer as to why he viewed her life as expendable. Did he? Did he think Ashley would kill her? Surely he at least knew he might. He'd killed Michael.

A sharp tug on her collar brought her back. It seemed that Ashley still felt she was of some value even if Kelvin didn't. She growled but didn't take her eyes off Kelvin, willing him to acknowledge her. He stared passively, if uncomfortably, past.

Silence descended. A brief silence. A painful and hate-filled silence – at least on one-half of the plateau's edge. And then, in one sudden burst, the silence, the hate, the unease was ripped apart.

None of them noticed it in time. They'd been too carelessly preoccupied. Certainly, Steph cursed herself for not being more careful. She cursed Martina too for not keeping up the nervous vigilance she had shown earlier. Each of them had allowed themselves to be sucked into the moment. Now the moment was being blown apart by the cave bear imposing itself upon them all. It had exploded down the slope and onto the plateau as if the ambush had been his to set all along and they were merely playing his game.

Steph turned her head in the direction of heavy, grunting

breaths and thudding paws. Everything slowed down. She noticed the whole thing with a clarity that had been missing just two seconds before. Her primitive brain was forcing a rapid assessment of the situation, absorbing detail in the hope that something might save her. What could save her? Perhaps the shape coming from her right. Perhaps that could. It was certainly on a trajectory to meet the bear, but what was it?

Steph's brain caught up with what her eyes were seeing as the shape crashed into the pumping back legs of the bear, another second later and it would have missed – it was Davey. He had launched himself in what could only be described as a shoulder-barge against the animal's flank. What he hoped to achieve was hard to say. What was clear was the result. The bear's back legs stumbled. Not a lot, but enough to slow it. For the briefest of moments, there was a mildly confused expression etched across its face. Its eyes widened and its focus fizzed quickly away from Steph and the others and around to whatever had interrupted its intended trajectory.

The moment was all that Kelvin needed. Steph noticed movement on the left of her periphery. She turned to see Kelvin and Martina whipping down the hill. She knew she should follow. Ashley seemed rooted to the spot, his mouth half open as he took in the bear's enormity. She should definitely run. But what about Davey?

In what seemed an intelligent move, Davey had allowed his momentum to carry him. He had crashed into the bear's hind legs in a sort of half spin. This spin, along with running into a weight far greater than his own, sent him tumbling behind the bear. As the bear spun around to look over its left shoulder, Davey was already tumbling over the ground to its right. This allowed him a precious extra second to get to his feet before the bear got its bearings. Even so, it didn't seem obvious to Steph how he'd escape. The whole move had been suicidal. Why do it?

Whatever little time Davey thought he had bought himself from the move evaporated as quickly as it had come. The bear launched itself at Davey, half-rearing up in sheer, explosive power. Then Davey did the next unexpected thing. In one desperate spring of flailing limbs, he leapt over the lip of the small plateau and down a particularly sharper part of the slope. He vanished from sight. The bear, again momentarily taken by surprise, roared after him. And just like that, the noises that had shattered the tautness of the moment, trailed off downhill.

Steph instinctively intended to follow the bear and Davey, but her legs remained rooted. She felt that she should do what she could to ensure he was OK. She owed him that. Her eyes flicked in the other direction. Ashley was still there. He was still seemingly transfixed, staring at where Davey and the bear had disappeared.

His mouth was the first thing to revive itself. "What the fucking hell just happened?"

His words seemed to break the leash that had held Steph. She turned to her right. She walked away at first, to her shame, in the opposite direction to Davey and the bear. After a few steps, she stepped it up to a light jog. Then she broke into an all-out run. She skidded down sections of the slope, leaping over tree roots. Her lungs burnt and the muscles in her legs cried for rest, but still, she ran.

She noticed a noise behind her. Something was following her. She allowed a quick glance over her shoulder. It was Ashley. He wasn't chasing her exactly – it certainly didn't seem that way – but he was definitely following her.

Steph didn't stop running until she had burst from the trees that littered the slope and out onto the same open grassland she had witnessed the wolves kill a deer on days earlier. Her hands clasped her knees as she tried to force oxygen into her chest, sweat tickling her temples.

The heavy breathing behind her announced that Ashley had also blown his lungs. She turned her head. He turned his. They looked at each other.

FORTY-FIVE

There was a lot to take in. Too much to absorb when just stood still. So Steph walked. Her heart still hadn't got the message that her legs had stopped pumping, and the air hurt her tired throat with every inhale. Where was she walking? She didn't know. There was just some innate part of her that knew she must walk. She was dimly aware that Ashley was trailing behind her, his own heavy breathing even more clearly audible than hers. It didn't bother her that he was following. She assumed he would follow. She was not sure that her being a hostage was really still a lucrative option for him if she was one. Either way, she didn't care as long as he was quiet. She needed to walk. She needed to think.

Something had snapped within her. She wasn't broken – there was nothing that dramatic going on – but something had definitely shifted. An understanding. An expectation. An assurance that she thought she had was now gone. When had it happened? Had she noticed it before? Was it when she saw Michael bleeding to death with a bullet in his guts? Stumbling on the tattered human remains of Fergus? Kelvin throwing her life away for that of his own interest? Davey sacrificing himself for... for what?

"Where are we going?"

Steph ignored the voice.

"Hey!"

A hand on Steph's arm tried to stop her. She wrenched it free and continued walking.

"We need to come up with a plan!"

"*We?*" Steph shrieked, surprising even herself as she spun around to face Ashley. "What the hell do you mean *we*? There is no fucking *we*! If you've forgotten, you just had a knife at my throat negotiating for some bloody car keys!"

She stalked off once more. Behind her, she could hear Ashley's heavy footsteps.

"Look, whatever was going on, we still need to talk. You knew the situation. You pretended that you didn't, but you knew. We all just acted in the circumstances as it was. It was business. Business for you; business for me."

Steph snorted.

"Business? What the hell do you even mean by that? It literally doesn't mean anything. People are dying! How was this business? Even if by some twisted grasp on things you thought it was business for you, how was it for me? What business was I getting from all this?"

"Book sales," Ashley shrugged.

The next barrage of words suddenly caught in Ashley's throat.

"Excuse me?"

"Hanging around longer would make for good material, I'd guess," Ashley said, looking around and unslinging the rifle from his back.

"How do you...?"

"It's my job to know," Ashley replied, checking the rifle.

Ashley's words were as sobering to Steph as they were shocking. They raised questions. Questions that distracted her from feeling sorry for herself.

"Who do you work for?" she asked, her hand dropping to the hilt of her knife as she pretended to tie her laces.

"That's not important," Ashley replied, a practicality

returning to his voice. Steph could see that he had sensed his in and was going to be efficient with his words.

"Look, despite appearances, I have nothing against you. Here is the situation and it is nothing you do not already know. I was hired with Baz to collect sample specimens for my employer. Michael was working on the inside looking for a quick payday. Personally, I thought the man was a rat and couldn't be trusted, but it was Baz who shot him, not me. He tried to be smart; thought he was owed more than he was. Our boss was quite clear on the cost of his previous blunder."

There was a slight pause. Steph wondered whether Ashley knew about the boy who had paid the price for the blunder; the family that were still paying the price.

"Anyway, the point is that we were to collect samples as and when the opportunities arose. If it was just the lion, then it was just the lion. However, we saw an opportunity for the bear and then you came along. Maybe we were a bit blinded by previous bad feelings with Kelvin, but we allowed you to take us into what we assumed was at least a half opportunity. I thought it was anyway. Goodness knows what was going through Baz's head, poor man."

"What was the previous business... with Kelvin?"

Ashley wrinkled his nose for a brief moment. Then he sighed. "All you need to know is that it was a rather well-preserved specimen from Siberia."

"Of what?"

Again, Ashley paused before saying, "That's for me to know."

"How well preserved?" Steph asked, her investigatory habits kicking in.

"Very," Ashley said, with a slight smile, "if you get my meaning."

"Wouldn't something like that make the news?" Steph replied. What could it have been? A mammoth? She knew mammoths were often found in Siberia under the ice. A rhino?

"Usually," Ashley replied with a knowing look.

Steph nodded. She assumed that she was thinking correctly. The black market was far more powerful and wider reaching than she had ever thought. Then again, had she ever actually thought about it? Not really. Her recent experiences were her first real ones except for friends talking about some tiger hides and ivory. It was scary in a way. It made her more aware of how much of society lived in a comfortable bubble of ignorance whilst others worked dark arts on the peripheries, seizing opportunities and forcing openings.

"Anyway, as I was saying, you brought us to an ambush – I don't blame you as it was your business – and we went thinking we could either overcome whatever you had planned or that you actually were working in good faith. Either could have been the case. Your ambush worked. Baz died. Kelvin took the keys and thus control of the lion that we all knew was in the back of the truck despite your pretence. Kelvin – coldly if you ask me but again understandable considering who he is – valued the lion and his work over your life. The curveball was the bear coming out and that guy – I assume it was Davey – sacrificing himself. I can't explain that bit. But the result is that Kelvin and Martina have got the truck and the lion, whilst you are now here with me – I thought it safer to follow you as I don't know who else Kelvin could have hidden with a gun pointed at me. You have reason to dislike Kelvin and I have no reason to hold you hostage anymore... from a literal transactional point of view. Your value is apparently not that high."

When he'd finished talking, he held his rifle under one arm and looked at Steph expectantly.

Two things bothered Steph: how he could talk about death in such a matter-of-fact tone, and why he knew so much.

When Steph could not find anything to say, Ashley then said, "So that all being the case, I suggest we stick together for now until we get out of here."

"Together?"

"Look, whether you like it or not, we have somewhat been put in the same boat."

"How?"

"Kelvin has thrown you under the bus and can't trust you now, so you're not safe. He'd obviously have me killed – just look at Baz," Ashley said, taking a few steps past Steph and looking into the distance.

"Yeah, but he wouldn't kill me!" Steph said. Did she believe that? "He might kill me with lawyers but not literally."

Ashley turned towards Steph. She didn't like the dark smile on his face.

"I'm not sure how well you really know Kelvin. I'm not sure anyone *really* knows him. Whatever happened to him all those years ago brought about a change in him. With one step at a time he has become who he is today. The man is *ruthless*. I don't like him, but I do appreciate that he is both brilliant and ruthless." Ashley looked at the ground, smiling. "But also a complete bastard. You can trust that you can't trust him. Besides, death by lawyers could be just as bad as literal death, unless you keep your mouth shut. Of course, it would be more convenient for him if you simply disappeared."

Steph wasn't convinced. She was still pretty sure that her life was in no real danger. Not from Kelvin at least.

"Surely the police would hold him accountable. In the end, the system would get him. It has to."

Ashley laughed. "Look around. Why aren't the police here

now?"

"Well, I suggested that we contact them but..."

"But they aren't here, are they? Whatever the reasoning, they aren't here! Instead, two guys intent on stealing and who aren't afraid to put a bullet through someone are here! Well, one of them is still here."

This was factually correct. Put to her in that way, it was no wonder parts of her assurance on what was and what wasn't had started to break.

Steph took a deep inhale of air and exhaled through her nose. "Considering you are one of those men happy to put a bullet in someone, why should I trust you? Especially as I helped set you up?"

"Firstly, it is *willing* to put a bullet in someone, not *happy*. I'm not a psychopath. Secondly, because the situation has changed. Like I said, you were just conducting your business as I was doing mine, but now we are somewhat in the same boat. Besides, you can trust me as much as you can trust anyone right now."

"Fair enough."

"And I have a gun which is somewhat useful given the circumstances."

"True. But why do you need me?"

"You know your way around here better than I do. I also don't think you have anything against me personally. Not relative to Kelvin anyway. Not anymore."

It was an odd assessment. Yet Steph supposed it was accurate enough. He was right: she found that she didn't really have anything against him despite him putting a knife to her throat.

"So what's your plan?" she asked.

Ashley looked out into the distance once more.

"I have lost both the truck and the lion, so getting out of here feels preferable. But that lion and truck are rather valuable and I would quite like to see my next birthday. That might be tricky without one or the other. I need you to take me to one of the cabins. One with people in preferably."

"What? Why? To take more hostages? You've seen how Kelvin valued me. He won't value who is left, I can promise you that much."

"Irrelevant. I just need to find them."

"Why?"

"That's my business."

"Then what's in it for me?"

"I see you safely out of here afterwards."

"Hang on. One minute you're saying that Kelvin would have me dead, the next you're saying I can be walked to the gate and everything will be all right after."

"I never said that. What happens afterwards is up to you. Anyway, you're the one who thinks Kelvin won't have you killed so what's the issue?"

"He won't!"

"Then there's no issue, is there?"

Steph's head was spinning. What did she actually think? Something didn't feel right; she just couldn't put her finger on it. Then again, what else could she do? She needed to escape the whole situation; that much was obvious. What then? How strongly would Kelvin hold her to her contract? There was a contract after all, and it was lucrative.

Steph sighed. She knew what she should do was get out of the place and write it off as a bad experience. She should release herself from any contract by mutual consent. She should forget that Kelvin saw her life as less valuable than that of his project. She should even accept it when Kelvin inevitably sent lawyers to tie up her story. All of these were things she knew that she *should* do.

"Follow me," Steph said slowly. "And I'd keep that rifle handy – I was serious about what I said about the wolves earlier."

Ashley nodded and held out an arm encouraging Steph to lead the way. She looked around. She was pretty sure that she knew the way from where they were. She had a general sense of the direction at least. As long as she hit a landmark that she recognised, they'd be fine.

FORTY-SIX

It turned out that Steph should have been less optimistic with her sense of direction. She did find she remembered certain landmarks and physical features of her surroundings, but unless she was wrong again, they were not quite where she thought they'd be.

The pair continued to walk in near silence. It became awkward after a while. In the end, it was Steph who broke the impasse. She tried to discover more about who Ashley was. Nothing doing. She asked about what went wrong when the cave lion killed that little boy. Ashley stopped talking again at that. It appeared he was fine killing men as part of business transactions, but he drew the line at the death of children being collateral damage.

A sound in the distance made Steph freeze. She held out a hand as a signal to stop. She listened. Her heart was beating faster because of the walk over woodland terrain, and she could hear the blood pumping in her ears. Then she heard the noise again. The howl. Slightly closer than before.

Steph looked around. The trees surrounding them were large Caledonian pines. Some, Steph noticed, had low enough branches to climb. Nothing comfortable for an extended period, but fine for an escape. She began to climb.

"What are you doing?" Ashley asked.

"Being cautious," Steph replied, eying her next foothold.

"What?"

"Didn't you hear the howl?"

"Well, yeah, but I have a gun..."

"And how do you fire your gun?

"What? By pulling the trigger! How do you think you fire a gun?"

"My point is, unless I am mistaken, that you pull the trigger, then pull back the bolt to load another bullet into the chamber."

"So?"

"So by the time you shoot one of them, the rest will be on us."

Ashley snorted.

"They'd be running scared with their tails between their legs... no?"

"No! Not these wolves anyway."

Another howl sounded through the trees. This time closer. Ashley gave one look over his shoulder and then finally accepted that following Steph's caution might be the most sensible course of action.

Steph made sure to climb high enough that there was a chance the wolves would miss them completely if they came through the trees to where they were. She needn't have worried, however; the nearest wolf she saw was still some distance off. They were, quite concerningly, moving through in the same direction that Steph believed they needed to go in, but it was unclear whether they had picked up a scent or were merely heading in that direction for reasons of their own. The wolf's leisurely padding stopped as it paused to gnaw its leg, suggesting it was in no real hurry.

To be safe Steph insisted they wait ten minutes before coming down to give the wolves a head start. Steph noted that Ashley had his rifle from his back and in his hands as soon as his feet touched the ground. Steph patted him on the back and gestured in the direction of Roger's cabin – or at least where she thought it lay.

"Those wolves," Ashley began as they walked, his voice notably quiet.

"Yes?"

"They're... well... they're rather on the large size, aren't they? Or was I just tricked by the distance and the one we saw was closer than it looked?"

Steph scratched behind her ear as she walked. "No, they're big. I assume Martina's doing."

Ashley nodded, mouthing Martina's name under his breath and shaking his head. Steph wondered how well-known Martina really was in the circle of genetics and how she was regarded. She had clearly achieved something monumental. However, who really knew about it? Was she seen as some sort of inspiration by her peers or a criminal maverick sailing too close to ethical winds?

It was not too long after having descended from the tree that they came across the beavers. They were out of the lodge and busy working on repairing their dam. Steph watched as they worked, gently carving through the water with large logs held by strong jaws. She also noted how another couple of trees had been felled since she had last passed by. The beaver's ability to shape its environment never ceased to amaze her. More interesting was how everything could be going on around the beavers, yet their little world seemed relatively unaffected. The beavers were focused on themselves. Everything else could do as they pleased.

Sounds from the trees made the last few hundred yards a nervous walk. Every so often Steph would find herself looking around, not for danger, but for any potential escape route. Fortunately, Roger's cabin soon loomed into view before

Steph had any need of a desperate escape route.

Steph puffed out her cheeks as she approached Roger's cabin... again. Circles. The last few days were nothing but circles. No. A downward spiral was more apt. It was as if she had revisited places over and over again but each time at a lower ebb in her life. Even so, she couldn't deny that the cabin made a welcome sight despite her desire to be far away from where she was, so she could put everything behind her. Far behind her. So far they couldn't even catch up with her on the sofa of some psychiatrist she was sure she'd have to end up paying in the aftermath of the whole ordeal.

Perhaps publishing the book would be therapy enough – whatever she was able to publish. Better to have commercial therapy and be paid than to pay someone else and have them judge you.

Steph stepped tiredly onto the decking outside the entrance. She found her right leg almost giving way from exhaustion. She ignored it and knocked on the door. The heavy door eased open.

"Steph, I see you've found a friend," said Roger, standing in the crack of the door, his face impassive.

Steph didn't even look over her shoulder. She merely shrugged and pushed past Roger who opened the door a little wider to let Ashley in too.

"This is Ashley," Steph said when she got inside and sank onto the sofa. She noted that Calum was no longer on it. He was probably lying in the bedroom making a meal of his bung knee.

Roger looked Ashley up and down.

"And, um, where exactly did this Ashley come from?"

"Hired to take the cave lion," Steph replied, deciding to lie on the sofa as sitting was just not cutting it.

"I see," Roger said, staring at Ashley who stood awkwardly staring back. "And he is with you because?"

"Because Kelvin's an arsehole. So is this guy, to be honest, but really I'm past caring. What was it you were banging on about, Ashley? People getting on with their own business? Well, my business is now just about getting out of this place."

"Kelvin won't agree to your leaving your post before your contract is up," Roger said, leaving Ashley to go and sit down.

"Possibly, although I suspect he has potentially relieved me of some of the contract, if not all of it already."

"What do you mean?"

Steph turned to look at Roger. The man looked confused. His mouth was partially open as if it was on the verge of forming its next question despite the current one still awaiting its answer. That was fair enough. Steph had come back with a strange man but with no Kelvin, Martina or Davey. Of course, there would be questions. It was just that Steph found she couldn't be bothered to answer them.

"Don't worry about it," Steph said. "Just know that he places little value on any of our lives.

To Steph's surprise, she heard Roger give a short bark of laughter at this. He still had a grim smile on his face when he sat down.

"Well then, Ashley, is it? You had best make yourself useful and make us all a coffee. You'll find some in that second cupboard from the right. Milk's in the fridge obviously."

Steph raised her head slightly to see how Ashley would react to being ordered about. He rolled his eyes a little but then unslung his rifle, propped it against the wall and went about making the coffees.

"So, Steph, what are your plans now?" Roger asked.

He was far too jovial for Steph's liking. She was too tired

and angry to have anyone behaving in an upbeat manner around her. She lay back and closed her eyes.

"Well, once I have had a brief rest, I'm getting the hell out of here. Ashley said he would guide me to the fence. Well, I suppose I would lead the way and he would ensure I don't get eaten."

"Said he'd help you to the fence?" Roger parroted. "And why would he do a thing like that?"

Steph opened one eye and rolled it in Roger's direction to see him looking over at Ashley, his last question clearly indirectly addressed to him.

"Because I guided him here," Steph said, not waiting for Ashley to answer. He had his back turned anyway, too busy measuring heaps of instant coffee.

Roger turned back to Steph briefly before turning around to address Ashley more directly this time.

"Why were you so desperate to come and see us in the cabin?"

"Oh, it was not wanting to see anyone in particular," Ashley said, continuing to make the coffee. "More just that I assume Kelvin will lose focus and turn up here at some point. He will likely secure the lion, perhaps go back to his little control centre and then come here with his public relations face on thinking that I will have tried to escape whilst I can. Essentially coming here means I can sit in a bit of comfort whilst he comes to me."

"Uh huh," replied Roger, his eyebrows raised. "Well, whatever you say."

Steph looked at the ceiling. Something didn't feel right. She could not say what it was exactly, but there was something. Was it the ease Ashley and Roger found themselves whilst in each other's company? Hard to say. Roger seemed at ease in most people's company. Ashley... well, he seemed to behave outside the normal laws of social convention too to some extent anyway. Perhaps it was nothing. But did Roger fully appreciate that Ashley was one of the men they had initially set out to stop?

"Well, it all seems to be quite the mess," Roger said, sinking back into his chair after accepting a coffee from Ashley. "I don't suppose this little experiment of Kelvin's can really carry on."

"Not if I can help it," Ashley said, quite politely as he tapped Steph on the shoulder and pointed to a mug that he was placing on the floor beside her.

Steph noticed Roger frown at the hot mug being placed on bare wood.

"Do you think Kelvin was actually trying to achieve what he said he was trying to achieve?" she asked, suddenly thinking about the whole *experiment*.

"What do you mean?" Roger asked.

"Well," Steph said, sitting up, "I mean, do you really think this was/is a whole rewilding experiment?"

"Hard to say."

"Why?"

"Because of the prehistoric animals running around. What was the purpose of them except for his own vanity? Rewilding in itself I can understand. Bringing in animals that were native to these lands in years gone by is fine. But everything else..."

"So you think he had two motives?"

"Possibly. Who is to say? You'd have to ask him. He's a clever enough man and I don't doubt that he genuinely believes there needs to be some rewilding, or that the planet and people would benefit from it to some extent. Whether he is right or not is another matter. Do people need to learn to live with extinct cave bears and cave lions though?"

"But then why would he pay people like you to see whether

you could live alongside them?"

Steph looked intently at Roger who took a sip of his coffee, grimacing slightly at the heat of it.

"I have ideas," he said. "That's all they are, of course. But I have them."

"And they are?"

"One is that he is and must be a competitive man to have made the riches he has for himself. As such, he wants to be the first to do what so many have talked about but not yet achieved. In short, it is vanity and getting people like me involved gives it some fake face of genuinely trying something for the *greater good*. Another idea is that he just thinks the whole thing is quite cool. It is, I suppose. It was enough to lure poor Daniel in, away from his fledgling career. However, there is also the possibility that he has done all this because of Martina. That's the other likelihood."

"Martina?"

Roger laughed.

"You will often find that, throughout history, men have tended to push themselves when a woman is involved. Whether to impress them or simply prove them wrong out of spite. Either way, they achieve. In fact, some only ever achieve anything when there is someone to impress or beat in some twisted way. However, it wouldn't surprise me if this whole enterprise was a mixture of my speculations. It also wouldn't surprise me if he was simply trying to tie in the extinct animals with something he truly believes in."

Steph picked up her coffee. She let the heat rise against her face as she digested what Roger had just said. Would someone do all this for love? Was love even the right word?

"In short, I don't really know anything; I doubt he has fully crystalised what he will do long term with the lion and bear," Steph heard Roger continue. "But I'm sure he won't be far away from settling on something and, whatever it is, it will make him money. Owning Martina's research will make him money for sure. That's the key component in all of this really regardless of his motives."

"But it's Martina's research," Steph said, continuing to hold the coffee close to her face as she stared out the window.

Roger laughed.

"Kelvin will have her under more contracts than there are lawyers in the world. He may be taken by her, but he is no idiot. People sign prenups all the time; it makes sense that he'd have her sign things even if he is taking her to bed each night without the marriage."

Steph ignored the image evoked by the last comment. Instead, she found herself despising Kelvin. How could he have allowed all of this to happen for such flimsy reasons? Daniel, Thomas, Davey. Was it worth it? To him she supposed it probably was. The greater question was where his contempt for others came from and how he could hide it so easily day to day.

Although Steph was lost in thought, she started to become dimly aware of a sound outside. She stood up so that she could see out the window and over the porch. Outside was Ashley's sleek black truck pulling to a stop.

Steph watched Ashley swiftly sweep across the room to stand with his back to the wall next to the door. It was then that Steph became aware of another sound. It was Roger. He was stifling a chuckle.

"What's funny?" she asked.

"Nothing," Roger smiled. "Just that it is all about image and smokescreens with Kelvin. It's not really funny. It's just... I don't know; it is just my sense of humour."

Roger then looked at Ashley and back at Steph. Steph noticed from her peripheral vision that he wasn't taking his eyes off her. She turned to face him.

"So the question is, are you going to stop Ashley?" he said.

"What?"

"Well, it appears to me that we have somehow arrived at a situation where one more person will die today. If Kelvin comes in, it makes sense that Ashley would kill him. They have gone too far with their game of chess to call a stalemate now."

"We have?" Ashley whispered, standing tight to the wall.

"I would suspect so," Roger replied, his tone suddenly solemn.

Ashley raised his eyebrows and shrugged. Then both men turned again to look at Steph. Their faces looked more curious than bothered. What to do? After all, Ashley had caused the trouble. Or had he? Was he really any worse than Kelvin? Was Kelvin any better than him? Had either really valued her life? No. The difference was that Ashley had let her go free whilst Kelvin had been resigned to her losing her life as a necessary casualty.

Outside, a door swung shut.

FORTY-SEVEN

A knock on the door said Steph's decision time was up. She noted that she was still standing up. Ashley narrowed his eyes at her. She sat down. She was not sure why she sat down. Was it the threat in Ashley's eyes? Was it the need for self-preservation that clawed at her? Whatever it was, she supposed her decision had been made.

Ashley nodded at Roger who opened the door. Steph could not see Kelvin behind the door due to where she was sitting. However, she could hear the voices clearly enough.

"Have you taken care of business then?" Roger asked. Steph couldn't understand how he could keep his voice so steady. It was as if everything around him was perfectly commonplace. She tried to remember what he had said his life had been like before he had come to take part in Kelvin's crazy games.

"Everything is under control now," came Kelvin's reply.

"And where is the lion?"

"Currently on its way somewhere where it can't do any further harm here. Probably for the best at present. I'm about to do the same with the bear."

"I see."

"Are you going to let us in or not?" came a different voice. It was Martina's. "We saw wolves hovering around on our way here."

Roger stepped aside. In pushed Kelvin followed by Martina. Steph found herself wholly unprepared for what followed. Despite all that she had already seen, there was something far more disturbing, far colder and far more soul-shattering about what she saw Ashley do.

In one clean fluid movement, he stepped behind Kelvin and put a hand over his mouth. The image that seared itself onto Steph's memory was not Martina's gaping mouth as she screamed, it was the way Kelvin's eyes bulged in realisation and fear. He had no time to bring his arms up in defence as Ashley raised the knife, slicing through his neck. Rich blood gushed from the wound as Kelvin collapsed to his knees clutching at his throat in a pitifully futile attempt to stem the flow. Then he fell forward. Then he stopped moving.

Steph's stomach churned. She was only dimly aware that Martina had stopped screaming. Her own blood seemed to have left her face as quickly as Kelvin's had spilt – her face was as white as a sheet.

"Well, that was suitably unpleasant," Roger said, grimacing.

Martina's head snapped around at Roger, then towards the door. Ashley must have been watching because he shut the door behind him and then stood blocking it. Martina looked at Steph, her eyes wild. She took a couple of steps towards her. Steph braced herself.

She noticed Martina glance at the window. Steph turned to face the window too. There was only the truck. Then she heard darting footsteps followed by a tired groan.

Steph turned in time to see Martina springing for the bedroom door, with Ashley striding after her. The door swung open. Martina leapt inside just as Ashley got there to jam a foot in the doorway. But the door never swung shut. Steph assumed Martina was going for the window, but Ashley didn't have time to enter the room before another scream bounced around the cabin.

Ashley stepped in.

"Ah," he said.

Frowning, Steph got to her feet and slowly made her way over. By the time she had pushed gently past Ashley, Martina's scream had given way to a quiet sob. A sob of resignation. She was looking at the bed.

Steph followed her gaze. Then she shut her eyes, hands rubbing across her face hoping that what she saw would be gone when she looked once more. It was still there: Calum's lifeless body, a pillow where his sleeping head should have been visible.

Leaving Ashley to watch over Martina, Steph slipped back out of the room. She stared at the floor in an attempt to calm her mind just a little. She couldn't control what she had just seen but she could control what she was seeing now. The floor, at least, was bland. There was nothing to it. It was simple – some wooden planks doing the job of offering people a platform to walk on. Nothing more. Nothing less. There she could make sense of things.

"Why?" Steph asked, not looking up.

There was a thoughtful pause before Roger sighed and said, "He knew too much, I suppose."

Steph heard a heavy slump in front of her. She looked up to see Roger in a chair. He looked different now somehow. His facial expression seemed less warm. It was not necessarily colder, but it had definitely lost some of the friendliness that Steph had associated with him.

"Kelvin put you up to it?" she asked.

Roger looked up, a pitying smile on his face.

"Not exactly, no. You see, Calum was working for me."

"You?"

"Yes, me," Roger said, a small smile returning to his face. "There is a lot you don't know about me. Maybe it is for the best that you don't. It would be simpler if you just knew me as Kelvin's competitor."

Steph looked at the body lying in a pool of blood. Roger followed suit before turning back with a grimace. "Was his competitor."

"But... but that doesn't explain Calum?"

"Ah, I see. Well, there were two reasons for Calum's death, under the umbrella of knowing too much. Firstly, I had to take him out of the equation because he knew who I was to some extent. That's not necessarily so bad in and of itself..."

"But you won't tell me who you are?" Steph interrupted.

"More for your own protection," Roger smiled. "Anyway, he knew who I was, and for all Kelvin's flaws, he was as good at finding out who people were as I am... maybe even better at getting information from them. He was very clean when it came to that. Eventually, he would have put two and two together as to who had helped Ashley and Baz – I believe you had the pleasure of meeting Baz before his death – gain entry into the place. The smokescreen Michael provided wouldn't have lasted long. Of course, this was before I knew that Ashley was going to take care of Kelvin. It certainly was not the plan. A quick in and out was the plan."

"And the second reason?" Steph asked, disgusted by her own curiosity.

"He was a loose end," Roger replied simply.

This took Steph aback. After the more reasonable first explanation, the second seemed a cop-out.

Roger seemed to read Steph's thoughts as he then said, "I wouldn't worry about him. He was not the best of people. He killed someone himself, did you know? Hit and run on a pregnant lady in the Surrey Hills; why he came here actually. It's amazing what someone will let slip after too much to drink."

Behind her, Steph heard Martina being guided into the room by Ashley. She vaguely heard some sort of obscenity being thrown Ashley's way but wasn't really paying attention.

"What will you do now?" she asked, her heart beginning to race at the fear of the answer.

Roger put all his fingers together in front of him. "I suppose, we take Martina."

At this, Martina stopped sobbing and thumping Ashley's chest and turned to glare at Roger. Her look suggested that she had pieced enough together the same way Steph had, although Steph suspected, Martina had a better idea of the motives behind the actions.

"Like I would ever help you!" Martina spat. "People like you are nothing but pieces of shit!"

Roger laughed.

"Takes one to know one I would say."

He got to his feet and sighed.

"What to do with you though, Steph? I suppose you will be wanting some sort of financial compensation. I am not sure that Kelvin will be able to fulfil his contractual obligations. Then again, I suppose you have a copy of your contract somewhere back at the house."

She did. Steph vaguely recalled Kelvin giving her a copy to keep. She had flung it into her case of clothes. It hadn't really seemed important at the time seeing as there were large and interesting animals to document. Now she thought about it, she supposed she did want something financial from all of this. She'd earned it. Also, how would her releasing of information work now that Kelvin was dead? Was it a free-for-all, or was Kelvin the head of some sort of huge company with people ready to step in and take his place? Steph's stomach churned. She really did know nothing.

"The police will want to interview you as well, I would imagine," Roger said, itching his wrist before shaking it out and putting his hands behind his back to rock on his heels.

"Won't they want to see you too?" Steph asked. She heard how stupid it sounded as soon as it left her mouth.

Roger smiled. "Goodness, no! I won't be here by then. Besides, as I am sure you have worked out by now, you have no idea who I am, so they wouldn't know who they were looking for even if you did make them aware of my existence. I'm sure someone could work it out, but they would be someone who worked at dizzying heights. The type of person who has an interest in things being grey and needs people like me in operation anyway. Thus, nothing would happen."

Roger then headed towards the door before stopping and turning to say, "Not that I am a bad person! It is just that a lot of what I do is hard to complete in an ethical manner, if you understand what I mean."

Steph blinked at him. He nodded awkwardly to himself and then, satisfied he hadn't really got anything left to say, nodded at Ashley who ushered Martina towards the door.

"Are you not going to see me to the outer fencing?" Steph found herself calling after Ashley.

"Roger turned once more. He looked at Steph, looked at Ashley, and then back at Steph.

"Is that what you want?

She thought about it. Was it? She thought about the contract in the house.

"Yes. Yes, I think so. I think that... I think it's time to leave."
Roger nodded.

"Fair enough. We will drop you outside the fencing. I would love to drop you off at the hotel or somewhere similar, but as I am sure you can appreciate, I am in somewhat of a rush."

FORTY-EIGHT

They all got in the truck. Martina was muttering under her breath, but Steph couldn't decipher what she was saying except for the occasional curse. Ashley turned the key in the ignition. Nothing. He did it again. Nothing again.

"What's going on?" Roger asked, his voice quite balanced. Steph watched Ashley turn his head towards Roger, tilting it slightly. There was an audible sigh from Roger. "Well, go and fix it then!"

"I'm not a mechanic!" Ashley replied.

"Well, neither am I!"

Roger held his ground, staring at Ashley. It seemed as if Ashley was going to show the same stubbornness, but after a couple of seconds, he submitted to the other and got out of the car to open the bonnet.

From where Steph was sitting, she couldn't see Ashley anymore. Not with the open bonnet blocking the view. She let her eyes move in the direction of Martina sitting next to her. Martina's eyes kept flicking from the open car bonnet to her door. Her hand hovered over her belt buckle.

Somewhere outside, there was a howl. The animal was still a way off from what Steph could tell, although she had no way of knowing how well the windows were muffling the sound.

It was warm in the truck. Comfortable. Steph became acutely aware of how tired she was in the silence. Her eyelids felt heavy. She let them close.

A loud bang outside broke her momentary rest. The

bonnet was shaking in front of her. A few moments passed. The fiddling sound that had notified everyone to Ashley's presence seemed to have stopped. Steph was not the only one to have noticed.

"Ashley?" Roger called through the windscreen. Nothing. He knocked on the windscreen. "Ashley?"

There was no concern in his voice. It was as if everything that happened around him was nothing more than an amusing formality. Had he always been that way? Maybe that was why she had liked him. In a normal person, she supposed, a refusal to take life too seriously was endearing. However, in someone who held such power and moved in such shadowy circles it was somewhat unnerving.

Steph looked out of her window. Martina did the same, her hands no longer hovering over her buckle.

"Well, I can't see anything, can you?" Roger said, turning to Steph, ignoring Martina.

"No," Steph replied, undoing her seat belt to turn herself to look further back through her window.

"How strange," Roger replied jovially. "Inconvenient really, but interestingly strange nonetheless."

An indecisive silence fell. Steph became aware of her heartbeat starting to creep up as the blood pumped around her ears.

Suddenly, the car bonnet slammed shut. Steph jumped. The other two also snapped their heads forwards expecting to see the worst. They needn't have worried: it was Ashley rubbing his head.

Steph watched as he meandered back to the driver's door and got in, shutting the door and looking forward.

"Well?" Roger asked.

"Well, I think I will be seeking compensation for a

workplace concussion!"

Roger laughed.

"Don't be daft; you know how poor our HR department is. The engine?"

"Dead!"

"Dead?"

"Battery acid everywhere. It's cracked."

"Cracked?"

"Yes, cracked! Shoddy parts used on this thing," Ashley said lightly thumping the steering wheel.

"Bollocks!" Roger snorted. "Nothing wrong with the parts used on this thing. It is the way it has been driven that's caused it!"

Ashley raised a triumphant finger, "Ah, but Kelvin was the last one to drive it!"

Roger opened his mouth to retort. Paused. Shut it and then said, "That's fair enough; he was always careless."

Martina growled in the back. Roger ignored her.

"Plan B?" Ashley asked.

Roger thought for a moment.

"We all need to get out of here for our own reasons. Personally, I think a northern direction would suit us best, Ashley. That's where the others will be waiting – it is a shame they will be disappointed by the lack of an animal, assuming they didn't cross Kelvin's own men outside coming in to take the specimens away. I fear they won't appreciate Martina as the real driving force behind it all – see how big a catch she is."

"I'll kill myself before I work for you!" Martina snarled.

"No, you won't," Roger replied dismissively. "You're far too much of a narcissist for such a thing. Besides, your scientific curiosity is as great as mine and I can give you what you need to explore current boundaries. Anyway, Steph, I suggest that when we get to the fencing and go our separate ways, you head back towards the village. I suppose that means a trip south first, Ashley. Perhaps that's not an issue. I am sure someone will be awake to potential scenarios."

Steph had heard Roger but was busy looking at Martina, curious as to how she would react to what Roger said. Her arms were folded and her eyes were still, but behind them the cogs were turning.

Steph turned back to Roger.

"And the wolves?"

"Not much we can do about them," Roger replied. "We have Ashley though."

"She seems to think these are some sort of *super wolves* and that I won't be of much help," Ashley replied, scepticism dripping from his voice.

"If that is what Steph thinks, then I am inclined to trust her," Roger replied. "I have seen enough out my window to know they have something about them. However, I was more suggesting that you would make the tastiest meal out of us all!"

"Why me?" Ashley replied, allowing himself a smile.

"Simple; you are not as large as Baz, but you still have more muscle meat than either Steph or Martina, and you're younger and therefore less tough to eat than me!"

Ashley chuckled as he opened the door and got out. Roger followed. Steph looked at Martina who narrowed her eyes. Sighing, Steph got out of the cab.

Steph walked with her knife out. She decided that, in the current circumstances, it made more sense to be prepared. Ashley went ahead with his rifle unslung, scanning left and right. Martina had picked up a stick. Steph noted that she kept sizing up both Roger's and Ashley's heads. She was pretty sure that Roger was aware of it, but as with most things his smile suggested that he found it mildly amusing.

They followed a direct route southeast. There was no clear path, so it involved navigating through shrubbery and up and down small slopes, but Roger insisted it was the most direct route to the outer fencing.

"Shouldn't we head to a gate?" Steph asked. "I'm not sure we can scale an electric fence that has a voltage designed to subdue a one-ton bear."

"You could be right," Roger replied. "But if we are walking along the fence, we might see a conveniently placed tree and branch that could speed up our escape. If not, we simply follow it to the nearest gate. However, it appears to me, although correct me if I am wrong, most of the bigger predators don't spend too much time by the fencing. It's not the ideal place to hunt?"

Steph thought about it. She supposed he was right, from what she had seen.

"I guess that's true. Although, nothing ever follows one rule perfectly; there is always a chance the wolves are there."

"For sure," Roger replied. "But that's life, and we can deal with eventualities when they come up."

This felt like a fair assessment.

Ahead of them, Ashley kept turning his head left and right whilst Roger kept a close eye on Martina. He had no weapon that Steph could see, but he kept a firm presence around her. Steph was so focused on watching this strange non-interaction, that she didn't notice the figure lurking behind the trees. Neither did Ashley.

The shape of something bolted from its hiding place just feet from Ashley, sending him tumbling to the ground. Steph held back. Roger grabbed Martina's arm, seemingly more concerned with what she might do than his own safety.

Everything happened so fast. Steph was acting before her brain could think how to act. She suddenly realised that her knife was raised and that she had taken a stride towards the two figures locked in combat on the floor, with Ashley starting to get the upper hand. Then Steph's brain clicked into gear.

"Stop!" she shouted. "Just stop!"

The mass of grappling limbs seemed to slow itself until the two bodies untangled and got to their feet panting.

"Ah," said Roger, smiling. "I assume it was probably you who fiddled with the car battery?"

Ahead of him, Davey turned a scowling eye. He was bruised and filthy. His right cheek had a large gash on it with dark dry blood caking the area underneath. His left arm hung limper than the right.

Steph couldn't believe it. She didn't know how it was possible. Roger, on the other hand, seemed perfectly at ease with the revelation.

"But why didn't you simply steal the truck?" he asked.

Davey continued to look at him, his chest heaving. Then he looked at Ashley to check he was where he had left him. He too stood panting, a small cut beneath his right eye, his rifle somehow ten yards or so from where he stood. They had rolled some distance in each other's unfriendly embrace.

"I couldn't let you know I had survived otherwise you'd know I was coming."

Roger nodded.

"And has everything gone as planned since?"

"Sort of. Although, I had hoped to knock this one off." He flicked his head in the direction of Ashley who derisively snorted with laughter.

"Ah, I see. Well, that is an inconvenience for you then. However, I'm sure your plan was based on what I'd call 'old information'. I suspect that you'd find trying to 'knock off' Ashley now, to be quite a waste of everyone's time."

Davey frowned. He turned to Martina and then to Steph.

"What does he mean?"

What did Roger mean? Steph supposed he could mean a small number of things.

"Kelvin's dead," Steph replied.

Davey's facial expression slackened slightly as he digested the news. He looked from one face to another. Then he paused, frowning.

"Where's Calum?"

"Dead," Steph replied.

"How?"

"Murdered... just like Kelvin."

Davey turned his head towards Ashley, his upper lip rising into a snarl.

"He was not really the man he made himself out to be," Roger said, his voice full of appeal. "Neither of them were, in fact. There is an awful lot that you don't know, Davey."

To Steph's ear, Roger sounded sincere. Even so, Davey's face continued to contort.

"You despicable little prick!" he said, turning towards Ashley again. "You're probably the one who shot Michael!"

Ashley continued his look of malice.

"Michael deserved everything he got. So did Kelvin!"

Steph could see Davey's fists clench. She watched as Davey took a couple of steps towards Ashley. Both men's bodies tensed ready for the clash. Then, as suddenly as he had started moving – Roger's half-hearted pleas for calm echoed around the space between the trees – Davey stopped.

Ashley sensed the momentary weakness and began to step forward. Davey began to step back, his shoulders beginning to slouch slightly as he let his chest deflate. Ashley barked out a laugh as he stepped forward again. Then his body arched backwards as something heavy and grey hammered him forward, onto the ground.

Steph reached forward to grab Davey's arm, pulling him away. Her eyes spun left and right, expecting to see more figures appear from between the trees.

On the ground, Ashley writhed, desperately trying to fight off the massive wolf who bit into his forearm causing him to yell in pain and anger.

Martina, like Steph, had the sense not to run – she too was spinning her head left and right waiting to see where the next wolf would come from.

Roger, on the other hand, remained perfectly calm. Steph watched as he kept his eyes on Ashley rolling on the floor, now calling for help as the wolf lunged at his throat. All the time, Roger edged towards the fallen rifle.

Steph noticed that Davey did not pull himself from her grasp to answer the call for help. Either out of dislike for Ashley or simply because he was stunned into inactivity, she didn't know. Together they watched as Roger slowly and deliberately kneeled so that his shot would be more horizontal and have less chance of accidentally hitting Ashley. He edged closer still, the wolf oblivious to his intentions.

There was a loud bang followed by a whimper. The force of the bullet lifted the wolf clean off its victim. For one brief second, the wolf tried to stand on shaking limbs. Then it collapsed, its breathing shallow.

Steph watched as Roger pointed the rifle at Martina who had been edging towards the nearest tree.

"No silly shenanigans from you, please."

He then turned to look at Ashley on the floor; his face fell slightly.

"Oh dear."

Releasing Davey's arm, Steph ran to kneel by Ashley. His arms were torn, bloody and bruised. However, it was his wide eyes, pale face and the tear in his throat that really drew the attention. He was trying to speak but couldn't. Blood was pumping from the wound in his neck.

Steph tried to stem the flow with her hands, but blood oozed from between her fingers. She looked at Ashley's face. He was terrified. She took his hand.

Behind her, the sound of the wolf's breathing had ceased. There was only the uncomfortable sound of Ashley's rasping last breaths.

His hand weakened in Steph's. His eyes still moved about pleadingly in his skull as if there was still a way out, that his fate was not yet sealed. Then he took one slightly longer breath and blood gurgled from his mouth. Then he choked and died.

There was silence amongst the others.

FORTY-NINE

Steph stood up. Another death. Death seemed to be everywhere. It hurt her to admit it, but the feeling of disgust and pity in her stomach was not as strong as it had been the first couple of times.

A sense of self-preservation caused her to look around once again. It seemed the others had similar thoughts. Still, nothing else seemed to appear between the trees.

She gazed down at the dead wolf, blood trickling from its snout. It looked like it had gone through a rough time recently itself. It had wounds on its muzzle and flanks. They looked days old like the wolf had gone through one hell of a fight.

"I'm not sure that we should dwell on this," Roger waved a hand in the direction of the two bodies on the floor, "for too long. I imagine the rest of the pack will be here soon."

"Maybe," Steph said. "But maybe not."

"What do you mean?"

"I think that this one was an outcast."

"A lone wolf?"

"Not by choice. Something must have gone on. Maybe it challenged the alpha of the pack, who knows? It is just that the injuries it has don't look like they were caused by any bear, certainly not any lion."

Roger raised his eyebrows as he too studied the wolf.

"Even so, I'm sure that something will have heard the gunshot, and I am not sure I trust the behaviour of these creatures enough for them to be appropriately scared."

Steph supposed he was right. She looked at Davey who was still clearly at a loss as to what was going on. However, he was no longer quite so angry now that the target of his fury had just had his throat ripped out.

"Come on," she said, putting a hand on his back to push him into motion.

The group walked. They walked in silence until they reached the fence. As Steph suspected might happen, they were forced to walk quite a way further until they inevitably reached the path leading to the house. At this point, each had their own reasons to return to the house before heading back to the main gate.

They could have decided to rest there but none of the party were inclined to do so.

Steph and Davey retrieved a few belongings, including the contract that was shoved at the bottom of her bag. Roger allowed Martina to retrieve some of her own possessions, as well as insisting on various bits of research that she had saved onto numerous memory sticks. Then the group made their way through the gates and out onto the road that led to the house from outside the two fences. They would have each taken a quad bike if it wasn't for the fact none were in the vicinity, each lying motionless somewhere amongst the trees.

They headed back down the path that ran all the way to the main gate. From there, they followed the small road that connected the place to the outside world. It was empty. Empty except for the sound of birds singing.

After a longer walk than Steph had anticipated, they reached the main road. It was the main road in the sense that it was *the* main road to the area. Even so, the traffic on it was still sparse. A car drove past as they stood on the grassy side. It was almost surreal to see one go past, with people going about their business oblivious to the mess just a few miles through the trees. Steph wondered whether the driver had clocked the rifle Roger still held limply in his hand, ready to direct at Martina should the need arise.

"Well," Roger smiled, "this is where we part ways."

Steph turned her bleary face towards him. Despite the rings around his eyes, there was still an energy about him.

"I believe – correctly, I hope – that someone should be coming to pick me up any moment now."

"How could you...?"

"I contacted someone whilst we were in the cabin. Goodness knows when they actually got here. Probably been going up and down the roads so as not to draw attention to themselves by staying in one place."

"And they knew you would be here?" Davey asked.

"Not exactly," Roger replied. "Things rarely work out so perfectly. They're probably covering a whole stretch of road. My intention was to meet someone a little further north of here. I dread to think what the petrol cost will be."

Davey puffed out his cheeks and shrugged his shoulders.

It was oddly calm as they stood there.

"I would suggest that after you have gathered yourselves, you head towards the village. I am sure that Jackie will look after you in the hotel's bar. No doubt you are in need of a hot meal and an ale."

Steph smiled. Now the image was in her head, it did seem rather appealing.

"How can you two just stand there and let this happen!" Martina spat, looking from one person to the other. "How could you just let him take me away like this!"

Steph ignored her. However, Davey, to Steph's surprise, said, "Probably the same way you were happy to let that other guy kill Steph."

Martina's face, somehow, soured further.

"Ashley threatened to kill you?" Roger asked, his voice mild with interest.

"He did," Steph replied.

Roger chuckled.

"I doubt he'd have actually gone through with it. Always liked Baz to do the dirty work if he could help it. He had more of a moral compass than was probably apparent, more of one than was probably useful in his line of work.

"A compass that pointed south when it came to Kelvin!" Martina snarled.

Roger raised his eyebrows.

"Yes... he really did hate him."

Martina was about to say more when all four became aware of a Ford Galaxy indicating to park alongside them. It stopped and a window wound down. A middle-aged man in a simple jumper looked out smiling.

"You guys all need a lift?" he asked.

"Just the two of us," Roger replied, opening the door to the backseats and forcing Martina in with a bag thrown over her shoulder.

Roger was about to follow her in when he noticed the look on Steph's face. She could not help looking at the driver and then at the car.

"Were you expecting some Cadillac with blacked-out windows?" he laughed. "Helps not to draw attention to oneself at times. Look at what happened to Ashley's truck..."

With that, he ducked his head in, shut the door and the car pulled off.

Steph watched it drive up the road and slowly round the gradual bend that took it out of sight behind the treeline.

FIFTY

Steph walked with Davey up the side of the road. For a while neither said anything; they were tired both mentally and physically.

Eventually, Steph asked, "So what happened with the bear?"

Davey smiled.

"Nothing too spectacular, I'm afraid to say."

"What then?"

"Well, after I'd run into it – like running into a wall of concrete wearing fur, by the way – and I tumbled down the slope, I sort of just lost it."

"Lost it? But I saw it go after you!"

"Yeah, it went after me all right," Davey chuckled. "Although, I crashed into a rather thorny bush and the stupid thing bowled right on past me. Scratched myself up pretty badly, but in the circumstances, I'd say things could have worked out worse."

Steph nodded to herself as they walked. A small silence descended once more.

Then Steph broke it by saying, "Thank you, by the way."

Steph could sense Davey turn his head towards her as they walked but he said nothing. She was sure, although she didn't look, that he was still smiling.

"So what happened next? How did you know where we were?"

"I didn't," Davey admitted. "I heard Kelvin and Martina

going down the hill, but I didn't risk moving from the bush straightaway. I could hear the bear – or at least thought I could – so I just lay there. Fell asleep, actually."

"You fell asleep?"

"I was shattered! I don't know if you've been paying attention, but I haven't had much rest recently!"

"You said the bush was thorny!"

"It was! But I'd already scratched my face up and my body seemed to have settled into a position. I didn't mean to fall asleep! It wasn't planned. It just happened."

Steph puffed out her cheeks.

"What happened next?"

"I woke up."

"No shit. After that?"

"I went back to one of the quad bikes and headed for the cabin. I had seen what had happened between Kelvin, you and that other dickhead, and thought I had best help get Roger and Calum out of there. Charge ran out on my quad bike partway there and by the time I reached the place, that truck was outside. I thought I would inconvenience Kelvin so I could work out exactly what he was playing at, throwing away your life as a bargaining tool, so I broke the battery. Of course, I then sensed something wasn't quite right when he never came back out of the cabin. So I followed you all until I could ambush the dickhead."

"Ashley," Steph said.

"What?"

"The dickhead's was Ashley."

"Right."

Steph wondered whether Davey could sense her irritation at him calling Ashley a dickhead. She could understand it but thought it harsh. Ashley seemed like a reasonably fair person, just caught up in a rather unforgiving job.

She could tell Davey was looking for something to say as he kept flicking his eyes towards her and half opening his mouth.

Eventually, he settled on, "So Roger wasn't what he appeared to be then?"

"Apparently not."

"Ah, shame. I liked him."

"I still like him, I think."

"You do?" Davey asked, raising an eyebrow and stopping. Steph stopped too.

"I think so."

"Even after all the trouble he caused?"

"Did he cause the trouble or did Kelvin?" she asked. "I don't think Roger caused the problems; he merely waited for them to occur and then capitalised on them."

"No!"

"What do you mean *no*?" Steph asked, wiping some dirt from under her eye.

"I mean, how could he have possibly known things would go wrong? How would he be in a position to be ready for when they did? No. I think he probably had a bigger hand in things than you realise."

As if to punctuate his thoughts, he began walking again. Steph followed. Perhaps he was right. Perhaps Roger had orchestrated things to a greater degree than she realised. Even so, he seemed like a likable person. Likeable enough for whatever type of person he was meant to be. Was he the boss or did he work for someone else?

"So what will you do now?" Davey asked, breaking Steph's train of thought.

She looked up.

"I dunno. Go to Sheffield and see my parents I suppose.

Write a book about what happened to that poor kid."

"What will you say killed him?"

Steph thought about it. What would she say? With Kelvin dead would she be allowed to write whatever she wanted? Did she want to write the truth? Maybe the truth was so farfetched that it would discredit her more than it would boost her sales.

"I guess I'll say a big cat got him," Steph replied. Then she said, "Or maybe I will leave it open and not reach a conclusion. Sometimes people don't like to know the exact truth; it leaves them with nothing to imagine."

"What do you mean?"

"Well, in my area, it is other people's ability to draw their own conclusion that pays my bills."

A car drove past with a child's face pressed against the window. Steph stuck her tongue out.